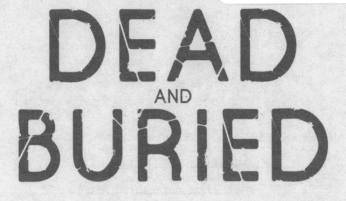

DEAD
AND
BURIED

ANNe
CAssiDy

BLOOMSBURY

LONDON NEW DELHI NEW YORK SYDNEY

Bloomsbury Publishing, London, New Delhi, New York and Sydney

First published in Great Britain in March 2014 by
Bloomsbury Publishing Plc
50 Bedford Square, London WC1B 3DP

A CIP catalogue record for this book is available from the British Library

ISBN 978 1 4088 1553 3

Typeset by Hewer Text UK Ltd, Edinburgh
Printed and bound in Great Britain by CPI Group (UK) Ltd, Croydon CR0 4YY

1 3 5 7 9 10 8 6 4 2

www.bloomsbury.com

To Alice Morey and Josie Morey
My favourite teenagers

ONE

Now, when Rose thought of her mother, the word *killer* came into her head. It conjured up pictures that she did not want to see, sounds that she did not want to hear. It was better not to think of her at all. She'd spent many hours remembering Kathy Smith, mother and police officer. She'd thought of her with Brendan, her partner, and his son, Joshua. She'd pictured the place they'd lived in, Brewster Road; the four of them sitting in the garden eating chicken wings and sausages from a barbecue that Brendan had spent hours trying to light.

Now she felt only grief for the loss of those days.

College work had become a priority. After a few months of lagging behind in her assignments she was now gaining high grades again and basking in the positive comments from her tutors. She was busy, busy. Her grandmother, Anna, had been pleased to hear that she was looking at the prospectus for Cambridge University. In eighteen months' time she would start her degree and begin to think of an adult and independent future. She would move away from Anna's house, away from London, away from everything that had happened recently.

Away from Joshua Johnson.

This thought gave her an ache across her chest. She once thought of him as her *stepbrother* but he wasn't that. Then she began to think of him quite differently, more as a boyfriend, more as someone to love. Now she hadn't seen him for almost two weeks. Their last meeting had ended in a terrible row and although they'd made up afterwards she had felt stifled by him. As soon as she'd got back to Anna's she'd sent him an email to explain that she was feeling overwhelmed by the things that had happened over the previous months and she wanted to pull back from it all and have a break from *him*.

As soon as she pressed the *Send* button she regretted it.

His email reply was brief.

Rosie, do whatever is best for you. Love, Josh XXX

She kept it in her inbox and read it every day. She wanted to contact him, explain why she'd said what she'd said, but with every day that passed the gap between them seemed to lengthen. She got annoyed from time to time at *him*. Why had he given up so easily? Was he so busy that she had just dropped out of his thoughts? Why hadn't he rung her or waited outside college for her? Why hadn't he come to Anna's house and insisted that he come in and that they talk it over? Instead of distancing herself from him as she had planned she now thought about him twice as much.

There was a knock on her study door. Then it opened.

'Rose, I found these in the Blue Room. It's your mother's old paperwork. Most of what's here is rubbish, I suspect, but you might want to keep some of it,' Anna said.

'Oh thanks, you can put them in the corner and I'll look through.'

Rose watched Anna as she placed some box files on the carpet. Anna was wearing *jeans* and a loose blouse and her hair was tied back in a headscarf. Rose had never seen her so casual. The jeans had a crease ironed into them, though, and the blouse was linen, crisp and fresh. Even Anna's dressing down was carefully coordinated.

'Oh, I found something else that I thought you might like. It's not part of the stuff I took from your mother's old house. It dates from long before then when she was about your age.'

Anna went out of the room and Rose heard her footsteps along the corridor. Moments later she was back holding a flowery top on a hanger.

'Katherine had this when she still lived here. It was quite expensive as I recall.'

Rose took the hanger. It was a silk top with a round neck and short sleeves. It was off-white with posies of flowers dotted over it. It felt fragile and looked sweet – not the sort of thing that Rose would ever wear.

'Keep it,' Anna said. 'It will only go to the charity shop if you don't. It's too pretty to give away.'

'Shall I come and help?' Rose said, hanging the blouse on the picture rail.

'In a while. I've a few things to organise before we start putting things in bags. I'll call you.'

When Anna went out of the room Rose's eyes flicked back to the blouse. She unbuttoned the shirt she was wearing and slipped it off. Then she put the blouse over her head and let it slither into place. She stepped into her bedroom and looked in the mirror.

She smiled.

The blouse fitted her perfectly. It meant that she was more or less the same size as her mother had been when she was her age. It sat on her hips and there was a small slit in each side. The button at the back of her neck was covered in fabric and fastened by a loop. The fabric had a sheen to it and the silk felt light on her skin. The posies were shades of pink and yellow, colours that she hadn't worn for a long time. She liked it.

The doorbell sounded.

'I'll get it,' she called.

She went downstairs, stroking the silk top, and opened the front door. A policeman was standing there. Rose looked out into the street to see if there was a police car.

'Yes?' she said, more abruptly than she meant to.

'Rose Smith? It's Henry Thompson. One of the police officers who dealt with the murders in Camden last autumn?'

'I know who you are, Henry.'

She was used to seeing him on a bike with a safety helmet. There was no bike and no car, though, so he must have come on foot.

'How are you?' he said.

'I'm fine.'

Rose stared at him remembering the grim things that had happened the previous October.

'Well, I'm fine too, Rose, since you ask.'

'Sorry. How are things with you?' she said. 'Are you well? Why are you here?'

'Direct as ever.'

'Is it about the murders in Camden?'

'No, not that.'

She was suddenly anxious. Was it about her *mother*?

'It's an enquiry that's taking place in East London that we think you may be able to help us with.'

He looked burdened, as if he had more to say than he could manage.

'Can I come in?'

'Of course,' she said, holding the door open. 'Come through to the kitchen.'

He walked slowly behind her. When she looked round

he was gazing at the huge hallway. He was impressed – she could tell. Most people would be, walking into Anna's wealthy home. In the kitchen he took his hat off and placed it on the table by a large bowl of lemons.

'You're still at college?' he said, sitting down.

She was leaning against the work surface. She nodded in answer to his question. Was he going to tell her something about her mother? She felt herself stiffen with tension. Henry Thompson was a decent police officer, someone she could trust. If he told her something bad she would have to believe it.

'You look different. You're wearing something that's, well . . . don't get me wrong . . . feminine.'

Rose looked down at the blouse. Henry had only ever seen her wearing black and white, her usual colours of choice.

'It's something of my mother's,' she said. 'I was just trying it on. It's a memento, not something I would wear out.'

'You should,' Henry said, smiling at her. 'You look really smart.'

Rose frowned. Henry wriggled around in his seat. He moved his hat to the corner of the table. He looked nervous.

'What's up, Henry? Why did you want to see me?' she said.

'I didn't know anything about your history when we met last year. I'm surprised, amazed actually, that you didn't tell me that your mother and her partner disappeared over five years ago.'

Rose shrugged. There were other things going on at the time.

'I thought we were friends?'

'We are friends, sort of . . .' she said.

'It does explain a few things,' he said, looking thoughtful.

She was irked. She didn't like the idea of Henry analysing her.

'What does it explain? Why I'm so difficult? So hard to get on with? Why I only wear black and white? Which bit of me does it explain?'

'Point taken,' Henry said, as his fingers tapped the table rapidly.

She sighed. She wished she wasn't always so touchy with Henry when all he had ever done was try to help her. She stared at the bowl of lemons. The colour of the fruit was sharp and cold, like sorbet.

'Sorry,' she said.

He waved it away with his hand.

'You and your stepbrother, Joshua Johnson. I think that was the lad you introduced me to? For this to happen to both of you is extraordinary.'

'It happened. We had to deal with it. I won't say it hasn't been hard but . . .' Rose felt her voice clogging up. 'But we've come to terms with it. We are getting on with our lives.'

It was a lie but Rose didn't want to talk about it any more.

'I hope what I'm going to tell you now isn't going to make things worse.'

'What?' she said, tensing herself.

He took a deep breath.

'You lived in a house in East London. Forty-nine Brewster Road.'

She nodded.

'You lived there firstly with your mother for two years and then her partner and his son moved in for three years. So in all, you lived in the house from August 2002 to November 2007? Just over five years?'

'Yes. What's happened?'

'Since you left the house was sold on. It's had three different owners and was recently bought by a Mr Kamath and his family. Mr Kamath had some building plans and . . . well, the blunt truth is that a body has been found buried under the back garden. Preliminary investigations suggest that it has been buried there for approximately five years.'

'A body?'

'Yes. The body of a young girl of eighteen.'

Rose pulled a chair out from under the table and sat on it. Her shoulders sagged. A *body*? Under the garden?

'Whereabouts?'

She spoke without thinking. As if it mattered *where*.

'Near the rear of the garden, I believe. I've not been to the crime scene myself . . .'

Rose pictured the back garden at Brewster Road. The end of it was overgrown, she remembered, big shrubs, some trees, long grass. She never went down there.

'I don't get this,' Rose said. 'It happened while we were living there? Someone came into our garden and dug a hole and buried a girl? It's mad. Why are you asking me about it? How would I know? Or my family, come to that?'

'This is standard procedure, Rose. If human remains are found in a garden then we have to speak to the people who lived in that house at that time. I'm here to let you know that the detectives who are following up the case might want to speak to you to see if you remember anything about the month of August 2007?'

'Why that month? I thought you said that the dates were approximate?'

'Dating human remains is approximate but in this case the body may be that of a girl who left home on 20 August 2007 and was never seen again.'

'Oh.'

'Anyway, I'm just here as a courtesy really. I think you've got my phone number? And I've got yours from last autumn. It hasn't changed?'

Rose shook her head. Her number was the same.

'So if there's anything you remember . . .'

Rose could hear footsteps coming down the stairs. Henry stood up and moments later Anna was at the kitchen door.

'Oh, hello,' Anna said, looking at Henry's uniform, a flicker of concern crossing her face.

'Mrs Christie. Police Constable Henry Thompson. We met last autumn . . .'

'Actually Henry was just leaving,' Rose said, standing up. 'Thanks for coming. It's good of you to let me know.'

'Is there a problem?' Anna said.

'Well . . .' Henry started.

'I'll explain to Anna after you go,' she said.

She chivvied him along the hallway. He started to ask about her college courses and she gave mumbled answers. When they got to the front door she stepped outside with him, closing the door behind her. She walked with him on to the street.

'I'll let you know if the officers from East London want to speak to you. Oh, one other thing . . .'

Rose waited.

'There might be some press interest in this case.'

'The press?'

'You know how the papers are. A body buried in a garden. It's big news.'

'What about Joshua? Are you going to see him?'

'Going there now. Camden, right? No doubt you'll be getting together. That might be a good thing. If the two of you talk it through, it might bring back some relevant memories.'

He walked off and she stood on the pavement, disconcerted. Part of her had wanted to say, 'I'll come with you!' But she hadn't and as she walked back up the garden path she imagined Henry standing next to Lettuce and Stuff, a cafe on Camden High Street, and knocking on Joshua's door. She saw Joshua come dashing down the stairs and frowning when he saw a policeman there. He would be guarded and surly because he had had his fill of policemen. Still, though, he would invite him upstairs and they would stand or sit in the small narrow kitchen and Henry would tell him about the body under the garden in Brewster Road.

How would he react? She couldn't imagine that part of the scene.

Indoors her grandmother was hovering uneasily.

'What was that about, Rose?' she said.

'It's just that house I lived in with Mum and Brendan and Joshua? There's been a report of a crime there. Years ago. Henry wanted to let me know. In case it upset me.'

'That's nice of him to think about you. It's got nothing to do with Katherine?'

'Oh no. Nothing at all.'

'He's a pleasant young man. Very well spoken. I liked him when I met him last autumn. If only more police constables were like that.'

Anna went into the kitchen and Rose drifted upstairs. Back in her room she slipped off her mother's silk blouse and placed it on the hanger. She put her shirt on and thought about Brewster Road. The thought of a girl's body under the soil, under the rocks and grass, made her shiver.

But this murder had nothing to do with her or Joshua. Neither did it have anything to do with her mother or Joshua's father, Brendan.

No, the murders *they* were involved in were quite different.

TWO

Rose spent time in the afternoon helping Anna sort out her mother's old bedroom. Anna called it the Blue Room and it hadn't been used since her mother quarrelled with Anna and left her house over twenty years before. As well as her mother's childhood and teenage things there were her belongings from the house at Brewster Road. Anna had kept these in case Rose wanted them. Rose added them to the things that were already in her room. While she was doing it she thought about Joshua and wondered how he had reacted to Henry's news. After a while she opened her laptop and glanced at her email hoping that Joshua had tried to contact her but it simply said: *No New Messages*.

She picked up her packet of chewing gum and took a stick out. She chewed as she looked up Google and typed in the words *Brewster Road* and *Body*. Several articles came up. Some of the headlines startled her.

Body of Missing Teenager Found in Back Garden of Police House; Mystery House Gives Up New Victim; Vanishing

Police Officers New Twist; Girl's Body Found in Garden of Missing Police Officers.

She sat stiffly, her eyes flicking back and forth across the print. She found herself holding her breath. The press were linking the two things: the body in the garden and their parents' disappearance. Should she be surprised? A dead teenager buried in August and months later, the two adults who lived in that very same house vanished.

This was why Henry had been so concerned. Why he had taken the time to come and see her. It wasn't only the press who had linked these two things but the police as well. The only reason it hadn't occurred to her was because she *knew* what happened to their parents five years ago and it had nothing to do with a body under the garden. From the police's point of view their parents' disappearance was unsolved but they were presumed dead. To them it was a 'cold case'. Rose almost smiled. Her mother and Brendan had been serving police officers themselves, working on a unit that dealt with cold cases. Now *they* were a cold case that would be opened up again, linked to some dead teenager buried under the garden of the Brewster Road house.

Rose clicked and opened up one of the articles.

The body of a girl has been found buried in the back garden of a terraced house in Brewster Road, Bethnal Green. Police sources suggest that the body was placed there sometime in the summer of 2007. The house was recently sold. Neighbours say they are shocked and saddened by the news. Police sources confirm that the house was once lived in by two serving police officers, Katherine Smith and Brendan Johnson. These officers disappeared in 2007. Police have not yet released the identity of the dead girl and are making no comment on the link between these two cases.

She closed her laptop down. She could hear Anna walking up and down the landing, busying herself in the Blue Room. How long before she noticed some of this press coverage?

The sound of her ringtone interrupted her thoughts.

She picked up her mobile and saw the word *Josh* on the screen. Her chest tightened.

'Hi,' she said.

'I've just been speaking to a policeman who you know.'

She was thrown by his abruptness. He didn't say, *Hi,* or *Hello, Rose,* or *Rosie.* She didn't know how to answer.

'Are you there?'

'Yes.'

'He said he'd been to see you.'

'Yes, it's Henry. I know him from last autumn.'

'How come you didn't let me know?'

'He said he was going straight to see you . . .'

'Maybe we should meet up. That's if you want to.'

His voice was guarded, unfriendly. It made her feel bad.

'Sure,' she said. 'Where?'

She could have asked him round to the house. She could have put the radiator on in her studio and then got some food for both of them. She had some new CDs she could have played but his tone of voice made her feel that he wouldn't be happy with that.

'The Dark Brew?' he said, mentioning a cafe that they had used in the past.

'Fine. When?'

'Can you make it this evening, about six?'

'OK.'

The call ended. Rose looked at the phone with consternation. It seemed impossible that she and Joshua should be distant and cool with each other. She sat back in her chair, pushing her laptop away and thought gloomily about the last time she'd seen Joshua and the row they'd had.

She'd been to the flat a lot since their friend Skeggsie had been killed. This time it was full of cardboard boxes. His things had been packed away and were ready to be shipped back to Newcastle where his father lived. Rose edged by the boxes and followed Joshua to his study. Before, when Skeggsie had been there she'd felt awkward, out of place, even unwelcome sometimes. Now she was just plain upset by his absence.

In the study her attention was taken by a huge Ordnance Survey map of East Essex that Joshua had placed on the wall behind his computers. Three towns were pinpointed with large labels beside them; Wickby, Southwood and Hensham. Between the three towns Joshua had fixed red tape with drawing pins. It made a red triangle. From somewhere within that triangle their parents had sent them a text message. It had happened just before the New Year and it was the only evidence they had of their recent whereabouts.

The previous two weekends she and Joshua had driven out to two of the towns and wandered aimlessly around all day long. Joshua hadn't seen it like that, though. From his point of view they had been *familiarising* themselves with the *territory*. It was as if they were hunters looking for prey. They'd walked up and down every street and small turning. Then they'd got in the car and driven around the country lanes and paused at gated properties while Rose marked them on one of several large scale maps that Joshua had brought along with them. The days had been long and Rose had developed a headache from the stop-starting of the car, her shoulders tightening with the tension of Joshua's demands: *Have you marked that one down? Write the name. Write the road, there, it's on the map further along. Make sure you spell it right.* By the time they were on their way home Rose's neck was aching.

Now Rose was staring at Joshua's back as he typed on to a spreadsheet.

'I'll pick you up at about eight on Saturday,' he said, without turning round. 'We need to make an early start because Wickby is the biggest of the three towns and so there's more ground to cover.'

There was quiet. Rose took a deep breath.

'I'm not coming on Saturday,' she said.

He stopped typing and let the chair swivel round so that he was facing her.

'You got something on at college? We could go on Sunday?'

'I'm not coming at all. I think it's a waste of time.'

'What?'

Joshua blew through his teeth.

'It's like looking for a needle in a haystack,' she went on. 'The area is too big. There are too many properties. We could go up to each town every weekend for a year and still not find them.'

'They're small towns, Rosie, not like London. When we've mapped it out then we'll start going round, into shops, showing our pictures of them.'

Rose looked back to the wall and saw, at the bottom left-hand corner of the map, two computer-generated images of her mother and Brendan. They were taken from old photographs that they had. They had been enhanced; Brendan had less hair and his face was thinner; her mother had heavy-framed glasses on that made her look stern and cold.

'Someone will recognise them.'

'They don't want to be found, Josh. We both know that. In any case I don't know if I want to find them any more.'

'Because of the murders?'

'What else?'

Joshua stood up. 'That's what makes it so important to find them. To stop them . . .'

'If this is what they've chosen to do why is it up to us to stop them? I've had enough. I've got no energy left. I want to move on with my life.'

Joshua huffed. He spoke under his breath. Rose didn't quite catch the words.

'What?' she said, becoming angry. 'WHAT?'

'You've never really wanted to look for them. You've always had to be dragged along. Every single thing we've achieved over the last few months has been in spite of you not because of you.'

'That's not true.'

'It is. You've always been half-hearted.'

'Only because I thought we'd get hurt. I didn't want to see me *or* you get hurt any more!'

He mumbled again, his hand in front of his mouth. Rose couldn't make out what he was saying. It made her angrier.

'What?' she said, her voice raised. 'WHAT are you saying? Spit it out!'

'You got over it, didn't you? Before we met, last September, you'd done your grieving and you were moving on.'

'No!'

'You'd forgotten about them.'

'No!' she said.

It wasn't true. She'd never forgotten. How could she? It was as if she'd lost a part of herself.

'If it hadn't been for me . . . and Skeggsie . . . we wouldn't have found anything out.'

'If it hadn't been for this, all this,' Rose said, pointing at the maps and photographs, 'Skeggsie would still be alive!'

Joshua flinched. He sat down.

Rose was rigid, her shoulders straight as a rod.

'Don't you think I know that?' he said.

She softened. 'I didn't mean it in the way that it sounded,' she said, her voice gentle.

Joshua leant forward, his elbows on the desk, and stared at the keyboard. Rose faltered. She looked around the room. Her eye settled on a giant glass bottle that was in the corner, the type that was usually used for plants. This one was three-quarters full with asthma inhalers: orange, purple and blue. It was something Skeggsie had done. Josh had called it an *installation*. It was not packed up waiting to go back to Newcastle. The sight of it touched her and made her feel worse about what she'd said.

'I know how close you and Skeggs were.'

A part of her wished she could walk out, leave the whole mess behind. Instead she went across and put her hands on his shoulders. He was hot and dishevelled. His hair looked greasy and needed a trim. His nails were bitten down. She stood very still thinking of Skeggsie, whose absence was present in every room of the flat, in every meeting they had, in every drive that they went on.

'Skeggsie would want me to go on,' Joshua said, his voice hoarse.

'I know.'

He was right. Skeggsie wouldn't have given up.

Then she noticed a picture up on the far corner of Joshua's noticeboard. It was a photograph of ex-Chief Inspector James Munroe. She felt herself harden at the sight of him; the man they knew was responsible for Skeggsie's death. It was a three-quarter view of Munroe walking along the street, other people in the background. He had on a suit and over the top the long dark Crombie overcoat coat he wore. He was carrying a briefcase and looked like a businessman on his way to an important meeting. She stared at it for a moment, her feelings stirred by his blank expression, his smart clothes and purposeful gait.

Skeggsie's life was over but James Munroe's was continuing.

'Where did you get that?'

'Munroe? I took it a week or so ago. I waited outside his offices in Chelsea. I was in a bus shelter and I was able to get a good view of him.'

Rose let out a sigh. This *mission* was filling up every waking moment of Joshua's life. If he had his way it would consume hers too.

'Then I followed him. He's got this flat in Docklands.'

'You *followed* him? Why?'

'I'm collecting information about him. I intend to find out everything I can about the guy. Then when the time comes . . .'

'You know what Munroe said. He told us to keep out of it. He said that Mum and Brendan would finish what they were doing and in time we would all be back together again. Why don't we just wait?'

'You think I would take any notice of what he says? He killed my friend. He lied to us about Dad and Kathy's death. He can't be trusted!'

'He could be dangerous.'

'You know what, Rose. You drop it if you want. I'll go on for as long as it takes. I have to prove that Skeggsie didn't die for nothing.'

Joshua left the sentence in the air. Rose was frustrated. Any argument she might make would just sound as if she didn't care about Skeggsie.

'I have to go home now,' she said.

Joshua turned away from her. She left him sitting at

the computer and went downstairs and out of the flat. As she closed the street door she stood for a moment listening for the sound of the bolts shooting across. It was something that Skeggsie had done when she'd first known him. He kept the door locked at all times. He'd been fearful of his own shadow. He'd changed, though, over the months, becoming more confident, ready to stand up for himself.

But on Christmas Eve he'd stood up to the wrong person.

She walked sadly away from the flat along Camden High Street.

When she got home she wrote an email to Joshua telling him that she needed some time on her own.

She stared at her laptop, flat and closed on her bed. For two weeks they hadn't been in touch. In the past they'd loved spending time together. Now it took a dead girl buried in their garden to make them get in contact with each other.

At just after five thirty Rose picked up her bag and her coat and made her way downstairs.

'Bye,' she called and heard Anna reply from the kitchen.

She left the house, feeling uneasy. What would Joshua say about this new development? As she walked along she pictured the garden at Brewster Road. There was a patio that they used to sit on. It had yellow paving stones and a small wall that divided it off from an area of scrubby grass that Brendan tried to cut occasionally. Sometimes Joshua set up goalposts there and he and Brendan would take turns trying to score. Beyond that there were dense shrubs and bushes. A path disappeared into the undergrowth and ended at a back gate.

'Excuse me.'

A voice interrupted her thoughts and she felt a hand on her arm. She stopped and looked round. A man in jeans and a parka jacket stood there. He took his hand off her arm and in his other hand he was holding something out to her. A card.

'My name is Jimmy Dobbs and I'm a reporter for a Sunday newspaper.'

She stared at him. He proffered the card.

'I wondered if you had any comments to make on the body that was found in the garden of the house you lived in with your mother and her partner, Brendan Johnson?'

Rose frowned. She turned abruptly and walked away. She heard him follow her.

'My newspaper is very respectable. If you speak to me first the tabloids won't come near you.'

She felt his hand on her shoulder. She spun round.

'Don't touch me!' she said.

'Just take my card and I'll go away.'

She stared at him. He had a streak of grey hair at the front and was wearing a single earphone as though he was taking instructions from someone else, like a TV news-reader. She snatched the card from him and walked off. When she got to the corner of the High Street she turned round and saw that he had gone.

She chucked the card into the first bin that she passed.

THREE

Joshua was already at a table when she arrived at the Dark Brew. He was drinking from a mug and nodded when he saw her. Even though the tiny cafe was almost empty he had his coat thrown over the chair opposite, saving it for her. She went straight to the counter and bought a peppermint tea. Sitting down, she started speaking quickly to get over the awkwardness.

'I've been on the web,' she said. 'The papers are linking this girl's body to Mum and Brendan.'

'I know,' he said. 'I actually read about it this morning before the policeman came.'

'Really? How come you didn't call me?'

'I didn't think you wanted to be called.'

'No, but with this development . . .'

'That's the only reason you're here?'

'Yes. No . . .'

She focused on his hair then. He'd had it cut very short, cropped almost, so that he looked like a soldier. He was wearing a scruffy maroon V-neck jumper that she hadn't seen before. The cuffs were turned back as if it was for someone bigger than him.

'The policeman asked me if I knew the dead girl,' he said, running his finger round the rim of his cup.

'He told you who it was?'

'The police think it might be Daisy Lincoln. She lived down the street from us.'

Daisy Lincoln. Rose knew the name and had a vague picture in her head of a teenage girl with long black hair walking down the street arm in arm with Sandy, Rose and Joshua's old babysitter.

'Daisy and her family moved to Chingford in the July.'

'That's awful. I sort of remember her . . .'

'I knew her a bit. She worked in a newsagent's on the High Street and I used to chat to her. I had a bit of a crush on her. I was fourteen, she was eighteen. Nothing was ever going to happen but I thought about her a bit and I used to hang round the shop where she worked. Then when her family moved she stopped working there. Later, I heard through the grapevine that she wasn't living at home any more. I guess I forgot about her. The policeman asked me if I was *involved* with her. I just laughed in his face.'

Rose pictured Henry sitting across the table from Joshua in the narrow kitchen of the flat. No doubt Henry had said something like 'Point taken!' when Joshua laughed.

27

'They can't seriously be linking this to Mum and Brendan.'

Joshua shook his head.

'I know they probably don't have the information that the Cold Case team have but even so this happened in August. They disappeared in November.'

Joshua shrugged.

'And,' she continued, 'this will probably be . . . well, a sex crime maybe . . . And Mum and Brendan were . . .'

'You mean,' Joshua said, lowering his voice, 'they didn't murder eighteen-year-old girls? Just gangsters and child killers?'

Rose stiffened. She looked round, aware of the young man behind the counter staring at them. Had he heard what Joshua just said? His hair was gelled so that it stood bolt upright and he had a piercing in his lip. It made him look slightly sinister. Joshua was drinking his coffee, unperturbed. His hair was bristly; it looked sharp as if it might hurt her if she touched it. Inside she was all screwed up. There was so much she wanted to say to him and yet broaching it was like opening a door she did not want to go through.

'How've you been?'

'Good.'

'Have you . . . Did you go to Wickby?'

He nodded.

'How did you manage? On your own?'

'I wasn't on my own. You remember that girl, Clara? From uni? She came with me.'

Rose was instantly stung. She remembered Clara. The one time she'd seen her she'd been wearing a duffle coat and her long blonde hair had been loose over her shoulders. She had been looking adoringly at Joshua and it had plunged Rose into a fog of jealousy.

'You didn't tell her anything about Mum and Brendan and the notebooks?'

He shook his head firmly. 'I told her I was researching something about population distribution in rural areas and that I was using that village as an exemplar.'

Rose pictured them driving through country lanes, Clara with the maps on her lap, highlighting properties along the way, changing pens and writing down streets and lanes and approximate locations. Maybe Clara was all buzzed up about helping her boyfriend with his college course.

'Did you find anything?'

'I thought you didn't want to know. I thought you were moving on in your life.'

Moving on in your life. He said it with sarcasm as if she was doing something ridiculous.

'Of course I would want to know – it's just that I don't think you'll find anything.'

'Why ask then?'

'Why are you being so vile to me?' she whispered. 'All I did was back off. I wanted a break. After what

I've . . . we've been through over these last months anyone would need a break.'

'Then the trail goes cold.'

'You're talking like a *hunter*!'

Rose remembered thinking that very thing earlier.

'In a way I am. I'm going to find them. Everything I've done over the last few months has made me more determined, not less.'

Rose drank her tea, using the long spoon to move the peppermint leaves around the glass. Why were they fighting? She had missed him. She had regretted her email saying that she wanted to *back off*. Why was she keeping it up now?

'Are there any bridges in Wickby?' she eventually said.

He looked up quickly and his face broke into a smile.

'Actually there is one. Constructed in 1829 and built of coursed squared granite. It has these two segmental arches which are brick. Very impressive. It's only wide enough for one car to cross at a time. Perfect for 1829. A little outdated now but very pretty.'

Bridges. It was the one firm thing she knew about his engineering degree. He planned to design them. She could always cheer him up by talking about them.

'So you and Clara are *together*?'

'We're friends. A bit like you and me are friends.'

Rose stared at him. What did he mean? The friendship they built up in the months after he came to London? Or did he mean the physical stuff; the hugs and the touching and the hand holding and the kisses. Or the nights, after Skeggsie was murdered, when they slept tightly together in the same bed? She wanted to ask him but couldn't.

'I'm sorry about the email . . .'

'It's all right. You needed some time. I understand. How are things at college?'

'Good. My grades are up and I'm looking at the prospectus for Cambridge.'

'You won't have any trouble. And Cambridge is close to London so I'll still see you a lot. That's if you want.'

'I do. I really do.'

Her hand moved across the table. Her fingers were splayed out on the wood centimetres from Joshua's. He moved his hand so that their nails touched.

'I sent Skeggsie's stuff back to his dad,' he said.

'Oh.'

It seemed like the end of something. Another line drawn under the past. The belongings of Joshua's closest friend in boxes. Would his father actually unpack them? Or just leave them to moulder and collect dust?

It seemed every bit of Skeggsie was now in Newcastle.

'I'd like to go back to Brewster Road,' Rose said.

'Why?'

'I'd like to look at the house . . .'

'The police will have it taped off.'

'My policeman friend, Henry, might be able to arrange it. He told me that you and I should talk about those days. Try and jog our memories. Going back to the house might do that.'

'You want to see the grave?'

'No! Yes . . . Maybe. If we went back, we might remember some things about that summer before they went missing.'

'What difference does that make? We know what happened that summer.'

'I mean things that led up to it. Maybe we might even remember some more about Daisy Lincoln. I don't know. I'd go on my own but I think it would be better if we went there together.'

Joshua looked thoughtful.

'I'll make a deal with you. I'll come to Brewster Road if you'll come to Wickby with me next Sunday, tomorrow week.'

Rose shook her head.

'Hear me out. There's an antiques and collectables fair in the market square. It's apparently quite an event. People come from miles around. Kathy loved that sort of thing.'

She found herself looking straight at him. His eyes were soft and dark like they'd always been. Just because his haircut was brutal it didn't mean he had changed.

'She might be there, Rose,' he said softly. 'We might see her. And Dad maybe.'

'After the things they've done? You still want to see them?'

'None of it is clear-cut. They're still our parents.'

She didn't speak but had an image her of mother, Kathy, walking along a row of stalls her hand drifting from one item to the next; an art deco brooch, a Victorian shawl, a piece of Clarice Cliff pottery. The stallholders would look up hopefully as she passed. She only bought inexpensive things, though – a silver ring or a cup and saucer or a bag.

'Come on, Rosie. We're a team, you and me.'

She nodded. When she looked round the man behind the counter was singing quietly, cutting up slices of cake from a large slab. Now he just looked happy, the piercing on his mouth simply decorative. When she turned back to Joshua her eyes focused on the tatty old jumper he was wearing. She remembered that it was his dad's. He used to sleep with it, he'd told her once. Now he was wearing it.

'You'll come to Brewster Road first?' she said.

Joshua nodded and she gave a tiny smile.

FOUR

When Rose got back to Anna's she could hear voices from the drawing room. She was about to make her way upstairs when the door opened and Anna stood there smiling at her.

'Rose, we have a visitor. Chief Inspector Munroe has called by.'

Rose walked towards the drawing room. Sitting on the sofa was James Munroe. She stared at him, hardly able to believe her eyes. His face looked tanned. She had a flash of memory of the first time she'd seen him over five years before. He'd been in full police uniform then and looked as though he'd just come back from a foreign holiday, his skin bronzed. Now he was in plain clothes but still looked tanned as if he'd recently been lying on a sun lounger somewhere hot.

'Hello, Rose. And please, Mrs Christie, I'm not in the *police* any more.'

'So sorry! *Mr Munroe* has been telling me about the

awful business in East London where Katherine used to live with you. I had no idea . . .'

'Why is Mr Munroe telling you this if he's no longer in the police?' Rose said sharply.

'Rose!' Anna said.

'No, Rose is quite right to ask. When I saw the story in the newspapers I rang an old colleague of mine. He knows some officers from Bethnal Green and he was able to give me the details of what they'd found. I knew, well, I felt sure, you would be concerned as soon as you saw it in the press. What with it being Kathy's old house. So I thought I'd call in.'

'That's really kind of you.'

'And Rose is here too,' he said, standing up. 'That's double the pleasure.'

He plucked a jacket off the back of a chair and walked towards her.

'But you don't have to go so soon? Surely not?' Anna said.

'I'm afraid so, Mrs Christie. I'm visiting some friends in the area, which is why I was able to drop by and see you.'

Rose kept her eye on him.

'Goodness, Rose, don't look so *unfriendly*,' Anna said, looking embarrassed.

'Not to worry, Mrs Christie. I'm sure Rose is just surprised to see me. Perhaps she'll walk me out to my car? We can have a chat along the way.'

'Sure,' Rose said, giving a wooden smile.

She walked ahead of Munroe out of the door, on to the garden path. She waited while her grandmother said goodbye to him and then turned towards the street. Munroe came alongside her.

'I had to park up a bit.'

'Why are you really here?' Rose said.

James Munroe was walking swiftly. He put his jacket on as he went along.

'You've got no right to come here, to my home.'

She was half running to keep up with him. He stopped at a parked car, fiddled in his pockets and pulled out a key.

'I came to reassure your grandmother about the unpleasant events in Brewster Road.'

'I don't believe you.'

He pointed his keys and the lights of the car flashed on and off.

'Of course I'm pleased to see you and it does give me an opportunity to reiterate some of the things I said after the disagreeable business in Newcastle. I wanted to make sure that you'd understood me clearly then.'

He was staring straight at her and she felt herself falter.

'How was your holiday?' she said.

'What?'

'Was it a winter break? The Canary Islands? North Africa?'

'It was Florida actually,' he said, leaning on the car, looking around the street, his eyes darting here and there. 'And it was very pleasant.'

He was so relaxed, so smooth.

'You're just a killer,' Rose said.

'No more so than your mother and her partner.'

'You're worse. You took our friend's life and Josh and I will never forget that.'

'No, no, no,' he said, grabbing Rose's hand and holding it tightly. 'That's exactly why I passed by today. Just to remind you of what I said in Newcastle. If you go to the police then I will make sure that certain parties know where your mother and Brendan Johnson are. They will not last long and I can assure you their death will be *particularly* ugly.'

Rose tried to pull her hand away but Munroe had it clamped, her fingers bent back from her palm.

'On the other hand you could just leave this. Get on with your own lives. Then one day, in the not too far away future, they will contact you. Believe me, Rose, this was always the plan.'

He let her hand go and she backed away from him.

'Goodbye, Rose,' he said and got into the car.

She turned to walk back to the house, hearing the car accelerating away from the kerb. She didn't look round. All the time she was gripping her hand where Munroe had hurt her.

When she got back inside Anna was watching the television. She sat on the arm of a chair. The report of the body found in East London was on the local news. It showed a photograph of Daisy Lincoln whose identity had been confirmed by dental records. No cause of death had as yet been found. The reporter, a woman whose hair kept blowing across her face, spoke to camera about the background of the case.

'What I can tell you,' she said, 'is that in 2007 this property was occupied by two serving police officers, Katherine Smith and Brendan Johnson. In November, just three months after Daisy Lincoln's disappearance, these officers went missing, leaving their children behind. Since 2007 nothing has been heard of them. The police are denying any link between these two cases.'

The screen was then filled with a large picture of Daisy Lincoln and underneath two small photos of her mother and Brendan.

'This is awful,' Anna said, looking pained. 'Mr Munroe said that Katherine and Brendan Johnson's death had had to be hushed up because of other cases they were working on. These police, involved in *this* business in East London, won't know any of this. Mr Munroe says they'll be told and then their names will disappear from the story.'

Rose didn't answer. It was best to let Anna believe Munroe. Anna had put the remote down and was now staring at the screen and gripping the gold chain that she always wore round her neck. An odd feeling was swirling round in Rose's chest. She felt a spurt of affection for this stiff woman who was her grandmother. It made her feel bad about not telling her the truth about Katherine, her own daughter. What would Anna say if she knew that Katherine was alive, living in hiding, spending her life on a personal mission to right the wrongs of society. What would Anna think of her daughter then?

It was better to let her think of her as dead.

'I'm going up to my room for a while,' Rose said and Anna nodded distractedly.

Rose walked upstairs agitated. She was already on edge but Munroe's appearance had further shaken her. She plucked out a stick of chewing gum from her pocket and put it on her tongue. Now, it seemed, was as good a time as any to work on her statement. She went to her study and opened the bottom drawer of her desk. At the back, in a file labelled *Solicitors*, she pulled out an envelope. On the outside, in her neatest writing, were the names *Myers and Goodwood* and an address in Finchley. It was the firm that her mother and Brendan had used for their affairs. Underneath the name was a paragraph that she had taken a long time composing. It was addressed to her grandmother. She closed her study door before sitting down on the armchair to read it over.

Dear Anna, if anything ever happens to me or Joshua or both of us please take this book to our solicitors. DON'T give it to the police or ANYONE else, just our solicitors. This is very important. Rose Smith.

Inside the envelope was a notebook that she had already written in. It was a deep red colour and had an art deco border. It was the size of a school exercise book and she must have been aware, when she was buying it, of how it differed from those *other* two notebooks that they had once had in their possession. She turned the pages. She'd filled up about six and she still had a lot to write. She opened the first page and read her message.

The following is a statement made by me, Rose Smith, February 2013. It was written on various dates and it outlines the things that Joshua Johnson, Darren Skeggs (deceased) and I have found out about the disappearance of our parents in November 2007. I write this in case anything happens to me or Joshua. I write it in this form, on paper, because computers and the internet are not safe. Most of what I write is from memory. Any evidence we had is gone.

Underneath she had signed it in an official-looking way. Reading it over made her feel a little silly as though she was play-acting. But what she'd stated was true. All of the communications they'd had via the internet, including her personal blog, Morpho, had had to be stopped. This, pen and paper, hidden away, was the only thing she could use to detail what had taken place.

In case anything happened to them.

It was something she was doing alone. Joshua had no part in it.

She couldn't help but read over the things she'd written on the first page.

On 4 Nov 2007 Kathy Smith and Brendan Johnson went out for a meal at the Tuscan Moon restaurant in Islington. They never returned to us. We found out what happened to them from a waitress who contacted us via the web. They left their car parked in a side street and took a taxi to a B and B in Twickenham. The next morning they went to Heathrow and took a flight to Warsaw. We do not know where they went after that.

We think that they may have come back to England and spent some time in a cottage at Stiffkey in North Norfolk.

The next sighting of them was in a photograph on Cromer Beach. This photograph was taken in June 2012.

Our most recent sighting of them was in a Skype

recording. This recording was made in December 2012.

On 29 December they sent us a text from a place in Essex. Somewhere in the area between the following three villages: Wickby, Southwood and Hensham.

Up to that time we know that they were alive.

The word *alive* gave her a jolt. How important that had been when she and Joshua first found out that they were not dead. They had Frank Richards to thank for that. Rose flicked to the end of the pages she had written and found the section where she had described the meeting with Frank Richards. She'd given it a heading – *The Notebooks.*

Frank Richards was a friend of Brendan Johnson's, a policeman who had been dismissed from the service. Joshua knew him by sight but I did not. In October 2012 we found him in a flat in Twickenham. He told us that my mother and Brendan were alive and he also said that my mother had asked him to look after me while she was away. He claimed he had done this over the five years that I'd lived with my grandmother, keeping an eye on what I was doing, checking that I wasn't being followed. When we found him he was packing to leave England. He had a pile of notebooks and Joshua stole two of them. When we looked at them we found the strangest thing. Each had a photograph of someone and then the rest of the book was full of coded hand-writing. These notebooks were ordinary exercise books and were both in the same handwriting. We believe the code was taken from an old hardback book called The Butterfly Project. *We had a copy of this for a while but were unable to decode the books, just scraps of pages here and there. We think that each of these two notebooks outlined the killing of a person. We believe, from things we heard afterwards, that one of the notebooks belonged to a series (the remainder held by Frank Richards) which docu-mented the killing of criminals.*

Rose had stopped writing there because she hadn't been able to find the words to go on. There was more to tell but she couldn't really state the blunt awful truth about what her mother and Brendan had become without explaining the rest. The whole story of The Butterfly Murder had to be told. Other people involved had to be described. The story of Viktor Baranski and his son, Lev. There was much more to say.

She looked down at the notebook in her hand. She could have written her statement on sheets of paper but somehow she had decided that a notebook was the right thing to have. In the shop it had taken her a while to make up her mind. There had been other colours but she had chosen red. The colour of blood. Was she being too dramatic? She closed it, flattening it with the palm of her hand. She had no stomach to write anything in it now. She slipped it into the envelope and then into the file and placed it back in the drawer.

Later she went to bed.

She was restless, turning her bedside light on and off, reading for a while, then listening to the radio. In the end she stopped trying to go to sleep. She heard Anna's footsteps on the stairs and then the sound of her door opening and shutting. There was no knock on Rose's door, no call of *Goodnight!* – just Anna, going about her day-to-day business as if she was living alone. Rose was used to it now but in the early days when she'd first been sent to live there after her mother and Brendan had gone missing it had been hard.

How long ago it seemed. Five years and four months.

She was twelve years old and felt wounded by the disappearance of her mother as if actual blood had been drawn from her. She spent a long time on her own in the rooms that Anna had set aside. Her frosty grandmother left her to her own devices and so she watched television and read and stared out of her bedroom window into the smart back garden. Each week that passed took her further from her old life. Joshua was in Newcastle, living with his uncle. There were some phone calls between them but they were always awkward. The easy intimacy they'd shared in the house on Brewster Road had disappeared and after she had asked him how school was she couldn't think of anything else to say.

Those first weeks it seemed as though *she* was the one who had vanished. It was as if she'd been out walking and suddenly spirited away into this other life. Now she was in a strange room, in a large house where the sound of her own footsteps echoed up and down the stairs and along the hallways. She was living with her grandmother, Anna, a woman who hardly ever spoke to her, whose eyes seemed to follow her round the room. She had a sense sometimes that her old life in Brewster Road was going on without her. That all the stuff about her mother and Brendan going missing had been some bad dream. It was she who had been taken, not them.

Now Rose sat up in bed. It was 1.03 a.m. She absolutely couldn't sleep. She put her dressing gown on and went through her study and into the hallway. She intended to go downstairs and make a hot drink but was distracted by a glow further along the corridor. It was coming from the Blue Room. The door was slightly open and there was light spilling out. She walked quietly towards it and heard an odd sound. She waited outside. It was Anna. She was sniffing and blowing her nose. And then she recognised the sound. Her grandmother was crying.

Rose stepped inside.

Anna was holding a child's nightdress. It was pink with

drawings of rabbits all over it. It looked old-fashioned and had lace around the neck and sleeves; real lace that someone had crocheted. Anna looked up.

'Are you all right?' Rose said, walking across.

On the ground, in front of her grandmother, was an open wooden chest. Inside it were toys and clothes and books.

'Katherine's childhood things,' Anna said. 'I collected them together. One day I thought I might show them to her, give them to her. But she left when she was eighteen and I never saw her again . . .'

Anna stopped and hugged the nightdress fiercely.

'I never got the chance to tell her . . . anything.'

Rose put her hand out and laid it on Anna's shoulder.

'You could give them to me,' she said.

Anna turned and stared at Rose. In an instant she seemed to pull herself together. 'You're a sweet girl, Rose. I haven't always been able to say how nice it has been . . .' She stood up, wiping her face with a hanky. 'I'm so sorry, did I wake you?'

Rose shook her head. 'I thought I might make a hot drink. Do you fancy a coffee?'

'That would be good. A latte, I think.'

Rose let Anna walk out of the room first. Then she glanced back at the wooden box, its contents unpacked, the nightie left lying over the side. Her mother's childhood possessions, left behind, just like all the stuff at Brewster Road.

FIVE

Henry Thompson made the arrangements for Rose and Joshua to go to the house in Brewster Road. Joshua drove there in the Mini and parked the car at the other end of the road away from the crime scene tape and the police cars and vans.

They sat for a few minutes while Rose told Joshua about Munroe's visit to her grandmother's. It had been four days since it happened and she'd considered telling him by text or email but both seemed too inflammatory. She was afraid that he might go back to Munroe's offices in Chelsea and have a row with him. So she waited to tell him in person. His eyes closed with annoyance as she described the things that Munroe had said to her. She left out the part where he'd hurt her hand. This, she thought, might enrage Joshua. She wanted as little to do with Munroe as possible.

'Just more proof of his guilt,' Joshua said. 'He's worried about what we might do. He's keeping his eye on us. One day he'll trip up and then we'll have him.'

Rose didn't answer. It was fantasy. Munroe had them where he wanted them. There was nothing they could do to him.

They got out of the car and headed towards the crowds. They walked along, weaving in and out of people who seemed to be simply milling round, pointing and looking in the direction of the house. They went up to a uniformed officer at the edge of an area that was cordoned off.

'Excuse me, we are due to meet Inspector Wendy Clarke. She made an arrangement with us for ten o'clock,' Rose said.

Before the officer could speak a woman who was nearby turned round and marched towards them. She was small, wearing dark trousers and a Puffa jacket. She had jaw-length ginger hair. She smiled and thrust out her hand to Rose.

'Rose Smith and Joshua Johnson?'

She shook their hands warmly, as though she was an old friend.

'Hi,' Rose said.

'I'm Wendy Clarke. Thank you so much for coming. If you don't mind waiting for a few moments while I make arrangements for you to go into the house . . .'

'Sure,' Rose said.

Wendy Clarke walked off in the direction of 49 Brewster Road. Rose watched her go and shifted her position to see if she could glimpse around the cars and people to the front of her old house. She could not. In any case the road looked completely different because of the commotion. It didn't look at all like the place she remembered living in. She was disappointed. She'd expected the trip to be an emotional one. She'd actually looked forward to seeing the houses and gardens and feeling the familiarity of her childhood surroundings. But standing here just felt strange as if it were any old place.

Joshua was quiet. Rose wondered if he was worrying about James Munroe. In daylight his hair was shorter than she'd thought, his skull showing through, his ears looking bare and cold. He was wearing a corduroy jacket that was lined with fake fur. He'd bought it in a charity shop in Camden. It replaced an overcoat he'd bought in the market just before Christmas. He'd got rid of it because it had been stained with Skeggsie's blood.

'Right.' Wendy Clarke was standing next to them again. 'I'll take you into the house. The family who live there now are in hotel accommodation for the rest of this week but I would ask you to respect their home and their privacy. Follow me.'

Joshua went first and Rose followed. They made their way through officers and people in plain clothes. When they got to the front of the house Rose felt a shock of recognition. Beside the front door was the metal number plate that her mum had found at a car boot sale. *What's the chance of that?* she'd heard her say. *A number plate for sale and it's the number of our house! Karma. I have to buy it!*

'This way,' Wendy Clarke said.

They followed her into the hallway. Rose noticed immediately that it had been carpeted and the walls painted a dark colour. The place looked considerably smaller or maybe she'd just got bigger. They walked past the front room door into the kitchen-diner. This room had also undergone extensive change. Where it had been wood everywhere it was now a white shiny kitchen with a black tiled floor. Rose felt like a stranger.

'We'll go out into the garden in a moment. We won't be going down to the crime scene but you'll glimpse it from a distance. I should say one or two things to you before we go. Firstly,' Wendy Clarke rubbed her eyelids with the tips of her fingers, 'I'm aware of your history and the tragedy of your parents' disappearance. I'm also aware that the press have tried to link the two cases. While we're not ruling anything out the information we have been given by the team who originally investigated your mother and your father's disappearance seems to suggest that there is no link.'

Rose nodded.

'The second thing I wanted to say was this; you two lived in this house when Daisy was buried here. You may have been out or away on holiday but still, when you came back, this young girl was in her grave not more than thirty metres away from you. If that makes you feel awful, then I'm sorry but the truth is it's not your feelings I'm interested in. I want to find out who did this to Daisy. I will find out and I'm hoping you will help me. I want to know anything you remember about that summer, no matter how small it is. I don't expect you to tell me anything today, just think on it.'

Wendy Clarke opened the back door. The first thing that Rose saw was a tent that had been erected down the back of the garden. It was white and went from fence to fence. It looked like a marquee; as if there were preparations for a party going on.

The three of them walked out on to the yellow paving stones, still there, a little brighter as if they'd been cleaned up. There was a smart garden table and chairs as well as a patio heater, standing like a standard lamp above it all. The garden itself had been worked on, the lawn flat and even, the shrubs neat, the earth around them dark and soft.

'The owners planned to build an outbuilding at the rear of the garden, a kind of office, I think. The builders were digging foundations when they found Daisy. She was well hidden. It was a properly dug grave, not something someone could just stumble on. Plus there was an old rockery nearby and a lot of the stones had been used to cover up the space.'

Rose frowned. She had no memory of a rock garden. She rarely went down to the overgrown end of the garden.

She hadn't liked the buzzing insects and the foliage and the grass was always too long and seemed damp and mulchy. She preferred to stay up on the patio.

'Did you ever use the door at the end of the garden?'

Rose shook her head.

'Not often,' Joshua said. 'It did open but it was stiff and anyhow we hardly ever used that part of the garden. Dad hated gardening. He liked barbecues but that was as far as it went with gardens. I went out of it a few times, on my bike. There's an alley there that runs down the back of the houses.'

'Do you think someone brought the body in that way?' Rose said.

'It's too soon to tell,' Wendy Clarke said.

The detective looked as if she was going to go off but then she placed her bag on the table and took a small tin out of it. Taking the lid off she picked out a roll-up. Rose could see several other home-made cigarettes there. Wendy lit it with a lighter. She inhaled.

'So, either of you two remember Daisy?'

'I saw her around a bit. She worked in a newsagent's on the High Street. She was mates with our old babysitter, Sandy Nicholls. She lived too far along to be a neighbour, you know, someone you see going in and out of their house,' Joshua said.

Wendy Clarke nodded. She held the cigarette tightly with her thumb and forefinger. It looked fragile – as if it might crumble at any moment.

'And you, Rose?'

'I saw her a few times. I've got a vague memory of her with Sandy out on the street but I never spoke to her. I was eleven. She wasn't someone who moved in my orbit.'

'*Orbit*,' Wendy repeated, nodding her head.

She blew out smoke and used the fingers of her other hand to pinch the end of the roll-up, putting it out. She replaced it in the tin as though she was saving it for later.

'OK, here's what I'm going to do. I'm going to let you two sit here for a short while. You absolutely mustn't come any closer because this is a crime scene. You shouldn't really be here, in this garden, at all. Your parents are gone, though, and you're the only two witnesses I have left so I'm pretty desperate. I'll be over there and I'll take you back out in a few minutes. That OK with you? Oh, here's my card, by the way. In case you need to get in touch with me.'

She gave one to each of them. On it was her name, email and a mobile number. Then she put the tin into her bag and walked off down the garden. She shouted out 'Tony!' and pulled back a section of the tent and slipped inside.

They sat down at the table, next to the patio heater. It felt strange to be there. It was not at all familiar and yet there was no doubt they had lived there; she had walked back and forth across that patio day in, day out; Joshua had fixed his bike there, turning it upside down, taking bits off and putting them back on.

'What do you remember about that summer?' Joshua said.

'It was my last summer before Big School. Mum and I shopped a lot for my uniform.'

She was reminded, fleetingly, of the denim cut-offs, edged with sequins, that she had lived in that summer; she had loved them and had hardly ever worn anything else.

'I remember you were supposed to look after me when Mum and Brendan were both at work.'

'I did look after you!'

Those mornings or afternoons when Joshua was in charge of her brought a sudden smile to her face. Joshua was always asking if she wanted anything to eat, as if she might go hungry during the time they were together. He allowed her to play games on his computer and sometimes they would watch *Star Wars* movies. One afternoon they'd made strawberry ice cream with her mum's ice cream maker that had never been out of its box. Those days seemed full of sunshine, waiting for her mum to come home from work and Brendan to walk through the door, see her in the living room, and say, *Hi, Petal!*

'And then I used to play with a couple of girls from my primary school. They lived in the next street and I was allowed to walk round there on my own. That was when Mum bought me my first mobile. It was silver and opened up like an old-fashioned powder compact. And I stayed overnight with them a few times.'

There was a raised voice. It came from inside the tent at the bottom of the garden and it made her feel instantly guilty. Thirty metres away from where they were sitting reminiscing there was a hole in the ground where a girl had been dumped. *Grave* was too nice a word for it. Rose stared at the tent, still and calm on the outside and yet inside were police and forensic officers searching painstakingly to find a strand of hair or a spot of blood that would have the killer's name on it.

'That mobile phone,' Joshua said. 'You never remembered to charge it.'

'Do you remember anything about that summer?'

'Apart from having a massive crush on Daisy Lincoln?'

'I noticed you didn't mention that to the detective.'

'Too embarrassing. In any case I had crushes on lots of girls that summer. I was fourteen and just finding out that there were other things in life than fixing bikes and playing computer games.'

'I don't remember any of this.'

'I wasn't going to tell you!'

Wendy Clarke had come out of the tent, her mobile ringing. She turned her back on them as she answered it. A conversation followed and Rose tried not to listen.

'I do remember Dad being away a few times. I mean, this isn't the first time I've thought about that summer. In my head it's all lumped in with Before, you know, *Before* they went missing. And the reason I remember him being away is that I was allowed to stay at Jon Kerrigan's house. He was my best friend until I went and lived in Newcastle. Anyway, I spent quite a few nights at his house. Dad went on courses, I think, and Dad and Kathy went away on a short holiday. I remember that.'

'Yes, I remember Mum and Brendan being away. They brought presents back.'

Wendy Clarke had finished her phone call and was walking up the garden towards them.

'I have to go now,' she said. 'I'll see you out. Don't forget my number's on the card I gave you.'

They stood up and followed Wendy Clarke back through the carpeted house, past the unfamiliar prints and wall decorations, past the hallstand that held a host of different coats. Then they were out on the street on the other side of the cordon and the police officer was walking away towards a car.

They made their way down the street. The number of people who had been hanging round had dwindled. Rose stepped aside to avoid bumping into a young woman with a pushchair. She walked on.

'Sandy?' Joshua said.

Rose looked round and saw that Joshua had stopped and was talking to the woman with the pushchair.

'I thought it was you! It's Josh Johnson. And here is Rose.'

It was Sandy, the girl who had babysat for them when her mother and Brendan went out at night. Rose looked at her with surprise. When she was younger Rose had idolised her, her trendy clothes and her spiky fringe and talon-like nails. She used to spend most of the evening staring at her and listening to stories about her love life. She was babysitting for them on the evening their parents disappeared. Now she was in her early twenties but she looked older. Her hair was pulled back into a pony tail and she had no make-up on.

'God! Joshua and Rose. You're here because they found Daisy's body? How awful. How are you both? You left in such a hurry no one had time to say anything to you.'

In the pushchair was a baby, fast asleep. It looked young.

'This is Jade. She's three months old and quite a handful. I have to walk the pushchair round to get her off to sleep.'

'She's yours?' Rose said.

Sandy nodded. 'You've grown up, Rose. You're so pretty. And Josh! A man now.'

Rose felt her cheeks flush with embarrassment. She looked down at her shoes. Sandy continued talking.

'Poor Daisy. We were in the same groups at college. We were quite friendly for a while then her mum moved to Chingford and I never saw her again. We heard she'd left home, of course. One of the girls in my class told me that she had run away with a man old enough to be her father but I don't know if that was true or not.'

Sandy put her hand into the pushchair, straightening the blanket that was over her baby.

'You still live round here?' Joshua said.

'Yes,' she pointed to the sleeping baby. 'Jade wasn't a planned thing. Her dad doesn't know she exists so I live with my mum.'

'Sorry to hear that . . .'

'Don't be. I didn't like him. Well, I must have liked him at one time . . . Rose, you're so quiet. When I looked after you you never stopped talking.'

Rose gave a shrug. 'We ought to go.'

'Bye. Oh, I suppose I should say this even though it all happened so long ago. I was really sorry about Kathy and Brendan. I liked both of them a lot.'

'Thanks,' Joshua said.

'You should come and see me some time. It's not like you don't know where I live!' Sandy said.

'Bye.'

They walked on and a second later Rose heard the sound of someone running up behind them. She turned just as a man with a camera took several rapid photos of

Joshua and her. It only took a fraction of a second to put her hand in front of her face but by then he'd managed to get a number of pictures.

Joshua swore at him and turned away, pulling Rose by the arm.

'Have you any comments on the discovery of a body in the garden of your parents' house? Was this girl's murder the reason that they disappeared?' a voice called out.

They walked swiftly on, heads down, away from the reporter. When they turned the corner and it was clear that he hadn't followed them they slowed up. Rose blew air between her teeth. She looked at Joshua. He shook his head.

'Now it'll be in the newspapers,' he said.

'Maybe Mum and Brendan will see it,' Rose said.

Joshua nodded as if that wasn't such a bad thing.

SIX

On Sunday morning they set off for Wickby. Joshua had a copy of a newspaper in the car when he came to pick Rose up. She looked at it. On the bottom of the front page was a photograph of the two of them. The headline was eye-catching: *Abandoned Children Revisit House of Death*.

'This is awful,' she said.

The photograph showed Rose's profile and Joshua's face as he turned to look at the photographer. Neither of them had any expression. Underneath, the caption read *Rose Smith and Joshua Johnson after their visit to the scene of crime*. The report repeated everything that had been said in the other accounts she had read and ended with a question: *Do Rose Smith and Joshua Johnson have the key to what happened at the house of death?*

Rose tossed the newspaper on to the back seat.

'Oh, I saw Margaret Spicer yesterday afternoon,' Joshua said.

Margaret Spicer?

'Did you?'

'She was at Munroe's Chelsea office. It's the first time I've seen her since . . . So I thought I'd speak to her.'

Margaret Spicer, the wife of James Munroe. The last time Rose had seen her had been in a hotel room in Newcastle. Munroe had just told Joshua and Rose some unpalatable truths about their parents while Margaret had walked around the room, packing things so that she and Munroe could leave.

'I taped the conversation. Well, not exactly a *conversation*. She gave me these short and to the point answers. The recorder is in the glove compartment. Listen to it.'

Rose reached into the glove compartment and pulled out something that looked like a mobile phone.

'When did you get this? What's it for?'

'Skeggsie had it for college. He used to record some seminars. He didn't like taking notes. I found it in his room a few weeks ago. I meant to pack it but forgot.'

'I don't understand why you were at Munroe's office again?'

'I thought I might see him. I was going to try and get him into a conversation and record it. For evidence. You know, when he spoke to you making threats? I thought if I could record something like that . . . Anyway, he wasn't there. Margaret Spicer was so I thought I'd speak to her. Play it.'

Rose worked out what to press. The sound came on, piped music in the background.

'"Margaret, it's Joshua Johnson. I just want to talk to you for a minute."

"I've got nothing to say to you."

"About Munroe. I want to ask you about . . ."

"Please leave these premises."

"Just a couple of questions. About what happened in Newcastle."

"I have nothing to say."

"How come Munroe –"

"I have nothing to say about James Munroe. He and I are separated."

"When did that happen?"

"That's not your business."

"Was it because of what happened to Skeggsie?"

"Don't be ridiculous."

"But why?"

"James Munroe and I have irreconcilable differences."

"Is that because he arranged to have my best friend killed in a dark alley and he used you to do it?"

"You can stand there all day or you can leave. I have nothing further to say to you."'

The piped music continued light and flowery but there was no voice. Then there was a clicking sound and silence.

'She wasn't going to utter another word so I left.'

Rose replaced the recorder in the glove department. There didn't seem to be anything to say. Munroe split up with Margaret Spicer. Was that before he went to Florida or after?

They saw signs for Wickby. The traffic on the roads was light. It was just after nine. Joshua said it would take about an hour to get to the village where the antique and collectables fair was being held.

Rose thought through the work she had to do for college the next day. As well as that there was a pile of her mother's things that she had to sort so that she and Anna could spend time deciding on the decorating for the Blue Room. Then it would no longer be the Blue Room but a room that Rose could use as a sitting room, somewhere to bring friends. Not that she had many friends.

'You're quiet,' Joshua said.

'Thinking of stuff I've got to do.'

When they got to Wickby it was busy. They drove slowly through the small town and passed lines of stalls being set up and signage pointing in all directions for *Art Deco*, *Victorian*, *Thirties*, *Vintage Clothes* and, strangely, *Bathrooms*. They parked beyond the town centre and walked back among crowds heading for the stalls. Rose looked around and was reminded of Holt, the town in Norfolk where she had been a regular visitor when she was at boarding school.

'Told you this was really popular.'

They walked around the stalls for a while. Joshua stopped at some and Rose found herself looking at the items. Her eye was taken by a tiny chest of drawers. It was the size of shoebox and the drawers were only big enough to fill with jewellery. She opened and shut each one.

She could buy it. It was sweet and she could put it on her desk. She didn't have a lot of jewellery but there were other things it could hold: keys, bits of make-up, memory sticks, combs and hair ties.

She hesitated then walked on. Joshua followed her. They headed for some benches at the top end of the market. They stopped and sat down. It was possible to watch people passing through the market from there.

'Oh!' he said, after a few moments. 'After going to Brewster Road I remembered something about Daisy Lincoln.'

'What?'

'It was the conversation with Sandy that triggered it. You remember she said that there was talk that Daisy had run away with a man old enough to be her father?'

Rose nodded.

'I remembered this day when I went into the newsagent's on the High Street just as Daisy was getting ready to leave work. While I was paying for my can of drink or whatever it was, she was looking into a mirror that was on the wall behind the counter and she was doing her hair. She was pushing her fingers through the front of it, using them like the teeth of a comb? To make it stand up?'

Joshua stopped for a moment, as if he was picturing the scene. Rose gazed at the people walking past, her mind on what Joshua was saying.

'She must have noticed I was looking at her and she turned round and said something like, *I got a hot date, Josh. It's the love of my life!* Then she got this lipstick out of her bag and opened it up in front of me. It was almost like she was teasing me. I was fourteen, secretly mad about her and it was as if she knew it.'

He was quiet again.

'And?' Rose prompted.

'She put the lipstick on without looking in the mirror. Just using it like a crayon across her mouth. Then she came round the counter and went out of the shop. I remember she seemed to bounce along. I watched her go and stayed at the shop door while she stood at the edge of the pavement waiting for someone. A car passed and it let out a little bibbing sound and then pulled up across the road, further along so I didn't see who was driving. Thing is, I do remember looking at the car. It was a Saab, a Swedish car. I was into cars when I was that age and I knew that Saabs were not the kind of car that young people drove. Too heavy and serious. It was something an older person would choose. An old Swedish car, solid but not stylish. Anyway, I didn't think any of that at that moment. I was too busy pining for Daisy. I watched her walk across the road and get into the car. I remember she gave me a little wave.'

Rose felt unsettled by this story even though she had no strong memories of Daisy herself. All she could picture was a laughing girl with long black hair. Daisy had never babysat for her and her house was just too far along the road for the families to be acquaintances.

'Anyway, shall we walk around again?'

Rose stood up.

'We'll split up,' he said. 'You stay in this general area and I'll go to the far end of the market. There's an auction there. It might be something that Kathy or Dad would be interested in.'

Joshua went off and Rose took a long slow walk round the edge of the market. She passed by the stall with the small chest of drawers and lingered for a few moments. She asked about the price. It was affordable but did she really need it? And in any case wasn't she meant to be concentrating on other things? Such as bumping in to her mother and Brendan.

But what was the likelihood of that?

She found herself wandering away from the stalls towards a small humpback bridge. She remembered then that she and Joshua had spoken about this bridge. It was certainly tiny. On the brickwork there was a plaque with a date: 1829. A footpath along one side meant that there was scarcely space for one car at a time to cross it.

She walked on to it and looked down at the stream that flowed underneath. It was glassy, moving slowly.

Through the water Rose could see layers of pebbles and rocks.

Daisy Lincoln came into her head. She pictured the girl walking across the street towards an expensive, older man's car. She wondered if she had been wearing jeans or a skirt or even a dress. It had been summer so she might have had sandals or flip-flops on. Her hair was black and long, must have been lying loose across her shoulders. In her mind Rose saw her pause before getting into the car, pushing her fingers into her hair to make it stand up then waving at Joshua, the fourteen-year-old boy who had a crush on her.

Rose had begun to feel some kind of connection with this girl. Daisy had been eighteen years old when she went missing, just a little older than she was now. Rose had a lifetime ahead of her but Daisy's life had been cut off and her body hidden away. This chilled Rose. She had seen death in the last few months but it had been carried out in a moment of passion or anger or just pure evil. The hiding away of Daisy's body meant that the deed had gone unknown. It meant that her family had lived with hope for weeks and months and maybe years. It meant that her friends may have suspected that Daisy had gone off with *the love of her life* and was living somewhere else, happy and contented.

Instead she was in a hole in the ground, in Rose and Joshua's back garden.

Rose sighed and turned back to the market. She'd go and find Joshua. At least if they were together it made the time go more quickly. She pulled her coat tightly round her and headed back in between the stalls. As she did so a man bumped into her. He was going swiftly past her on a narrow stretch of pavement and his elbow hit her arm. She found herself saying 'Sorry' and then *tsk*ed because she hadn't been the one who had caused the collision. She looked with indignation at the back of the man walking ahead and saw the holdall he had slung over his shoulder. It was a red bag with a chequered flag on it. The kind of flag that is used at the end of a car race. A victory flag. It gave her a start.

She knew that bag.

The man disappeared into the market and she went quicker, following him. Once in the crowds milling round the stalls, she couldn't see him but she caught glimpses of the red holdall. The market was busy and there were pushchairs in the way and elderly people standing in groups talking, their dogs straining on leads.

'Wait,' she called out. 'Frank, wait . . .'

The name came out of her mouth as if it was an old friend she had just spotted. But Frank Richards was anything but a friend.

Frank Richards left the stalls area and crossed the road, forcing a car to pull up sharply. He headed away from the market towards a lane. Rose had to wait while a family on bikes passed by. She shot across the road and went up the lane. She saw him twenty metres or so down, opening the back door of a black car and slinging his holdall in.

'Frank,' she called.

He stood by the driver's door as she ran up to the car. He was holding a set of keys in one hand. He looked the same as she remembered, tall and thin. His head was completely bald although today he had a shadow on the bottom half of his face as if he hadn't shaved for a while.

'What are you doing here?' she said.

'Rose,' he said. 'I trust you are well.'

'Are you following me again?'

'No, no, not this time.'

'So, what are you doing here? Are you with Mum and Brendan?'

'Just at the market. That's all. I have to go, Rose. I'm sorry.'

'But you know they're here? In this area.'

'Rose,' he stepped forward, keeping hold of the driver's door. Rose saw that the sleeve of his jacket and jumper had fallen back and that his butterfly tattoo was visible on the back of his wrist. Her eyes clung to it. He saw her looking and used his other hand to tug at the sleeve so that it was covered up.

'It's not long now,' he said. 'You just have to be patient. You'll see your mother and Brendan soon. Sooner than you think.'

'But . . .'

She heard her name being called from behind. She spun around and saw Joshua at the top of the turning. At the same moment the car door clicked shut.

'Wait,' she said.

But the engine had started, the indicators were blinking and the wheels were turning on the cobbled street. She stepped back as it pulled away from the kerb and headed down the lane, passing Joshua as it went. Joshua stared at it and then recognition registered on his face. She walked towards him.

'Was that who I thought it was?' he said.

She nodded. She wondered where he had gone. Was he staying close by or somewhere else? Was he with her mum and Brendan or just keeping an eye out from a distance?

'Did you speak to him? What did he say?'

'He just said that it wouldn't be long until we saw them.'

Joshua tutted. 'Why can't he just be straight?'

As they walked back to the car Rose looked at the market stalls. She was picturing her mother browsing at a stall, maybe the one with the small chest of drawers. Her mother wouldn't have hesitated like Rose. She would have bought it. She felt a rush of emotion. Joshua took her hand in his and held it firmly.

'It was worth coming. We're getting closer and closer,' he said.

SEVEN

On the journey home, after they'd been going for an hour or so, Joshua began to talk about Skeggsie. He had been dead for almost two months.

'I know you still get upset about him,' Rose said.

'I think about him a lot. Especially when we're trying to find Dad and Kathy. I keep thinking, *What would Skeggs do?* I know you weren't very fond of him but I miss him.'

'It's not that I wasn't fond of him,' Rose began.

She stopped, though, because she was never actually sure what her feelings had been for Skeggsie. Darren Skeggs, two years older than Joshua, his friend from school. Joshua and Skeggsie had come together through a fight against bullies and then became firm friends. Skeggie's generosity had allowed Joshua to live in his London flat virtually rent free. When she'd met up with Joshua the previous autumn Skeggsie, it seemed, had come as part of the package. He was always awkward when she was around. He wore tight shirts that were fastened up to the top button as though he was locking himself in, just as he had been keen on bolting the door of the flat. He was awful at small talk and had been critical of Rose from the start. Somehow, though, they'd made their peace with each other and before Christmas, they'd come together to try and locate the owner of a car that they thought had been following them to Newcastle.

Then Skeggsie had been murdered.

Rose thought back to the events of that terrible night. It was late on Christmas Eve and Skeggsie had walked into an alley and met someone with a knife. There was an argument, a fight, then Skeggsie had been stabbed. A single wound to the heart. He'd bled to death on the ground amid rubbish bags and fast-food wrappers. She and Joshua had discovered him there but it had been too late to save his life. There'd been no witnesses apart from some CCTV footage of a young man in a hoodie walking away from the alley. What the police got was DNA evidence. In the struggle Skeggsie had scratched his attacker and had hair and skin under his fingernails.

Rose knew, in her heart, that the person who organised that murder, James Munroe, would never be caught.

Out of the blue she noticed Joshua's hand on hers. He stroked her skin for a few moments then pulled his hand back to the steering wheel. She glanced at him but he seemed engrossed in the driving. Her hand was very still and she was sure she could feel the sensation of his touch from seconds before. It gave her a powerful memory, a physical flashback to the way things were between them after Skeggsie died. They had reached out for each other. They had held on to each other and she had kissed him until her lips were swollen. Then they had become more than friends but not quite lovers. Had talking about Skeggsie brought some of those feelings back for Joshua as well?

There were things she wanted to say but now was not the time to say them. It didn't seem right to talk about their relationship while this search for their parents was going on. She laced her fingers through each other and sat quietly. One day she would hold him still, make him look at her and tell him that she loved him.

They drove on.

'Why don't you come in for a while,' she said, when they eventually pulled up outside the house in Belsize Park. 'Anna wants me to bring friends home. She's redecorating a whole room so that I have somewhere to take them.'

'OK,' Joshua said.

He looked tired. He left his jacket in the back of the car. She took his hand, lightly, as she would if he were a small child, and pulled him up the path. The front door opened before she had a chance to put her key in. Her grandmother stood there.

'Rose, that policeman's here to see you again. Oh, hello, Joshua.'

Anna looked a little pained. She was still in her 'Clearing Out the Blue Room' clothes.

'What does he want?'

'I don't know. He said he tried to ring you.'

Rose tutted. Her phone had been on silent.

'He's in the kitchen. I gave him a drink. I'll be upstairs. I'll leave you to talk to him.'

Rose walked towards the kitchen. Joshua was behind her.

'Shall I go off home? This might be personal.'

'It's probably to do with the house in Brewster Road. Come on. It'll include you as well.'

Henry was in off-duty clothes: a checked jacket and brown trousers. He looked as though he'd dressed up to go to church. Rose wondered if he had, if he believed in God. He stood up as they came in.

'You're both together. That's good. I just called at your flat, Joshua. When you weren't there I took a chance and came here. I've got some information for you. Why don't you sit down.'

He was acting as though it was his house, not the place where Rose lived.

Joshua pulled out a chair and sat on it, slouched. Henry's face was drawn and Rose felt a pang of fear. She sat down on the edge of the chair. The thought came into her head that he had come because something had *really* happened to her mum or Brendan. They'd seen a Skype recording of them after Christmas and had a text message from them days later. They had been alive then. Could it be that something had happened to them since?

'The detectives in East London have asked me to liaise with both of you regarding the situation at Brewster Road. I hope that's agreeable. It saves them coming across to see you and as I know you, Rose, I thought you wouldn't mind.'

Rose felt a shiver of relief. It was to do with Daisy Lincoln, unconnected to their parents. She sat back, an image in her head of Daisy running across to the road to the car in which the *love of her life* was sitting. This picture of a girl she hardly knew seemed to have taken root in her thoughts.

'The cause of Daisy Lincoln's death is not clear. It's hard after so much time to ascertain exactly how a person died. There was no bullet found near the body and the skeleton has no signs of violence, no broken skull or cracked bones,' Henry said.

'So we'll never know?'

'Strangulation, asphyxiation, poison. Until the crime is solved, the perpetrator found, it will be hard to identify the cause.'

Henry was pulling something out of a bag on the floor that Rose hadn't noticed. It was a black leather briefcase.

He opened a file and took out a colour photograph and placed it on the table so that they both could see. Rose leant towards it. It was a picture of a man's tie. It was mauve with blue stripes and there was a crest of some sort in the middle.

'What's this?' she said.

'It's a West Ham tie,' Joshua said.

It looked scruffy, the edges of it dirty and frayed.

'Do you recognise it?' Henry said.

Rose shook her head. 'What's this got to do with Brewster Road?'

'If you could just have a good look at it. See if it rings any bells for either of you.'

Rose looked closer. The tie had been laid on a white background, a table of some sort. It had been stretched out but still it seemed wrinkled in some places. It reminded her of the girls' ties that hung in Lost Property in her old school; they looked as though they'd been through a mangle. She had no memory of this tie – why should she?

Joshua started to speak.

'I bought a tie like this for my dad one Christmas. He wasn't really a West Ham fan. He supported Newcastle but he never went to their matches. He never went to *any* matches but he always watched *Match of the Day* on television and he said that West Ham were his second team so I bought it for him. He wore it a couple of times, I think.'

'Like this tie.'

'Yeah, exactly like it.'

Henry put the photocopy back into the folder.

'I'm sorry to tell you this but we believe that this *is* your father's tie. We think this because DNA was extracted. It's the DNA of Brendan Johnson.'

There was a puzzled silence in the kitchen.

'DNA?'

'Yes, saliva, hairs, something of that sort.'

'OK. So?' Joshua said, a sudden surliness in his voice.

'When the body of Daisy Lincoln was found some items of clothing had survived. A lot of natural materials, cotton, silk and so on would decay over time. This tie, made of synthetic fibres, did not. There were a couple of other items as well . . .'

'What was Daisy Lincoln doing with my dad's tie?'

'Ah.'

Rose stared at Henry. She was feeling irritated. Why couldn't he just blurt it out, whatever it was?

'We think that before Daisy was killed she had her hands tied behind her back. They were bound up with Brendan Johnson's tie.'

Joshua sat up, his forehead wrinkled, his shoulders straight.

'Naturally this puts a different slant on things. It opens up the case to other interpretations. I felt it was only right that I should tell Joshua as soon as possible and you too,

Rose. There may well be a completely innocent explanation about this and if there is the police will find it . . .'

Henry's voice seemed to dwindle and he stood up, grabbing his briefcase.

'I gave you my number, Joshua, and Rose has it too. Get in touch with me if there's anything you need to talk about.'

Joshua was still silent, his eyes staring hard at the table. Rose followed Henry out of the room and into the hallway.

'It'll take a while for this to sink in, Rose. You know where I am.'

Rose closed the front door. When she went back to the kitchen Joshua was standing up and looked as if he too was about to leave.

'Josh, I . . .'

He shook her arm off. 'This is rubbish. It's crap.'

'I agree but . . .'

'But nothing, Rose. My dad is not a murderer!'

Rose stared at Joshua. His eyes looked dark and cold. The words he had just spoken hung limply in the air. There were things she wanted to say but didn't. The truth hung around them like a bad smell.

'My dad did not kill Daisy Lincoln. It's because of murders like this that my dad . . . took the path he did. Decided to right wrongs, to get justice for the innocent.'

'You're making him sound like a superhero! He has *killed* people!'

'Yes. Baranski. Someone who didn't deserve to live!'

She stepped back, startled.

'But not Daisy Lincoln,' he said, a crack in his voice. 'Never some eighteen-year-old innocent girl. Never.'

He walked away from her and she stood there and let him go. He opened the front door and closed behind him. From upstairs she could hear Anna humming. She thought of Brendan's tie knotted around the wrists of Daisy Lincoln. She thought of Brendan, when they lived together, smiling at her. *All right, Petal?* He often picked up a packet of her favourite sweets when he bought a newspaper.

She knew Brendan wasn't capable of such a thing.

He had killed Viktor Baranski and maybe others.

But an eighteen-year-old girl?

Brendan couldn't do that.

EIGHT

In the corner of Rose's study were her mother's things which had been cleared out of the Blue Room. It had made the area temporarily untidy. Anna said that Rose should look through the paperwork and keep anything that she wanted. Rose had a feeling that she would keep it all, every sheet of paper, whatever it was.

On Rose's pinboard was a photo of her mother that she had recently put there.

It was a head and shoulders close-up and for once she didn't have her glasses on. Her hair hung round her face and she was wearing a black dress which was low at the front. Rose thought she must have been going somewhere formal. Around her neck was a pendant on a chain. The pendant was silver, quite heavy, in the shape of a heart. At the centre of it was a red gemstone. Rose remembered that this pendant had been a gift from Brendan but that her mother hadn't liked it much. She'd worn it now and then but had told Rose *It's not really my kind of thing. Don't tell Brendan.*

Her mother's jewellery box was on her desk. Rose had looked in it over the years when it sat in the Blue Room. Most of her mother's jewellery was not valuable but it was still precious to her. It held an eclectic mix of rings, necklaces, bracelets and earrings. Rose had looked at these from time to time, hoping for some connection to them, some stories to emerge from them but nothing much resonated. They were just items that she had bought or other people had bought for her. She looked at the photo again, at the pendant on her mother's neck. The gemstone looked dark, the colour of a bead of blood. Rose had looked for this pendant over the years but hadn't been able to find it. She wondered if, perhaps, her mother had secretly got rid of it.

Rose closed up the jewellery box and tucked it away by the rest of her mother's things. Then she stood up and walked across to the window and looked out into the street.

Half an hour before Joshua had got into the Mini and driven away in anger. Now he would be at the flat in Camden, upset, disbelieving.

Everything seemed to have come to a standstill.

Over the last few months it seemed as though they were always moving towards something: some revelation or a reunion with their parents or simply the absolute truth about what had happened. But now everything was muddled. They seemed to be wandering alone, in circles.

Now Joshua had another reason to be angry with her; she had failed to rise to Brendan's defence.

She bent down to her desk drawer and pulled out the brown envelope that held her statement. She slipped the red notebook out and opened it to a clean page. She moved her keyboard to the side of her desk to give herself space and she put a date as she had with the other entries. Then she began to write.

For a while I've wondered exactly how much my mother is involved in the notebooks and the murders. I've had a feeling for some time, much stronger recently, that she was a reluctant participant. That she went along with it because she loved Brendan.

Rose thought back to the Skype recording they'd seen around Christmas. Her mother and Brendan had been speaking directly to them. It was the first sight of them they'd had for over five years. The quality of the film hadn't been good but still Rose had hung on to every moment, her eyes searching the screen for facial expression, eye contact, hand movements. Brendan had done most of the talking. He'd explained the life they'd taken on before and since disappearing; her mother behind his shoulder, in his shadow, had said very little. She'd looked strained and grim. Brendan had talked earnestly about their choice, about the things they had done, but her mother had just looked burdened by it all.

Right from the beginning, Rose wrote, *on the night they disappeared my mother left her glasses case behind in the restaurant. In it there'd been a card for a Bed and Breakfast place in Twickenham. It had seemed like a clue left on purpose. Then, the false surname they had used in the B and B had been Brewster, the name of the road we had lived in. On top of this my mother had not tried to disguise her handwriting when she'd signed the guest book, her ornate lettering giving away her true identity.*

It seemed as if she was leaving a trail for me to find.

And then there was the Butterfly Murder.

It was the crime that started the whole 'mission'. Her mother had *not* been part of this. Rose turned back a few pages in the notebooks. There, a week or so before, she had written about it.

The Butterfly Murder was the beginning of everything.

In 2002 ten-year-old Judy Greaves was abducted and murdered, her body left in a room full of mounted butterflies. She was discovered by a police-woman. A man called Simon Lister had been arrested and tried but was acquitted through lack of evidence. Brendan's brother, Stuart, had known the girl's sister, and had become obsessed with this miscarriage of justice. He'd contacted his brother and asked him to look into the case but Brendan couldn't. Brendan went up to Newcastle in 2004 to visit him, taking my mother, his new girlfriend, with him. Stuart had gone to Simon Lister's house and stabbed him. He got back home with blood on his hands. Brendan had been shocked. In order to save his brother from a life sentence he'd rushed round to the crime scene, removing the weapon and any trace that his brother Stuart had been there.

When the dead man was found the police searched his home and his computer and found evidence that he'd murdered Judy Greaves as well as others. They also found photographs and plans to abduct a further young girl.

It seemed to them that the murder had been a good thing.

The experience changed Brendan. Other police were involved in the cover-up and they must have stuck together. Policemen and women who were tired of criminals getting away with major crime. They decided that they would mete out justice and if that meant taking the lives of killers and those in organised crime then they would do it.

When exactly had her mother become involved?

Had she ever actually killed someone?

The only murder they knew about in any detail was that of Viktor Baranski. And as far as Rose knew her mother had played no part in that case. She turned forward a couple of pages and found the section of her statement that dealt with it.

The Second Notebook.

The photograph at the front of this book was of Viktor Baranski, a Russian businessman. He was linked to people trafficking and in 2003 the bodies of five teenage girls were found in the back of a container lorry. They had suffocated and the youngest was thirteen. They were being smuggled into Britain in order to become prostitutes. Viktor Baranski was never charged with this crime although the Cold Cases team (who were already investigating Baranski for other crimes) were convinced that he was responsible.

In 2006 he disappeared and his body was found near Cromer pier. His hands had been tied behind his back. It is my belief that Brendan Johnson and others carried out this assassination as a form of justice for the girls.

How willingly had her mother become part of this group within the police force? This was the question that had begun to play on Rose's mind. It had been *Brendan*'s brother who had committed the first murder, *Brendan* who went and tidied up the crime scene. It was *Brendan* who had been part of the group who killed Viktor Baranski.

It was Brendan who did all of the talking on Skype.

Had her mother simply been pulled along by Brendan?

Did she regret her involvement?

Did she wish she had never got involved?

If only . . . Rose thought as she continued writing her statement.

NINE

Rose sat opposite Sara and Maggie before class started. Sara had an arm linked through Maggie's. They looked like twin sisters but they were just friends who'd been around each other for a long time. Now and then they saw it as their job to look after Rose.

'Come out with us on Friday to the Pink Parrot. It'll be fun,' Sara said. 'They, like, have talent spots. People get up to five minutes on stage to show what they can do – comedy, singing, dancing . . .'

'This guy read his poems out!'

'I liked them.'

'Embarrassing!'

'He had the bluest eyes.'

Rose looked from one to the other. 'It doesn't sound like my kind of thing.'

'I'm sure you'd enjoy it. And, anyway, Jamie Roberts might come. He likes you.'

'Jamie Roberts? From Law?'

Maggie nodded excitedly. 'He asked us about you. We told him that you're, like, a special girl.'

Rose had to smile. Sara and Maggie wanted Rose to live the kind of life that they did. They were both fiercely intelligent and they worked hard in their classes but outside they liked to play. They wanted Rose to have a boyfriend and come to the pub and go to parties. It was an alien life to Rose but they didn't stop trying to persuade her.

'Here's a leaflet. The Pink Parrot is not a gay pub. Well, there might be, like, gay people in it, but you know what I mean. It's in Kentish Town, about two minutes from the tube. Loads of kids from college go there.'

'Not the rough lot,' Sara said. 'Nor the druggies.'

'Just intellectuals like us,' Maggie said, smiling.

Rose took the leaflet. The bell sounded for the last afternoon class and Sara and Maggie headed off while she sat finishing her tea. She looked at the piece of paper in her hand. *Variety Night! Readings, Comedy, Drama, Singers, Dancers. All Welcome. Every Friday, 8.30 start.* She couldn't picture herself out on a night like this. Getting ready at home, deciding what to wear, meeting Sara and Maggie outside the tube, the three of them laughing and giggling on the way to the pub, getting a table or standing around watching the cabaret while keeping an eye out for Jamie Roberts from Law. Could she have a regular night out with college friends? With a frisson of possible romance thrown in?

This wasn't the sort of life that Rose lived.

Sometimes she wished it was. Every now and again she *longed* to be ordinary, like Sara and Maggie. Each of them was comfortable in their long-term friendship, their days in college, their nights out in North London, their plans for university (the same one for both, of course). But Sara and Maggie didn't have a history to carry round with them. How could she go out, have a laugh and joke with people, watch a show, flirt with Jamie from Law? How could she enjoy herself when these other things were happening in her life?

She folded up the leaflet and put it in her pocket.

Her phone beeped. She had a message from Joshua. It was two days since she'd seen him, since Henry had told them about Brendan's tie. Two days of silence. She was apprehensive as she looked at the text. **Come round to the flat after college. Something exciting to show you. BTW sorry for the other night. XXX**

Three kisses. She felt herself soften. She sent a reply. **See you just after five. XXX**

She rang the bell to the flat and heard Joshua's footsteps coming down the stairs.

'Hi!' he said. 'Come up.'

She followed him. In the kitchen he helped her take off her coat and put it and her bag on a chair. She looked round and saw, with dismay, that it looked bare. The pots and pans that Skeggsie had lined up on the shelves had gone. The pictures that had been on the wall were gone. The work surface was clear of his mugs and the giant see-through salt and pepper shakers. None of it was there any more. Joshua saw her looking.

'A bit empty now. I'll have to buy a few things . . .'

Rose noticed something on the work surface behind Joshua. A large padded brown envelope. On the outside were the words *Private and Confidential. Joshua Johnson.*

'This arrived,' he said, picking it up.

Joshua looked excited. Rose sat down at the narrow long table where she'd been on many occasions before.

'It came by post.'

Joshua put his hand inside the envelope and pulled out a number of exercise books. This made Rose sit up. She didn't speak but watched as Joshua laid the books out on the table. There were four of them. Rose stared at them one after the other.

'The rest of the notebooks,' he finally said.

'Frank Richards must have sent them,' she said, her voice low, 'after he saw us in Wickby. He must have decided to send them.'

Joshua nodded.

She pulled one of the books towards her. She frowned. It was exactly the same as the two that they had once had in their possession. When she opened the first page there was a photograph there. The rest of the book was full of coded writing, page after page of unreadable prose. She closed it and pulled another one across. Then another. In the end the four books were lined up in front of her.

There was, however, something different about these books. They had a name and a date written across the cover in neat black capitals. The one she was holding had *2005 GEORGE USHER* on it. She picked up the others – *2007 MICHAEL McCALL, 2008 RONNIE BINYON, 2010 JAMES BARKER.*

'Frank Richards has given us more information,' Joshua said. 'He's identified the men in these notebooks, the men who were executed.'

Executed. Rose flinched at the word. It brought to mind a man with an axe or a hangman, an anonymous person who dispassionately ended the life of someone else.

'You remember what James Munroe said when we were in Newcastle?'

She dragged her eyes away from the books. The printing on the covers was precise in a straight line, as though Frank Richards had written the names with a ruler underneath. She must have looked blank because Joshua went on.

'He said that *six evil men* had been removed from our society. If you count the Butterfly Murder as the first one plus Viktor Baranski, that leaves four. These are the four other men who have been *removed*. If you look at the inside of the back cover of each of the books you'll see some other information.'

Rose took the first one and opened it up at the back. The word *Judgement* was there and underneath the details of the death of George Usher. It was blunt and cold. She picked up the second book and saw the word *Judgement* again and the name of Michael McCall. Again the cause of death was stated. A single word. No emotion at all.

'I've made a list of them, here, look. I've included Baranski even though we don't have his notebook any more.'

On a piece of A4 paper was a bulleted list.

- *2005 December George Usher: Shot.*
- *2006 August Viktor Baranski: Drowned.*
- *2007 July Michael McCall: Stabbed.*
- *2008 June Ronnie Binyon: Hit and Run.*
- *2010 December James Barker: Fell under a tube train.*

'What about the other two? The boy from my college and Skeggsie?'

'They don't count. They're not part of this project. You know that. These are the people who they *meant* to kill. I've researched them. George Usher, sixty-two, big hotel owner in the West End. Possible cover for drug dealing and prostitution. Police arrested him for the murder of one of his own girls but couldn't make anything stick.

The newspapers hinted that his murder was drug related. Viktor Baranski we already know about. Michael McCall, forty-three, walked away from a prison sentence for the manslaughter of his second wife due to a technicality. His first wife died in mysterious circumstances years before and there's even a suggestion that his mother died an unnatural death. Ronnie Binyon, fifty-four, money lender and property owner. High profile case of two brothers who lived in one of his flats beaten to death by his workers. Then the mother of the brothers commits suicide. Binyon stays out of prison. Lastly James Barker, thirty-nine, a serial rapist and killer out on remand awaiting trial. His victim kills herself so no trial. He falls in front of a tube train weeks later.'

Rose didn't know what to say. She stared at the notebooks in front of her.

'Why did Frank Richards give us these?'

'I don't know. Munroe said Frank was a maverick. Munroe was dismissive of the notebooks. Maybe the notebooks were Frank's way of collecting the evidence. He had once been a policeman. While Munroe was trying to cover up what they'd done Frank Richards was trying to record it in some way. I just don't know . . .'

Rose thought of the red notebook she had back at Anna's. She was trying to record things in much the same way.

'So the mystery of the notebooks is solved.'

'There's one more that I haven't shown you yet.'

Joshua got up and disappeared for a moment. Rose heard him moving about in his room. He came back holding another notebook. This one looked brand new, unused. There was still a name written across it, though; *2013 MACON PARKER*. She opened it. Inside, on the first page was a photograph of a middle-aged man. His hair was receding a little but it was jet black, as if it had been dyed. The rest of the pages were blank.

'What does it mean?' she said.

'It means that Macon Parker is the next person to be killed off.'

'Oh.'

'I looked him up,' Joshua said excitedly.

'What is he? Murderer? Rapist? Drug dealer?'

'He's an American businessman. Used to be a doctor specialising in organ transplants. Now he's in private medicine as well as a number of other things.'

'Why is he a target?'

'There's a hint that one of his companies was involved in illegal organ transplants. You know – paying people to give their kidneys. I don't know any more than that. One thing I do know, though, is where he lives.'

Rose waited. She knew that Joshua was bursting to tell her.

'In Essex just outside a village called Two Oaks. That village is about three miles from Wickby. Don't you see,

Rose? If he is the next target then Dad and Kathy might be there.'

She looked at him sadly. He was keen again, buzzing. And yet the things he was talking about were grim and awful.

'So what does this all mean?' she said. 'What do you think it means for *us*? I don't understand why you're so fired up?'

'Because you and I are going to find Kathy and Dad.'

She looked at the notebooks. Coded stories of premeditated murder. Why should they have anything to do with this?

'We're going to stop them carrying out this murder. We're going to get them away from all this.'

'I don't want to be part of it any more. I've told you that.'

'But this must change your mind?' he said, pointing at the notebooks.

'No.'

'When we're finally getting somewhere you give up!' he said stiffly.

'You think what you like,' she said.

She'd had enough. She picked up her coat and bag and left him at the kitchen table.

Waiting at the bus stop she shoved her hands in her pockets. In one of them she felt the leaflet that she'd picked up from college earlier. She thought back to the conversation she'd had with Sara and Maggie, the invitation to go out on Friday night. How nice it would have been to tell Joshua, to arrange to meet him outside the pub. To open the doors and feel the heat and the noise and the bonhomie of a local bar full of young people like them. Why couldn't they shake off all this stuff, leave it behind, get on with their lives? Go to the Pink Parrot and get drunk every Friday night?

Why couldn't both of them just be regular teenagers?

TEN

Early the next morning Rose got up, wandered into her study and found an email on her laptop from Joshua.

Dear Rose, Some weeks ago you sent me a message saying you wanted a break from me, from what I was doing about Dad and Kathy. I was hurt but I understood. We've been through a lot together, you and I. You mean a lot to me but at the moment your lack of commitment to this search is holding me back. So I'm going to say I need a break from you for a while. I am determined to continue and feel that I'm getting close but your reluctance is pulling me down. I care about you but I can't be with you right now. Josh

She sat down and read it again, the words sinking in.

Joshua was breaking off with her.

She crossed her arms tightly, feeling the thump of her heart deep in her chest. She shook her head. Joshua could not distance himself from her. She walked back into her bedroom and picked up her mobile. She would call him, explain, persuade him not to be so dramatic. He'd most probably sent it in the heat of the moment. No doubt the minute she'd walked out of the door yesterday he'd hammered out the email just to show he was angry with her. She accessed his number and stood very still for a moment, thoughtful. She turned back into the study and looked at the email to see what time he'd sent it. Thirty-eight minutes past six. It had been sent just over an hour before. He'd had all night to consider. He'd thought about it, weighed up the pros and cons, slept on it and decided to push her away.

Hadn't she done the same thing weeks before?

She sat back down in front of her laptop. She remembered the message he'd sent her when she told him she wanted a break. She tapped out her own reply.

Whatever is best for you, Rosie.

She pressed *Send*.

Anna was getting ready to go out and Rose, still in her nightclothes, took her time over her breakfast, telling her she had a late start at college. When her grandmother left she went back up to her room.

She lay on the bed for a while, feeling confused.

Wasn't this what she had wanted? To be left to get on with her own life. Hadn't she been pining for this ever since they'd got back from Newcastle? She made herself sit up. She straightened her back and flexed her shoulders and then ran her fingers roughly across her scalp, mussing her hair. She needed to pull herself together. Get ready, go to college, keep her studies going strong, build up momentum for Cambridge. She picked up a towel and went into the en suite and put the shower on. She let the water soak into her hair and drill into her face. This was what she had wanted. To leave the troubles of her family behind her.

Once she was dressed she went into her study and began to pack her bag for college. She put it over her shoulder and looked round her room for stray books. Her eyes settled on her mother's things in the corner.

She let her bag slip down her arm. Energy drained from her.

She walked across and picked up the top box file, labelled in her mother's handwriting, *Legal Papers*. Rose sat cross-legged on the floor and opened it. Inside was a pile of papers covered with the small print of legal documents: pension plans, work contracts, tenancy agreements, life insurance. Rose closed the file. She pulled the second box file across. It was labelled *Old Photographs*. She looked inside and saw wallets of photographs. She plucked some out and saw colour photos of groups of people and places that she didn't recognise. Her mother looked young enough to be at university. All pictures from before Rose was born or when she was a very young child. She found herself looking through these for what seemed like a long time.

Then she picked up the last file which had *Miscellaneous, Old Correspondence* written on the label. Inside were a number of envelopes – *Job Applications, Health* and *Car*. Underneath them was one that said *Personal*. Rose opened it. In it were four short letters and a number of birthday cards. They were all from Brendan to her mother. They were more like notes than letters, no address at the top, only dates. The first was 15 April 2007. The others were written soon after, one in May and two in June. How odd that Brendan would write to her mother after they'd already been together for almost three years. Rose put them down, feeling that she was prying, but after a few moments she picked them up again. She read the first one.

Kathy, my love, I'm sorry about the row last night. I had to leave early this morning so I thought I'd write this and try and explain my feelings. I can't seem to put into words how sad I am about the baby. When you first told me that you were pregnant I was surprised because you and I had no intention of extending our little family. It took me some time to get used to the idea and this upset you, I know.

Rose narrowed her eyes and read on.

I know how depressed you've been since losing it. You think I am pleased but I'm not. It's just that with everything else going on I don't see how a baby can fit into our lives. We're all right as we are. Love you lots. See you in a few days, Brendan

A baby? Her mother had lost a baby? Rose picked up the second letter dated 12 May 2007.

Dear Kathy, I'm sitting in my hotel room with an empty bottle of wine next to me. I'm sorry you're so down and I'd do anything I could to make you happy but we can't change what's already happened. It was out of our hands and we have to move on. We have our family, my Josh and your Rosie. That has to be enough for us.

You should never accuse me of not loving you. I do. You know it.

Brendan.

The next letter was on 8 June 2007.

Kathy, I'm not sure how we can go on like this. I feel that you don't love me any more. It was not my fault that you lost the baby. I'm just trying to look forward. We have a lot going on right now so I have to be away. You know how important our project is. I have to think of the bigger picture. I'll be back by the week-end and then we can talk about what to do. Brendan

The last letter was also dated 21 June 2007.

Dear Kathy, I'll be away for almost a week and I think this will give you time to think things over. I don't agree that our relationship is 'tainted', to use your word. I still love you but I am beginning to doubt that you love me. If everything we had depended on this accidental baby then I've misread things between us for years. We have our family and we have our project. If these things are not enough then I don't know what to say. Ring me. Yours, Brendan.

Rose replaced the letters in the envelope marked *Personal*.

Her mother had been pregnant with Brendan's baby and she had had a miscarriage. Then she and Brendan started to have troubles in their relationship.

Rose wondered whether Anna had read these letters. She had had these papers for over five years. She must have looked through them, analysed them, tried to work out what had happened to her estranged daughter and her partner. It would certainly explain the things she had said about Brendan the previous autumn. She had accused him of murdering Kathy and running away from justice. Maybe these letters had made her think in that way.

Anna had never seen Brendan and her mother together. They had been happy. Rose was sure of that. And yet the letters suggested something different, things that had happened of which Rose had no memory It had taken place in 2007, their last summer together in Brewster Road.

A golden time.

And sometime during that summer Daisy Lincoln had been killed and buried in their garden. She had been suffocated and her hands were tied behind her back with Brendan's tie.

With a heavy heart Rose put her mother's things back in the corner.

She went to college but only stayed for a couple of classes. In the early afternoon she found herself on the tube heading for East London. Just after four thirty she walked up Brewster Road and stood across the road from the house that she had once lived in. It was a strange feeling to be there on her own. The police were no longer around and there was no crime scene tape. The street looked normal, like any other street – cars parked along each side, people walking, groups of young people standing talking. Further along a removal van was parked with the back open and a ramp sloping down to the tarmac. Men were walking up and down it carrying boxes. A woman in a shalwar kameez was standing at the gate holding the hands of two small children, a beaming smile on her face. A family was moving in, starting their new life in Brewster Road.

Rose pulled her eyes away from her old house and walked along the road until she reached number fifty-four. She went to the door and rang the bell. Loud footsteps sounded along the hall and there was a shout of 'I'll get it!' A woman of about forty-five answered. She had short dark hair and half-moon glasses which rested on the end of her nose. She looked quizzically at Rose.

'Mona?' Rose said. 'I'm Rose Smith, Kathy's daughter.'

Sandy's mother looked puzzled, then she took the glasses off, pushed each of the arms closed until the glasses lay flat in her hand.

'Rose Smith. Goodness. Sandy told me she'd seen you and Joshua last week. Come in, come in. Sandy's just upstairs bathing Jade. Come in.'

Rose stepped into the hall. She placed her bag alongside a pushchair and took her coat off and let it hang over her arms.

'It's so nice to see you, Rose, and you're so grown-up. Of course you are. You'll be . . . seventeen?'

Rose nodded.

'Come and have a cup of tea. Sandy will be down soon.'

From upstairs there was the sound of a baby crying. Rose looked up and Mona rolled her eyes.

'I love Jade to bits but she was an unexpected surprise, I can tell you!'

'I saw her. She's very sweet."

'I know! Sandy was in the third year of her degree

course and came home one weekend and told me she was giving it all up. I couldn't believe it. I still can't. But still, if it hadn't happened we wouldn't have little Jade.'

Rose followed Mona into a large kitchen. By the radiator was a clothes horse covered with vests, socks, trousers and tops, as well as sleepwear and blankets.

'Babies generate an awful lot of laundry! Will you have some tea? Coffee?'

'A cold drink if you have it. A glass of tap water is fine,' Rose said, laying her coat over the back of a chair and then sitting down.

'How is Joshua? Sandy said he's back in London.'

'Yes, he's at Queen Mary doing Engineering. He's well.'

'That is good.'

There was a moment's quiet when Rose realised that the baby wasn't crying any more. She glanced up at a noticeboard on the wall and saw a card pinned there. It was white and the front had a series of deep red hearts overlapping each other. At the bottom it said, *You're My Valentine.*

'I'm sure Sandy won't be long,' Mona said, sitting down at the table opposite Rose.

'Actually, Mona, it was you I came to see.'

Mona handed Rose a glass of water. The outside of the glass was still wet to touch and Rose placed it on the table.

'I know that you and Mum were quite friendly.'

'Rose, I'm so sorry about your mum and Brendan and whatever happened to them. It's all such a mystery. Everyone in the street was upset. We often wondered about both of you, how you were doing. And now all this . . .' Mona gesticulated towards the street. 'Have the police said anything to you? Do they know what happened?'

Rose shook her head.

'Mona, I wanted to ask you about that last summer when we were living here. I wondered if you'd known about Mum's baby.'

'About her miscarriage, you mean? I did know. I didn't think she had told you . . .'

'She didn't. I found one of her old letters the other day. I was reading through it and she mentioned it. I had no idea.'

'Well, I suppose it's all right for me to tell you this. Now, after so long. I'm sure she would have told you herself eventually.'

Rose leant forward, her forearm resting on the table.

'You know, Rose, it's funny you should say that your mother and I were close. It must have seemed like that to you, as a child, but we weren't really. Your mother kept herself to herself. She hardly spoke to anyone round here. Most people thought it was because she worked for the police and that she didn't want people to take advantage of that. She spoke to me from time to time but I always thought that was because she needed Sandy to do the babysitting. Then she mostly talked about you. How brainy you were, how well you were doing at school, how you'd bought something for her. She just beamed when she talked about you. But she never really talked about herself. Anyway, she was over here arranging for Sandy to babysit and I think I asked her if she had plans to go on holiday – just small talk – and she burst into tears and told me about the baby. She said she hadn't meant to get pregnant but once it had happened she said she thought it would be a fresh start for them. I remember her saying *fresh start* which I thought was kind of funny. As far as I knew she and Brendan got on well, they always seemed to be together. 'Course he went away now and then but whenever I saw them in the street they were smiling, happy. That's why I allowed Sandy to babysit. I saw them as a completely – how can I put it – a completely secure couple so that when she said it would be a *fresh start* I was surprised.'

Rose nodded. Mona was describing exactly what she remembered. Her mum and Brendan happy and yet the letters seemed to suggest that things had been rocky.

'When they disappeared I was so shocked. It was as if the ground had opened up and swallowed them. Lots of people round here had their opinions. They thought that the pair of them had been caught doing something bad and had made a run for it to another country. All very dramatic but I just didn't believe that. I knew she'd never leave you of her own free will.'

There was the sound of a voice calling from upstairs. Mona looked towards it.

'It's Sandy. I'll just go up and take over with the baby. Do stay and talk to her for a while. She doesn't have a lot of non-mum-and-baby company.'

Mona went out and shortly after Sandy appeared at the door.

'Rose! Nice to see you again.'

'How's the baby?' Rose said.

Sandy gave a long sigh. Her hair was still pulled back and she looked tired. She plonked herself down at the table.

'Jade's fine. You at college, Rose?'

'In Camden. Doing four "A" levels. Applying for uni next year.'

'Well, make sure you finish your degree. Don't be an idiot like me!' she rolled her eyes exaggeratedly.

Rose didn't know what to say. She had never had a conversation like this before. Babies were alien to her; she'd never known one, never been in close contact with anyone in her own generation who had one.

'I love her, though. It's only sometimes I wish . . . well, things were different.'

Sandy's hands were together and Rose looked at her fingers and remembered what her nails had once been like – long, shaped and glittery. Sometimes they had designs stuck on them, black and white check, stars.

'Nice card,' Rose said, pointing at the noticeboard.

'Yeah. Single dad I met at the medical centre. He's got a boy of four. You don't think he'd be interested in me otherwise!'

'I'm sure that's not true.'

'Enough about me! How've you been? I thought about the two of you ever such a lot when you first left. And now with this stuff happening. I was the first one who saw the police cars. I was walking Jade round in the pushchair and then they turned up. One after the other. Three cars and a white van parked all over the place, the police running towards the house as if there was a bomb waiting to go off.'

'Did you know who Daisy's boyfriend was?'

Sandy shook her head. 'No. I hung around with her but I wasn't a *close* friend. No one was that close to her. Her sister, Esther, might have known.'

'I don't think I ever saw her sister.'

'No, she was away at college then. She's a teacher now. She teaches primary school kids in Walthamstow. I was in touch with her on Facebook recently. She's doing really well. Expecting a baby. Daisy talked about her. She looked up to her.'

There was the sound of footsteps coming down the stairs. Rose could hear Mona's voice. She was talking in the silly way that adults did when small children were around. The door opened and she stood there holding Jade. The baby smiled as soon as she saw Sandy and put her arms out in the air.

'She wants her mummy,' Mona said.

Sandy stepped forward and took her. Rose put her coat back on.

'I have to go,' she said, edging past them.

'I'll come to the door with you,' Sandy said.

'Bye, Mona.'

Rose's bag was by the pushchair and she picked it up. At the front door she stood for a moment. Jade was making sounds, her fist in her mouth. There was a strong smell of talcum powder. A strand of Sandy's hair had come loose and was hanging across her eye. She used her hand to push it back but it fell forward again.

'Tomorrow night I'm going to a pub in Kentish Town called the Pink Parrot with some friends.' Rose said. 'Why don't you come along? There's some entertainment and my friends are really nice. You'd be welcome.'

Sandy made a face. Rose thought it was because she was so much older. A twenty-two year old in a pub full of sixth-form college students.

'It'll be fun,' she said, remembering Sara and Maggie's words to her.

'I'm sure it will be,' Sandy said. 'And thanks for asking. I could come. Mum would look after Jade but I don't want to leave her. Thing is, Rose, I *like* being with her, looking after her. I did all that stuff. Standing in pubs, mooning after boys. Now it's just me and Jade.'

'Don't forget the Valentine's card.'

'And him too, maybe.'

Rose opened her bag and pulled out her phone. 'Give me your number so I can stay in touch. There could be something on at college that you might like.'

Sandy smiled and handed the baby to Rose, taking Rose's phone from her. Rose, startled, grasped the child awkwardly, a little away from her. The child stared at her with interest and Rose felt she should say something or rock her up and down. She didn't, though, she just held her stiffly, feeling awkward while Sandy tapped her number into the phone.

'Here,' Sandy said, holding it out to her. 'Let's swap.'

Relieved, Rose handed the baby back.

'Bye, then.'

'Look after yourself, little Rosie!' Sandy said.

ELEVEN

The Pink Parrot was definitely a student pub. As soon as Rose walked in she saw Maggie and Sara standing by the bar. They both smiled at her and then gave each other a secretive 'I told you she would come' glance. The place was crammed with vaguely familiar faces and once Sara had got some drinks the three of them headed for a table in the back room. It had a stage which cut across one corner and the rest of the floor was full of chairs and a few tables.

As they sat down Sara and Maggie were talking about Jamie Roberts from Law.

'He broke up with his girlfriend just after Christmas.'

'They'd been together since, like, Year Ten.'

'He's into vintage, music and stuff. He's an interesting person.'

'And he's got that jet black hair.'

Rose held in a sigh. Sara and Maggie had clearly decided that she needed a boyfriend and Jamie Roberts from Law was fitting the bill.

'What time does the entertainment start?' she said.

'Soon. Any time.'

The back room filled up in dribs and drabs. Some other girls joined their table and made small talk with Rose. Music was playing and the room seemed to get darker and warmer at the same time. A young man started to fiddle with a microphone that was on the stage. Not long after there were a couple of acts. A man with a guitar sang four songs which Rose quite liked. Next was a comedian who told some complicated jokes which she didn't like. After that there was piped music and she sat back in her seat and watched Sara and Maggie dip in and out of animated conversations with the new girls who had come. One of them, a girl from her English class, started to talk to her about an essay that had to be in. When they'd exhausted the subject she looked down at Rose's clothes and said, 'Like the black and white look. Quite sixties.' Rose smiled and fiddled with the buttons on her jacket. Sitting back, finishing her drink, she realised that she was enjoying herself.

Maggie and Sara were collecting money for a round of drinks. Rose got hers out and dropped it into Maggie's cupped hands. As Maggie went through the door into the other bar Jamie Roberts came in with some lads from college. He came across to them. Maggie's seat was empty and Jamie sat in it and started to talk to the others. Rose stiffened with apprehension. She'd spoken to Jamie before but it had always been about work. She reached out and picked up her glass even though it was empty.

'You won't get any more out of that,' he said.

'No,' she said, putting it back down again.

'Someone told me you have a tattoo?'

Rose frowned. Then she remembered showing the tattoo to Sara and Maggie when she'd first had it done.

'Is it somewhere that I can see? Without embarrassing everyone?'

Rose hesitated but took her jacket off and crumpled it up on her lap. Then she rolled the arm of her T-shirt up. There on her skin was her butterfly tattoo.

'Not bad,' Jamie said.

Rose was immediately reminded of Joshua's tattoo, a more strident image than hers. His butterfly had been imprinted on to one side of his ribs and looked as though it was moving in flight.

'I've got a tattoo,' Jamie said.

He rolled his sleeve up to show an ornate diagram of a dragon. The tail stretched most of the way down his arm. A couple of the other girls were *ooh*ing and *aah*ing at it but it had irritated Rose. It was as if he'd asked her about her tattoo so that he had an excuse to show off his own. She put her jacket back on and looked away towards the stage. He kept talking to her, though. She *mm*ed but kept her head turned away.

'People say you're stand-offish, Rose, but I didn't think that was true.'

'Who says I'm stand-offish?' she said, turning back.

'Um . . .' he said as if thinking hard. 'Just about everyone. Barring Maggie and Sara.'

'I'm not,' she said sharply. 'Just because I'm not desperate to talk to people doesn't mean . . . If people had interesting things to say then I might want to listen!'

'OK, fair enough. I won't speak. You speak. Tell me about yourself. What bands do you like? Which universities are you applying to? What was the last really great movie you saw and who's your favourite writer?'

Rose opened her mouth to say something sharp and suddenly she couldn't. She smiled and felt her shoulders slacken.

'Is this a test?' she said.

'Maybe.'

'Of what?'

'Sociability.'

'What if I fail?'

'Retake it.'

Maggie returned with the drinks. She placed the tray on the table and beamed over at them.

Loud music came on and Rose saw a DJ behind some turntables. He was dancing from side to side on the stage. His eyes were closed as if he was carried away with the music. Actually the songs he played weren't bad and she

115

felt herself loosening up. Her elbow touched Jamie's and she didn't move it away. She drank another beer and listened while Jamie talked about a movie he had seen. It was a movie she had thought looked good but recently going to the cinema had not been high on her agenda.

'I'm going for a smoke,' he said. 'Be back shortly.'

When he had gone she felt her phone vibrate. She pulled it out of her pocket and looked down at the screen in case it was Joshua. The name *Henry* showed. Puzzled, she put it back in her pocket. A comedian came on at the same time that Jamie returned. It was a lad from her college. She recognised him and laughed at some of his jokes. Her phone vibrated again. She looked at the screen and saw the name *Henry* again. What did he want? At eleven o'clock on a Friday night?

'I've just got to make a call,' she said to Jamie.

She walked out of the room and through the main bar, heading for the door to the street. She edged through the throng of people and went outside. Once there she was in the middle of a dozen or so smokers so she found a space against the wall and returned the call. It was cold and she pulled her jacket tight. Henry answered after a couple of rings.

'Rose? I'm at A and E at Whittington Hospital. It's near Archway. Do you know it?'

'Not really. Maybe. I'm out with friends, Henry.'

'I was called here because of a serious RTA.'

'What?'

'Road traffic accident.'

'OK. What's that got to do with me?'

'I was walking round, waiting to speak to a witness, and I saw your stepbrother, Joshua. He's been in a fight of some sort. I'm afraid he's pretty badly hurt.'

Rose held her breath. Beside her a couple were kissing passionately, the girl on tiptoes, the boy's arms around her back, gathering her up towards him. The girl's hand was in mid-air, her cigarette glowing in the dark.

'Did you hear me, Rose?'

She felt sick. She put her hand out to lean on the brick wall.

'How badly is he hurt?' she said.

'I can't say for sure but I thought you'd want to know. Do you know where the Whittington Hospital is?'

'No, but I'll find it. I can get a cab. I'll be there soon.'

'I don't know if I'll still be here . . .' Henry was saying but Rose ended the call.

She stood very still for a moment. Joshua had been in a fight? It wasn't possible. She went back into the pub and made her way through to the back room. A girl was singing on the stage. It was mostly quiet apart from a few murmuring voices.

'I've got to go,' she said in a low voice.

She leant across Jamie and pulled her coat from round the back of the chair.

'Why?' Jamie whispered.

'Personal stuff. Sorry, I'll see you in college.'

She left before anyone could say anything to her, Outside, on the street she asked a couple of smokers if they knew where a cab place was. She walked briskly along until she came to it. The cold air freshened her up. When she got to it there was a long queue and she swore gently. Just then a black cab was coming along. She stepped out into the traffic and confidently hailed it. She'd seen Anna do it often enough.

'Can you take me to Whittington Hospital A and E?'

The cab driver looked suspiciously at her.

'Just you. I don't want no one injured in the back of my cab,' he said.

'It's just me.'

'It'll be about twelve quid. You got that?'

'I can give it to you now if you like.'

'Hop in,' he said.

She got in and sat in the corner of the seat, pulling the seat belt across her. She didn't look out of the window but closed her eyes and tried to keep calm.

She paid her money and ran into the A and E department. She sidestepped people who were standing round to get to the reception desk. There was a queue and she had to wait. She looked around, bursting with frustration. Then she saw Henry. He was in uniform and was standing by a pair of swing doors talking into a mobile phone.

She walked swiftly towards him, waited until he'd finished and then patted him on the arm.

'Henry, where is Joshua? Can I see him?'

Henry took her arm.

'I can take you to him in five minutes or so. It's not my case. I'm here for something else but I've got a few minutes so I can show you where he is. He's being stitched up at the moment.'

'He's having stitches? He's been cut?'

'He said he'd been in a fight.'

'Joshua isn't like that!'

'I asked him if he'd been attacked and whether he knew the boy concerned but he just wouldn't say. He says it was nothing and he didn't want to talk about it. I've seen this before, Rose. Teenage boys attacked by others. They won't press charges – they just have some idea of revenge and that could lead to even greater injury. Maybe you could talk to him. We could press charges. If he needs any reconstructive surgery then someone could go to prison for this.'

'Reconstructive surgery! How badly has he been cut?'

Rose's voice was squeaking with alarm.

'Don't upset yourself, Rose. I spoke to the doctor very briefly. Like I said, it's not my case but . . .'

'Henry, *please* tell me what's happened to him.'

'It looks as though someone has tried to cut off his ear.'

Rose felt faint. She stepped backwards and felt the wall behind her. Henry put his hand out to keep her steady.

'It's horrible, I know. I've never heard of a gang round here using this method but maybe it's a new thing. I hope it isn't,' he said grimly.

TWELVE

Rose felt sick. She made as if to move past Henry but her step faltered. She didn't know where to go. The rest of the waiting area was packed, all the seats taken and with other people standing around. Straight across from where they were a man was sitting on the floor, his legs splayed out. He had only one shoe on and the other foot showed a grey sock. He had a towel held to his jaw and a woman was kneeling down beside him, mumbling something. Rose looked about hopelessly.

'I can't believe it,' Rose said. 'Joshua's ear?'

'They don't know how bad the damage is . . .'

'Who would do such a thing?'

But even as she spoke she knew who it was. A feeling of absolute certainty held her. She would have sworn an oath to it. Henry looked pained and she realised that she was crying. She pulled a tissue out of her pocket and pressed it against her eyelids. In her head she saw a deserted cottage on the mudflats in North Norfolk. She and Joshua had been there months before. It had been cold and dark and the two of them had been hiding in an outbuilding. They had sat very stiff, hardly drawing breath while Viktor Baranksi's son, Lev, together with his men, searched the place. They'd been discovered and dragged out to the front of the cottage. Joshua was bruised and battered and she had stood weak and useless beside him. The lights of Lev Baranski's silver SUV had been turned on them as if they were being interrogated. He spoke icily. *You tell your father I will never stop looking for him.*

'I know this is upsetting for you. I wish I could find you a seat but . . .' Henry held his hands out at the crammed waiting area. 'I'll go and check on Joshua. Probably better if he doesn't see you upset like this. When you're calmer you can make arrangements to take him home.'

Rose watched him go and thought back to that night at the cottage in Norfolk. Lev Baranski and his men holding them prisoners, threatening Joshua. *I have not forgotten my father's death and I never will.* Mikey, the man who had pulled out a knife, pointed it at Joshua and said, *You want I should rough him? Hurt him? Just a little message for father? An eye? An ear?* Lev Baranski, who thought that his father had been killed by Brendan, had taken a minute to think over Mikey's question. *No, not this time. This time I want him to go to his father and say that Lev Baranski wants to see him . . .*

Henry came through the swing doors.

'You can see him now. He's a bit drowsy and numb. But he's awake.'

Rose followed Henry through the doors into a wide corridor. They passed a number of cubicles, some with their curtains drawn, some open. Doctors seemed to wander round in their scrubs, looking as though they'd been called out of an operating theatre. There was a group of people studying a whiteboard which had been divided into sections and had names scribbled on in untidy black felt-tip.

When they got to the end of the corridor Henry paused by a cubicle. Rose looked inside. Joshua was sitting on a chair. He was dressed, his elbows on his knees. As he turned to her she saw that his ear was bandaged. On top of the bandage, sticking plaster stretched across his cheek and down his neck.

'Oh no,' she said.

'Rosie,' he said, cupping the injury with his hand as if to hide it.

'I should get back to my RTA,' Henry said.

'Thank you so much,' Rose said, gripping Henry's hand for a moment.

When the policeman had gone Rose pulled up a chair and sat alongside Joshua and put her arm around him, turning him towards her so that she could look at his face. It wasn't just his ear. He had a black eye and there was blood on his lip. His neck looked red or bruised. He had on a checked shirt and it looked as though the top buttons had come off.

'Baranski?' she whispered.

He nodded. He paused a moment as if making sure no one but Rose was listening to him.

'He came to the flat. I answered the door and there he was. I tried to close it but his minder – the guy with the knife, Mikey? He was behind him. He dragged me into his car.'

'When did this happen?' she said, pointing to the bandage on his ear.

'He drove up to Hampstead Heath. We got out of the car and they spent a lot of time questioning me, being nice, joking with me. Then it turned nasty. Mikey got his knife out.'

'Oh . . .'

She grabbed his hand and held it tightly.

'It was awful, Rose. Pain like I've never felt. It was red hot, like my head was on fire. I think I might have passed out. When I woke up I was in the car and they drove me here and dumped me outside. There's a split at the top of my ear. Some cartilage has been damaged and I've got stitches,' he shrugged.

'I can't believe it!' she said. 'You can't go back to the flat. You have to come back to Anna's. Stay with us for a while.'

'Your gran's?'

'She'll be fine about it,' Rose said.

A picture of Anna's worried face came into her head but she pushed it away. Just then the curtain was pulled back, making a sharp sound that rang in her ears. She looked up to see a young male doctor. He looked tired and had a pen nestled behind one ear. While he was speaking he fiddled with it.

'Mr Johnson, I have your medication here. Antibiotics and painkillers.'

Rose stood up.

'He'll be ready soon,' the doctor said to her.

'I'll be outside, Josh. I'll just phone Anna and let her know that we are coming.'

Joshua nodded. Rose walked out through the swing doors and headed for the exit. She felt the tension of the last hour drain from her. Joshua needed to stay with her. She had to look after him. Outside, she stood next to the building in the glow of the light spilling from the windows. She got out her phone and was thinking of what to say to her grandmother when she felt a hand grab her arm roughly and hoist her away from the light.

'What?' she said.

She pulled hard, holding herself back, trying to dig her heels into the ground but another hand had gripped her free arm and in moments she found herself half dragged, half lifted round the corner of the building and pushed rudely into a recess between two pillars. In front of her were Lev Baranski and Mikey.

Even though she'd only seen them once she recognised them immediately. Lev Baranski was tall and thin, dressed in a knee-length leather coat over trousers. Mikey was shorter and wider and wore a large roll-neck sweater over jeans. He had her bag in his hands and she put her hand out to get it but he pulled it back like some tug of war.

'You see your boyfriend?' Lev Baranski said, ignoring what was going on.

He was staring intently at her. His hair was thin at the front. It made his forehead look larger than the rest of his face. Mikey was on the ground, picking up her things.

'Get off,' she said. 'Give me my bag.'

But Lev pushed her back and grabbed the front of her coat, pulling it towards him. His breath was hot on her face.

'You see what we can do? Next time the whole ear. Or maybe worse. You tell him that we want to speak to his father. Tell him that, for now, we just want to talk. If we have to wait much longer then there will be no talking.'

Rose heard a flicking sound and saw Mikey holding his knife up in front of him.

'Shame if pretty girl like you lose her looks.'

Rose stared hard at him. She would not cower. She would not flinch. He moved the knife in a circle in front of her face like a silly game. She was still as a rock, her heart thumping like a bass drum. He rested the tip of the knife on her chin.

She held her breath.

Then he took it away and retracted the blade and threw it into the air as if he was juggling it. Both of them turned and walked away, Lev Baranski pulling at his leather coat as if to smooth it down, Mikey out front, jauntily heading away from her.

Her bag was on the ground and she picked it up.

She stumbled around the corner and then went back into the hospital. She looked around for the toilet and headed there. It was a single cubicle and she locked the door and sat on the closed seat, making herself breathe slowly. She was thoroughly shaken up, her blood racing through her veins. The skin on her right arm was sore and she pressed on it with her other hand. She found herself rocking gently back and forward, a feeling of helplessness taking hold of her.

All she'd wanted to do was go out on a Friday night like other students. To have a few beers, a few laughs, maybe flirt with Jamie from Law. She'd even been enjoying herself, warmed up by the chatter and the music and the jokes. She'd felt comfortable in the Pink Parrot until Henry's call had come. What if the policeman hadn't been in the hospital? Hadn't stumbled on Joshua being treated? What if she had never known that he was hurt?

She might be still there in the pub or back at someone's house for drinks or maybe walking back home with Jamie from Law, waiting for him to lean down and kiss her. Then Joshua would have been on his own and it wouldn't have been anything to do with her. Not her responsibility.

Was there a little of her that wished this was true?

She stood up and leant over the tiny sink, cupping water from the tap and splashing it on her face. Then she looked into the mirror. At the point on her chin where Mikey's knife had rested was a bubble of blood. It startled her.

The door handle moved.

'Anyone in there?' a woman's voice called.

'Just a minute,' she said.

She got a wad of tissue and patted the blood. Her skin was clear for a second then it came again, bright red, scarlet. She held the tissue up to her chin and pressed it. She opened the door and without a word passed the woman who was waiting. She looked round. Joshua was over by the exit doors, looking for her. The sight of the dressings on his ear made her flinch. He looked like someone wounded in a war. He was in the checked shirt she had seen earlier, no coat. She walked towards him. He turned round to her. His face fell into a frown as she came closer.

'What's the matter?' he said. 'What's happened? Has something happened?'

She took the tissue away from her chin.

'I've seen Lev and Mikey,' she said.

'Rosie, you're bleeding. What did they do to you?'

'It's nothing. Let's get out of here.'

In the cab, on the way home, she sent a text to Anna and told her that Joshua had fallen off his bike and had been to A and E. She said that she was bringing him back to stay the night in the attic and that she hoped Anna wouldn't mind.

She sat back and watched the lights of the city zip past her. It was late, almost two o'clock. Joshua was slumped against her. He felt hot and heavy. She put her arm around him and kissed his head.

'Stay with me for a few nights,' she whispered. 'Sleep it off, get better. Then we'll think about what to do.'

He looked up at her sleepily. The side of his face was covered with dressings and plaster. His lip was swollen.

'What happened to your mouth?' she said, lifting her finger and running it along the swollen part.

'Punched.'

She winced and pictured Mikey and Lev Baranski marching Joshua along Hampstead Heath the same way they'd taken her from the front of the hospital, into the dark so that they could do what they wanted with him. She was filled with guilt. How could she have wished she'd not known about this?

She lowered her face and kissed his bruised lip. He stared at her.

'We'll sort this out,' she said.

He put his arm around her and held her tight.

The taxi sped through the empty streets towards Belsize Park.

THIRTEEN

Joshua slept late. Rose went up to the attic periodically but each time he was still in the same position, the duvet at a slant, a corner of it touching the carpet. She stood and looked for a moment. His chest was rising and falling, his face slumped on the pillow, his bandages bright and startling against the bedding. It gave her a twinge of nausea to think of what he had been through at the hands of Mikey. She touched her chin. Her cut had dried up quickly. Still it had shaken her. The flick of a knife had given this man power to maim her. It made her angry as well, her fists clenching at the memory.

It was gone twelve when Joshua finally woke. Rose heard him moving about and she dashed up the stairs and found him sitting on the side of the bed. He was taking some tablets, one hand holding his ear where the dressings were.

'I feel like someone hit me on the side of the head with a hammer,' he said huskily.

'Shall I get you some tea and toast?'

'Just tea,' he said. 'I don't feel much like eating. I'll probably lie down again.'

'OK.'

She brought the tea and then left him alone. She went down to her study and tried to get on with some work. From time to time she paused by the stairwell and listened then at just after five she heard the upstairs shower going. She waited and then crept up and knocked before opening the door very slightly.

'Are you OK?' she called.

'Come in.'

He was dressed, sitting on the side of the bed, his head in his hands.

'How are you feeling?'

'A bit dopey. Painkillers,' he said, pointing to a strip of tablets on the bedside cabinet. 'Those are strong.'

She sat on the bed beside him. She put her arm round his shoulder. He lifted his hand and placed it on hers.

'Will you come downstairs? Eat something?'

'Yeah. I'd best have something.'

She stood up and pulled him to his feet. He turned towards her and seemed to flinch for a moment, raising his hand to cover his injured ear. She made a sympathetic face and they went downstairs.

Anna was shocked.

'Good Lord, that looks dreadful!' she said.

Her grandmother was getting ready to go out. She had tickets for a concert, Rose knew. She had on a woollen suit and very high heels. She was holding some cream leather gloves.

Rose retold the story about the bike accident. It rolled out easily and she added a few details about a car being involved and Joshua being taken to hospital in an ambulance.

'What's happened to the bike?'

Rose looked at Joshua.

'It's written off, I'm afraid.'

'You're insured?'

'I think so.'

Anna nodded. 'Stay here for a few days. Until you're well.'

'No, I'll be fine.'

'I insist. Just till you're feeling better. Persuade him, Rose.'

Anna left them in the kitchen.

'You should stay.'

'Why? Baranski can find me here as well. He must know where you live. He's not an idiot.'

'Camden is so busy all the time it's hard to see if anyone is watching you. Here it's quiet. All the houses have good security and there are alarms. People would notice someone hanging round.'

Joshua didn't answer but she sensed he understood her point.

'I'd have to bring a few things. My laptop, files and stuff.'

'Sure. The room's private. Anna never goes up there.'

He nodded.

'We could go now. Get a cab. Drive the Mini back.'

Joshua shook his head.

'No, the Mini stays where it is.'

He said it sharply. She felt chastised as if she'd been insensitive. Of course he wouldn't be able to drive. The injury to his head may have affected his confidence or his balance and then there were the painkillers that were making him drowsy.

'OK. Why don't we go now?'

Anna insisted on giving them a lift to Camden on her way to the Royal Festival Hall. The car smelled of polish and as they drove there was classical music playing. Anna drove slowly and carefully, leaning forward, both hands gripping the wheel. Eventually she pulled up outside Lettuce and Stuff, just beyond a double red line.

A car tooted angrily from behind.

'Have a good evening,' Rose called, shutting the door.

Lights were on inside the flat. Joshua saw her looking up to the windows.

'Baranski grabbed me as I answered the door. They slammed it behind me. I didn't have my phone or keys or anything. The lights, the TV, my computer, it's all on up there. My beer bottle is sitting on the desk untouched. Wait here. I'll get my spare key from the cafe.'

He went into the cafe and came back out moments later. When he opened the front door Rose could hear the television from upstairs. She followed him up.

'Luckily I wasn't running a bath,' he said.

She went into the kitchen.

'Just going to pack a few things,' he said, heading off.

There were some dishes waiting to be washed and a jumper hanging over the back of a chair. The table had books and folders on it. Rose picked up one of them. It was a big battered paperback book, *A History of Engineering and Technology: Artful Methods*. It had several Post-its stuck to pages and a ruler lying through the middle of it like a bookmark. The kitchen still looked bare. The absence of Skeggsie's things meant there were gaps everywhere.

'Want me to pack up your college stuff?' she called.

Joshua said something but he was in the next room and she couldn't quite hear him. She went after him.

'I said do you want me to pack . . .'

On the bed was a holdall that he'd been throwing things into.

'No college stuff. College is on the back burner for the moment. I've got other things to think about.'

He had a large brown padded envelope in his hands. On the outside was written *Private and Confidential. Joshua Johnson*. It was the envelope that held the remainder of Frank Richards' notebooks. It was the last thing they'd talked about before he sent her the email to say that he wanted a break from her.

He saw her looking at it.

'Rosie, I need to tell you a few things. Maybe explain why I think Baranski came round to see me when he did. There's some stuff I didn't tell you about.'

Rose sat on the very corner of Joshua's bed. Her legs were tightly together and she crossed her arms.

'I know where Dad and Kathy are.'

She didn't respond. The words seemed to fall around her. The same old story – we know where they are, no we don't, yes we do.

'I've been researching Macon Parker. He was the name on the empty notebook?'

'I know. You told me before that he was a doctor and lived in Essex near Wickby.'

'Macon Parker is forty-eight, born in Denver, came to this country in 2001 to work in University College Hospital in London. Worked on the Renal Unit and then worked for a while as part of a kidney transplant team. He did various placements and ended up at St Thomas's in Westminster in 2006. He got a job there as a senior registrar and then a year or so later he went into private practice. Now he's a businessman with interests in private health companies. He has a house in the US and France and he also owns a house in a small village called Two Oaks.'

Joshua paused but Rose didn't say anything.

'He has a company website, Quality Lifestyles. It's an umbrella heading for a whole range of small companies to do with health. Anyway, that's where his legal income comes from. But I also found this article. It's from a Sunday newspaper supplement, just over three years ago. It's about the harvesting of organs.'

'What?'

'It says that there is a flourishing trade in organs. People from Third World countries travel to Britain on some kind of student visa and while they're here they sell an organ. They've been promised twenty thousand pounds for a kidney. Twenty thousand pounds is a fortune for these people – it's like winning the lottery. They come here, undergo an operation and then they get a few hundred pounds for their trouble. The rest of the money goes towards their travel, visa arrangements, medical care and so on. They go home with a few hundred pounds and only one kidney. And that's not the worst.'

'What?'

Joshua shrugged. 'Some of them don't go back at all because they don't just donate one kidney, they donate both, plus liver, plus anything else that's needed. Look at this.'

He handed her a printout. It was a section from the Sunday supplement article. It showed what looked like a family photo of a teenage girl. She was standing beside someone but that person's face was pixelated. The article was adjacent to the picture.

Polina Bokun, nineteen years old, from Belarus. The hairdressing student came to London on a student visa in 2002. She disappeared from her lodgings four weeks after her arrival. Months later her body was found in the Thames Estuary near Shoeburyness. A post-mortem showed that both kidneys and liver had been removed.

'This is horrible.'

'The article mentions Macon Parker by name. It says that one of his companies was involved in the visa scams and in organising travel and accommodation for these people. It hints that the British police were looking into his affairs.'

'Why wasn't he arrested?'

'I guess because there was no hard evidence. I found some later media references to him because he sued this newspaper for libel. The matter was settled out of court and a retraction was printed.'

'Is this why his name was on the notebook?'

'I would think so. A couple of days ago I drove to his house in Essex. It's like a mansion.'

Rose exhaled. 'Where does this leave us?'

She realised that she'd used the word *us*. Was it *us* again? The two of them *together*?

'It leaves us with a problem. I told you that Lev Baranski took me to Hampstead Heath? Well, he didn't beat me up straight away. He and Mikey questioned me and asked me why I kept driving out to Essex. They said that they knew that that was where my father was.'

'They're following you?'

'I think they must have. Maybe they've been watching me for a while. They know I drive a Mini. Mikey actually mentioned Two Oaks so they must have tailed me last week. Maybe that was what brought about the attack. The thing is they can't know about Macon Parker's house because I parked the car and walked to it. No one was following me then. This makes it absolutely imperative that we find Dad and Kathy.'

Rose didn't argue. It explained why Joshua hadn't wanted to drive Skeggsie's car. She sensed what was coming next.

'If we don't find them, Rose, Baranski will. It's a small village. If they are there, living in some cottage, biding their time until they can execute Macon Parker then Baranski will find them.'

'What do you think he'll do?'

'He thinks my dad killed his father. We know that's true. If he finds them he'll kill my dad.'

What about my mum? she wanted to say. But she didn't need to. Lev Baranski would realise that she was part of it and he would kill her as well.

'I tried to find them, Rose, because I wanted to stop them living this life that they're living. I wanted to stop them killing any more. And all I've done is bring Baranski to them.'

He looked pained. He shook his head and rubbed at his short hair. She couldn't say anything to make him feel better. She knew it was true.

FOURTEEN

They packed Joshua's things and tidied up the kitchen, throwing unused food into a black rubbish bag. Rose was about to call for a cab when the doorbell rang. It was almost nine o'clock. Joshua looked edgy and told Rose to stay where she was and he went downstairs. She saw him put the chain on and open the door slowly. He had an exchange with someone then he took the chain off and pulled the door back. Rose saw the detective from Brewster Road, Wendy Clarke, standing at the bottom of the stairs. She was pointing to Joshua's bandaged ear and asking him what had happened. Rose had recognised her at once even though she looked very different to when she'd seen her more than a week before. Her ginger hair was loose and looked frizzy and she had a long raincoat on over a suit that made her look like a businesswoman. She came up the stairs talking all the time about local gangs and the dangers of being a young man on the streets of London at night. She puffed when she got to the top, out of breath.

'Rose here as well,' she said. 'That's a stroke of luck. I wanted to see you both and I was passing by so I thought I'd have a word with Joshua and here you are too. Are you going somewhere?'

She was looking at Joshua's holdall and other bags that were lined up on the landing.

'He's staying at my grandmother's for a while. Just until he's recovered.'

'That's good of you. Have you made a complaint against these boys who attacked you?'

'I didn't get a good look at them.'

'That's a shame.'

They stood awkwardly on the landing.

'Well, could I just have a few minutes of your time? Before you go off?'

'Sure,' Joshua said, pushing open the kitchen door, turning the light back on.

Wendy Clarke walked ahead of them. She took a Black-Berry and a tin out of her pocket and laid them on the table. Then she slipped her raincoat off and placed it across the back of a chair. She sat down, making herself comfortable. Rose kept her coat on and sat on a chair with her hands in her pockets. Joshua was beside her.

'I half expected to hear from you – either of you – after your visit to Brewster Road.'

There was quiet and she seemed to look penetratingly at each of them. Rose began to feel uneasy. So far Wendy

142

Clarke had been friendly and polite but Rose sensed something else coming.

'I did give you my card.'

'I thought you only wanted us to ring you if we remembered something,' Joshua said.

'And you didn't remember anything. Not one single thing.'

'I was eleven going on twelve,' Rose said.

'I . . . We did remember some things. 'Course we did but nothing that we thought was relevant to . . .'

'What things did you remember?'

Wendy Clarke was smiling but Rose saw something rock hard behind her expression. She'd not come here just for a little chat.

'What is it you want us to say?' Rose said. 'I remember my mum shopping with me for my school uniform. Is that relevant to your investigation?'

'You mean the dead girl under the garden. You mean Daisy Lincoln who was tied up, killed and then buried under the ground. That investigation?'

'Why are you saying it like that? We've not done anything.'

Wendy Clarke took a deep breath. She picked up her BlackBerry and looked at it. Then she put it down again and opened the tin.

'You can't smoke in here,' Joshua said immediately.

'Just making a couple of roll-ups. That's all right, isn't it?'

143

Joshua didn't answer and Wendy took out a small green packet and pulled out three papers which she laid flat on the table. She used the tips of her fingers to smooth them out.

'I have a bit of a problem where you two are concerned. When I didn't get a call from either of you I was surprised. I thought you might come up with a load of irrelevancies – barbecues in the garden, Mum digging up plants, Dad painting the shed, noises in the night and so on. This is the stuff we get and sometimes, in the middle of all those memories, is an interesting nugget, something that might help the investigation. But what did I get from you two? *Nada*. Nothing at all. Just silence.'

She stared at them again. Then she pinched out some tobacco from a packet and laid it carefully on one of the papers. She carried on and did the same with the other two. She was concentrating, pulling the tobacco so that it fitted the papers. Rose felt she ought to say something to fill the uncomfortable silence but she didn't.

'So I had a quick look at your history. You both have this awful tragedy in your life. You lost your parents in November 2007. You were split up and you grew up in different cities. Then last September you, Joshua, came to London to study at Queen Mary College and you met up again. That's how I understand it. Am I right?'

Rose nodded, glancing sideways at Joshua.

'And since then your life reads a bit like a soap opera plot. I don't mean to be rude . . .'

Wendy Clarke pulled a pad out of her jacket pocket and flicked through the pages.

'Last autumn, Rose, you witnessed the murder of two teenagers from your college?'

Rose nodded.

'Then a friend of yours was killed. A girl from your old boarding school . . . I've got the name here . . .'

'Rachel Bliss,' Rose said.

'That's right. Then, Joshua, before Christmas, your uncle had an accident in Newcastle and then your friend, Darren Skeggs, was stabbed to death in an alley.'

Joshua's face was completely still, showing no expression.

'This is extraordinary. Two young people skirting on the edge of something dark. If I were a betting person I'd lay money on the fact that,' she said, pointing to Joshua's bandaged ear, '*that* is something to do with all these other things.'

'We've just been unlucky,' Rose said.

'Please. Most people go through their lives without touching on death at all. You two, between you, have made a pastime of turning up at murders.'

'I didn't *turn up* at my friend's murder. I was trying to *find* him. And I object to the tone in which you are

145

talking about this. My friend's life was snatched from him by some thug in an alley. This is no soap opera and no joke.'

'And neither is a girl buried in the back garden of the house you once lived in. I took time and effort to get you two over to that house to jog your memory and you didn't even have the courtesy to call me.'

'We should have, you're right,' Rose said, realising that they'd just put the visit out of their minds.

'But *why* should we? This is nothing to do with us,' Joshua said.

'It was in your garden and this poor girl's hands were tied together with your father's tie. It is linked to your family whether you like it or not.'

'But not us!' Joshua said, shoving his chair back so that it scraped along the floor.

Wendy Clarke used her index fingers and thumbs to pick up one of the cigarette papers and raised it to her lips. Keeping her eyes on them she licked the edge of the paper and began to roll it gently in her fingers. Pinching the loose tobacco from the end she added it to the next cigarette and picked that up and went through the same procedure.

Rose was agitated. She wanted to explain.

'I'm not trying to make excuses but that time, that summer, just blurs for me. Maybe for Josh too. I spent so long thinking about those days before my mum and

Brendan went missing, that November, trying to recreate that time to see if I could find a clue to where they were . . .'

Rose stumbled on her words. Now she knew where they were it didn't alter the fact that she had *once* thought like this.

'So my memories of them are always about those days in November. The previous summer just merges into lots of summers.'

She was lying. Since reading Brendan's letters she had more information about that summer but she wasn't going to talk about it *now*.

'OK. Well, here's a new question for both of you. Did your parents ever take you to a cottage in Norfolk?'

They both stared at her.

'No,' Rose said.

'No,' Joshua said.

'Did they ever talk about a cottage in Norfolk they might have rented?'

'No, they never talked about Norfolk.'

'Or any cottage anywhere. Why?' Rose said.

'I've been talking to Daisy's sister, Esther. She's a teacher, lives in Walthamstow. She said that they regularly spoke on the phone and she remembers her sister boasting about going away with her new boyfriend to Norfolk. She joked with her sister about this implying that he was *older* than a boyfriend. An older man.'

Rose couldn't speak. She didn't know what to say. She kept eye contact with Wendy Clarke until the police-woman looked down and began to pack away her finished roll-ups in the tin.

'We don't know,' Joshua said. 'We don't remember.'

'You're speaking for both of you now?'

'I don't remember either,' Rose said.

'You know what? There's something funny going on here. I'd say that you two know an awful lot more than you're letting on. And if I find that you – either of you – knew something that could have helped my investigation then I will have you up for perverting the course of justice. That's a prison sentence if you're asking.'

'We know nothing about the murder of Daisy Lincoln. Nothing.'

Wendy Clarke looked from Rose to Joshua. Her fingers were tapping on the tin.

'But there's something you do know, right? Something you're not telling. I can see it in your eyes. I interview hundreds of people and I know when they are holding something back. You two know something. You're sharing a secret that you think I don't need to know about. I hope for your sakes that you're right about that.'

No one spoke. Wendy Clarke stood up and took her raincoat from the back of the chair. She put her Black-Berry and pad in one pocket and the tin of roll-ups in the other.

'OK. We need to make this more formal. I want to see you, Joshua, Monday morning at ten, Bethnal Green Police Station. It's just off the Roman Road – look it up on the internet. Likewise, Monday at twelve for you, Rose. I want you there promptly and I want you ready to start opening up to me or else I could become quite a big problem in both your lives. Am I making myself clear?'

Neither of them moved or spoke.

'I'll let myself out,' she said.

They both listened to her going down the stairs, one heavy footstep after another. Then the front door opened and shut.

'The cottage in Stiffkey,' Joshua said in a low voice.

'How could Daisy know about that?'

'Unless it's a coincidence.'

'It can't be.'

'All the more reason to find them. Then we can ask them what they know about Daisy. We can demand to know.'

'You think that it might be part of . . .'

'No, no. No. Whatever they've done it was for a reason. It was for justice. I don't agree with it and neither do you but there was – is – a logic. This thing with Daisy, it's just *murder*.'

Rose looked at Joshua.

'And what they did to Lev Baranski's father? Tying his

hands up and throwing him into the North Sea. That wasn't *murder*?'

'Baranski had done terrible things. What about the girls in the container?'

'But where does it stop, Josh? He kills the girls. Brendan kills him. Lev Baranski wants to kill Brendan. Then what? Then you go and kill him? How many people have to die?'

'This is not a discussion we can have without knowing all the facts and we can't know those until we find them. That's what we have to do. Tomorrow. We have to go to Two Oaks and we have to find out if they are there.'

He was leaning his elbow on the table, his hand cupping his bandaged ear. His face flinched as though it was hurting him. Rose reached forward and touched his face.

'Let's go back to Anna's.'

He nodded. Rose got her mobile out and called a local cab company. Then they turned the kitchen light off and picked up the rubbish bag and the other bags from the landing and walked downstairs. Joshua locked the street door while Rose put the rubbish into the large wheelie bin along the way. They stood for a moment looking along the road for the cab. All the while Rose was thinking about Daisy Lincoln. She remembered Joshua's story about her running across the road to meet her older boyfriend. The car hadn't stopped where she'd been standing – it had driven past and she'd had to run up the road towards it. Joshua hadn't seen the driver.

Could it have been Brendan sitting in that car? Waiting for Daisy?

'Here's the cab,' Joshua said.

Rose picked up Joshua's bags and headed towards the car.

FIFTEEN

The next morning Joshua went to hire a car.

Rose was looking out of her study window, waiting for him to come back. It was raining, a steady drizzle. The street was empty and the house was quiet. Anna had gone out earlier. She was driving to Suffolk to see some old friends. Rose was relieved to be on her own. Joshua seemed frenetic in his wish to go and find their parents *that very day*.

The previous night, after returning from the Camden flat, Joshua had found out more information about Macon Parker. He had spent most of the evening in the attic. Anna had been pleased. *He's probably sleeping it off*, she'd said. *Sleep is the best cure-all*. When Rose went up to see him she'd found him feverishly working on his laptop, making notes by hand in a pad.

'I haven't got a printer,' he'd said when she commented on it.

'You can use mine.'

'I might later. I found out some interesting stuff.'

She'd sat down on the edge of the bed.

'Parker has a number of companies. The main one, Quality Lifestyles, owns a company called Aftercare Residentials. It appears to be a hotel in Brighton where people who've undergone cosmetic or other surgeries can recover. It's less expensive than staying in a private hospital but there are doctors on call, that kind of thing. Well, anyway, I put the addresses into Google to see if anything came up.'

Rose was listening and not listening at the same time. Joshua was talking fervently, pointing at his handwritten notes. The bandage on his ear was starting to look grubby, the plaster on his cheek flicking up. He didn't seem to be in such pain but he'd looked pale and harassed, his hand trembling slightly as he pointed to his notes. He needed to see a doctor she thought.

'So this newspaper report in Brighton says that two illegal immigrants were arrested in Travis Place – that's the road the hotel is in – and that they said they were legitimately in the country for renal surgery although no paperwork could be found for this claim.'

He'd looked at her. She'd nodded just to please him. They hadn't talked about DI Wendy Clarke and her mention of the Stiffkey cottage. It was as if they were simply ignoring it, getting on with other things.

'Organ transplants. That's what Macon Parker's work is about.'

'You look tired,' she'd said, wanting to end the conversation. 'Why don't you have an early night?'

'I will, I will," he said, staring at the notes.

She'd left him soon after. She'd closed the attic door and gone back down to her own room. Waking up that morning she'd felt a gloominess that was hard to shake. Today was the day that they were going to find their parents. Were they? Or was it all going to turn into another dead end?

Staring out of the window, waiting for Joshua to return with the rental car, she wondered what it would do to him if nothing came of their search. Since Skeggsie had been killed he had been a different person, edgy, manic, full of purpose and intent that seemed to lead to nothing.

And what would it do to *her* if they didn't find them?

Her feelings were unclear. Since seeing Brendan and her mother on the Skype recording she hadn't wanted to find them. Their lifestyle choices had been too much for her to swallow. And yet the things she had recently found out from Brendan's letters showed that relations between the couple hadn't been right. Could it be, as she had once feared, that Brendan had led her mother into this? That her mother hadn't really wanted to be part of it? And if so did it make her mother less guilty than Brendan?

A car came slowly along the street. It was a black Ford and it pulled up outside the house. Joshua got out. He fiddled with the dressing on the side of his head as if it was irritating him. Then he saw her at the window and waved up at her. Something in her chest seemed to unfurl at the sight of him. He had no jacket on even though it was wet and cold and she wanted to go out and put her arms around him to keep him warm. He pointed the key fob at the car and she saw the sidelights flick on and off as the car locked. Moments later she heard the front door open and waited as his footsteps came up the stairs. He pushed her study door open.

'Rosie?' he said. 'You ready? I'll get my stuff and we can go.'

His hair was wet. His shirt looked damp. She walked across to him and slipped her arms around him and put her face against his chest.

'What's all this?' he said in a half jokey way.

But she held on tightly and after a few moments he put one arm firmly around her, his hand gripping her ribs, the other hand holding her head, his fingers touching her hair. After a few seconds she tipped her head back and looked up at him.

He kissed her.

His mouth was warm and she felt the heat radiate through her, her head dizzy, her chest aching. After a few minutes he stopped and his mouth was at her ear.

'We should go,' he whispered. 'We can't do this now.'

She stepped back, her skin flushed and tingling. He walked out of the room and she heard him head up to the attic. Up above her he was moving around no doubt picking up his laptop and his maps and notebook. Distractedly she got hold of her things. Before going out on to the landing she closed her eyes and placed the backs of her fingers on her lips and ran her tongue along the skin. Why go out at all? Why not just stay here, the two of them together, in the warm, wrapped up in each other's arms?

Then she heard him coming downstairs, his footsteps determined. Later there would be time for just the two of them. Later. She picked up her coat and followed him out to the car.

The Ford was bigger than Skeggsie's Mini. She had masses of leg room and seemed to be sitting further apart from Joshua. On her lap were the maps that Joshua had previously printed out. The car had no satnav but Joshua was used to the journey and in any case he'd told her he preferred to find his own way to places. The radio was on and they drove mostly in silence. The drizzle was turning into rain, coming at an angle and pitting the windscreen, making it glitter for a second before being cleared away. Even though it was only twelve the dark clouds gave it a feeling of being later in the day and made Rose feel a little tired. She stared out of the side window and felt her eyelids heavy. Joshua was driving steadily, not too fast. Cars and lorries were passing them, sending spray up into the air which washed across the windscreen and blurred their view for a second.

They left the motorway and the traffic lessened.

Rose felt hungry and they stopped at a garage and bought sandwiches and coffee. The man who served them looked at Joshua's dressing and said, 'You been in the wars, mate?' and Joshua brushed it off with a mumbled reply. They ate the food sitting in the car. Then they were driving along country lanes and Rose recognised some of the landmarks from when they'd gone there before. She saw a sign for Wickby and they followed it and drove through the village, passing the green where the collectables market had been. Rose glanced to the side at the lane where she'd seen Frank Richards go a week before.

'We're going to drive through Two Oaks,' Joshua said, turning the radio off. 'Then we'll park up and take a short walk through the wood to look at Macon Parker's property. I want you to see how grand it is.'

She didn't answer. Joshua had worked out a plan and she would just follow it. There was silence in the car except for the squeak of the windscreen wipers. There were no other cars and it seemed for a moment as if it were just the two of them out on the Essex lanes. Two young people staring through a curtain of rain, searching for ghosts from their past.

They went through Two Oaks. A line of houses which bordered a winding road. There were no shops and no pubs. Then they were out in the country again.

'I told you it was small,' Joshua said.

The indicator was going and Rose saw a turning off the road. They turned into it and the lane narrowed. They slowed down as they followed the track. After a few minutes they came to a wood and then there was a pulling-in place that was deeply rutted with potholes. Joshua carefully steered the Ford into a space and then turned off the engine and they sat in silence as the rain pattered on the roof of the car.

'It's a five-minute walk, mostly under cover. Then we'll come back to the car.'

'How is this going to find Mum and Brendan?' she wanted to say. As if reading her mind he carried on.

'There are twenty-six houses in Two Oaks. We're going to knock at each one of them and show photos. If they are staying round here then someone will know. After that there are twelve houses in a one-mile radius. We'll do all of those as well. It'll be light until about five so we've got hours.'

They got out of the car. Rose put her hood up and shoved her hands in her pockets. She followed Joshua on to a foot-path which led them through some trees and then on to a straight path which was much firmer than the muddy terrain at each side. They walked for a while, mainly sheltered from the rain. Around them the trees were mostly bare so it was possible to see through them. Up ahead Rose thought she could see a solid wall. As they got closer something scuttled across the path and made her jump.

'That's the wall of his garden. If we go left here into the wood it takes us a bit higher and it's possible to see over the top.'

She followed him up a sloping path. It was less sheltered and the rain was heavier. After a while she turned around and could see the periphery of the garden and close by it a huge tree house with two platforms.

'Wow,' she said.

The tree house was the kind children fantasised about. It was wooden, as solid as the tree it was built on. The lower structure was like a playhouse with a veranda. There was a door and a window and someone had hung wind chimes on a nearby branch.

'Look at the size of that garden,' Joshua said.

It seemed huge with its own section of wood and lawn. On the lawn were swings and an elaborate climbing frame. In the far corner she thought she could see water shooting into the air – maybe a pond with a fountain.

'Where's the house?' she said.

'Beyond that wood. The garden's so big you can't see the house. That's the house of a millionaire businessman.'

Something moved at the corner of Rose's eye and she swung round to see a dog shoot out of the wooded area of the garden. It was a black Rottweiler and it stood its ground and began to bark. It was followed by three more dogs all running towards the wall and barking angrily.

'Get back,' Joshua said, grabbing her arm and pulling her into some bushes. 'Look, on top of the tree house.'

Rose looked. Her eyes focused on the roof of the tree house. She saw the camera then. It was small and black and, as she looked at it, it seemed to move as if making eye contact with her.

'Come on, we'll go back to the car on a circular route. If anyone is looking it'll seem like we're walkers.'

'In this rain?' Rose said.

'Walkers are a hardy bunch.'

She moved away, the sound of barking dogs in her ears. By the time they got back to the car she was wet through. She took off her coat and put it on the back seat. She got into the car and Joshua started it up.

'I'll put the heater on,' he said. 'Then we'll drive round to the front of the property.'

They reversed, dipping in and out of potholes and went back along the lane. Joshua headed towards Two Oaks and turned off before they reached the village. The road was barely wide enough for one car. He drove for a couple of minutes then pulled over into one of the passing places that had been put there in case two cars came face to face in the lane. He left the engine running and slowed the windscreen wipers so they cleared the glass intermittently. Rose could see, about twenty metres along on the right, two large wooden gates. On one side of them was an electronic keypad and above it an audio link. At each side of the gates sat cameras that were meant to be seen from a distance. It all gave a look of fortification.

'This guy's seriously rich.'

'Might he *just* be a businessman?'

'No, for two reasons. His name is on one of the notebooks. So they've picked him out for some crime or other. Two, he started work as a normal salaried doctor. No one rises to this kind of wealth in ten years. Unless they're doing something dodgy.'

Rose couldn't help but shake her head. It was a statement built on such slight evidence. A house of cards provided by a tatty notebook and a list of Google links.

'Shall we go and show the photos round?' she said, keen to get it over with.

'Yep,' Joshua said.

The lights of a car showed in the distance. It was coming from the far end of the lane. It had its headlights on and wasn't moving particularly fast.

'I'll just let this car pass then I'll turn around,' Joshua said.

It came closer. It was a large black car and when it got nearer Rose could see the three-pointed star badge of Mercedes. She tapped her fingers impatiently as they waited for it to pass. Now that the sightseeing was done she wanted to get on with the rest of the day. She wasn't looking forward to knocking on people's doors and holding up photos of her mum and Brendan but if it pleased Joshua then she was prepared to do it.

The car wasn't getting any closer, though. It had slowed down and stopped just before the gates of Macon Parker's property.

'Why has it stopped?' Joshua said lowly, as if talking to himself.

He switched the windscreen wipers to a faster setting so that they could see clearly out of the window. The Mercedes was almost level with the wooden gates. There seemed to be two people in it but Rose couldn't make out whether they were male or female. The car flashed its lights at them.

'They want us to pass. Maybe they're going into the property.'

'Do you think it's Macon Parker?'

'I don't know. Let's drive past and see. I'll keep my eyes on the road – you look around. The notebook is there, with his photo. Find it. Then tell me if it's him.'

Joshua moved the car out slowly as Rose rummaged through the papers and pulled out the notebook. She opened it. On the first page was the photo of Macon Parker. She looked up and saw that they were getting closer to the Mercedes. Their windscreen wipers were flicking from side to side. One moment the window was dappled with damp, the next it was clear.

'The man in the driver's seat is talking on a phone,' Joshua said. 'Maybe that's why he's pulled in. Maybe it's nothing to do with the house. He's just taking a call.'

Rose looked down at the photo and then tried to keep her attention on the man's face as their car approached the Mercedes. The Mercedes' windscreen looked steamed up but cleared as the wiper sketched a half circle and then went back again. They were a couple of car lengths away and Rose thought she could make out a woman in the passenger seat but she let her eyes go back to the man to focus on him and the photograph.

She was suddenly distracted, though. The wooden gates began to open. Small lights flashed on and off on the top of the gateposts and they inched back slowly.

'The car is going into the grounds. It *must* be Macon Parker,' Joshua said.

She leant forward as the Ford came up to the Mercedes. The man's head was turned to the woman and she could see his phone clamped to his ear. The Mercedes started to move forward. The woman was staring out in front. Then the man lowered the phone and looked out of the window.

Rose felt a jolt of recognition. It went through her like an electric shock. She turned forty-five degrees in her seat and kept her eyes clamped on the two figures in the car. The rain smeared the windscreen but then it cleared and she stared hard at each face for a few seconds until the Ford passed the Mercedes and headed slowly on down the lane. Rose unhooked her seat belt and turned round, hanging over the back of the seat so as to keep her eyes on the disappearing Mercedes.

'Was it him?' Joshua said, pulling into the side of the lane.

She couldn't answer. Her mouth was dry and she was holding on to the seat as though she might tumble back at any moment.

'No,' she said.

'You all right?' he said, puzzled.

She turned round and grabbed his hand.

'It was Brendan and Mum. They were in that car. Both of them. Together.'

Joshua's face tensed as the words sank in.

'In that car?'

She nodded.

'Are you sure?'

'I saw them on Skype. I know what they look like now. It was them, Josh.'

The rain came down, drenching the car. In the lane she could see small rivulets forming, water running down the side and across the middle. The surface of the road seemed to glow.

'It was. I'm not mistaken. I know my own mum.'

'And Dad?'

'He was driving. It was him.'

SIXTEEN

Joshua got out of the car.

'Wait,' Rose said.

He left the driver's door hanging open and walked quickly up the lane towards the wooden gates of Macon Parker's house. Rose leant across and pulled the door shut. Then she opened her door and followed him out. She called to him.

'Josh, what are you doing?'

He ignored her and in moments was standing in front of the gates. She looked around, up and down the lane. It was deserted and yet she felt uneasy, as if someone must be around. She focused on the cameras perched on each side of the gates. *Someone* was watching, she was sure. She slammed the passenger door and walked towards Joshua.

At the gates he was moving from side to side, staring up at each camera.

'What are you doing?' she hissed.

'I want them to see me. I want them to know that I am here. I've waited a long time for this.'

'You can't,' she said, grabbing the sleeve of his jacket. 'We have to hang on, to think this through. Remember that Munroe said they were working undercover . . .'

'I don't care,' he said, jabbing at the buttons on the entry pad.

The rain was less heavy now but she felt it on her face. A voice came from the speaker and startled her.

'Can I help you?'

It was a male voice but it wasn't Brendan's.

'I need to see someone,' Joshua said, looking up at the camera. 'I need to see the man who just drove in here.'

'Can you give me your name and the nature of your business?' the voice said calmly.

Joshua hesitated. He swore under his breath.

'What is your business?' the voice repeated.

Rose leant over and spoke into the speaker.

'The car that just came in here? It almost ran into us. Further along the lane. Really inconsiderate. We would like an apology.'

'I think you should just move on,' the voice said and Rose was sure she could hear a hint of a laugh.

'We're not going until we get an apology. Face to face,' Joshua said.

He was still moving around looking agitated. Rose put her arm through his to try and anchor him. What did he think he was doing? Insisting on some face-to-face meeting when they simply weren't ready for it? After five long years of waiting could they not have driven off and waited one more day?

There was a crackling sound on the intercom and the voice spoke again.

'Wait there. Someone will be down.'

They stood together, staring at the wooden gate. She couldn't quite believe it. Joshua's hands were clenching and unclenching. Was this it? Were the gates going to open and reveal her mother and Brendan ready to be reunited with them?

The noise of a car approaching made Rose look round. It had turned into the lane from the direction that they'd come from earlier. It moved slowly and in seconds she saw that it was another Mercedes, dark red with tinted windows. One minute it was moving and then it came to a stop a couple of hundred metres or so away from them. Rose couldn't see who was driving. The windows were smoky like giant sunglasses. She felt herself holding her breath. Whoever was in the car was most probably staring at them, wondering what was going on.

Was it Macon Parker?

The wooden gates made a noise and began to open slowly. Rose tensed. She didn't know what to expect. Joshua took a couple of steps backwards but she let her hold on him drop away and stood her ground. The gates shifted slowly and she peered through the gap wondering if Brendan would be standing there. From behind she heard the car along the lane moving again. The gates continued to open, creaking a little, and in moments the gateway was clear and she could see Brendan standing by the side pillar, staring at both of them in disbelief.

'Dad!' Joshua said, his voice dropping to a whisper.

'Josh, don't say anything!' Brendan said sharply.

The dark red Mercedes was beside them. Joshua hardly seemed to notice it. His face was twisted up. One of his hands was cupping his bandaged ear as if it was giving him pain. Brendan glanced at it and looked away. Rose swung round and looked beyond the gates to see if her mother was there. About a hundred metres up the driveway was the house. Her mother was not anywhere that she could see. Her eyes crept up the building, three storeys of it. The windows were too far away for her to spy anyone in them but she imagined that her mother was there at one of them, staring at the electric gates in shock.

To see seventeen-year-old Rose knocking for her.

From behind she heard the driver's window slide down and she looked round to see a man's face appear. The man in the photograph, Macon Parker.

'Everything all right, Ben?' he said.

Brendan walked to the side of the car.

'Fine, Mr Parker. Just a couple of young people who've got lost on the country lanes, I think.'

Macon Parker nodded and the car window slid shut. Brendan put his arm out to edge Rose back from the pathway. The arm felt rigid and she realised that he hadn't so much as made eye contact with her and he seemed to be ignoring Joshua completely. When the car glided past them he waited with his back to Joshua. He could have been a complete stranger.

Then he turned to both of them.

'What are you doing here? How did you find this place? My God, Joshua what's happened to your face?'

Joshua went to speak but Brendan shushed him.

'This is putting Kathy and me in danger.'

'Dad?' Joshua said, a look of incomprehension on his face.

'What *happened* to you? Rose, what's been going on?'

Rose couldn't answer. Joshua seemed distraught. Brendan looked back at the house, at the gates. He was becoming agitated.

'Listen, there's a village near here called Great Dunmow. Find a pub in it called the Three Kings. It's open all day. Go there and Kathy and I will come at four o'clock. Leave now.'

He walked away from them without looking backwards. The gates began to close as though an operator had been watching the whole conversation and knew it was over. Rose walked across to Joshua and took his elbow.

'Let's go,' she said.

He didn't move though. He was reluctant to leave. He waited until the gates had shut completely and they were faced with solid planks of wood slotted together, impenetrable.

He followed her to the car, looking back from time to time. When he got in he sat very still for a minute as if he didn't know what to do. He seemed to shiver a little as though someone had walked over his grave. She put her hand on his sleeve. It was damp just as hers was.

'Just drive,' she said. 'We'll find Great Dunmow.'

He didn't move.

'Josh, come on. We have to go there now.'

He seemed to pull himself together and started the car up.

It took about twenty minutes to reach Great Dunmow. It was bigger than Wickby, the largest of the villages they'd visited. There was a shopping area and several churches. They drove slowly, looking for the pub. After several false turns they found it on a turning off the main road through the town. It was set back off the street and had a small car park. They pulled into it and Joshua turned the engine off. The clock on the dashboard showed 3.16. They had just under forty-five minutes to wait.

'What do you want to do?' she said. 'Go for a walk?'

He shook his head.

'Sit here? Or go into the pub?'

He didn't answer. She turned to him. His face was a blank page. She had no idea what he was thinking. He was hardly breathing, as if conserving his energy.

'I'll tell him about Baranski,' he said.

'OK,' she said. 'And we'll ask about Daisy Lincoln?'

'I don't think we should bring that up as well. Not this time. Let's just make contact. We don't want to overload the first meeting. There's time for that stuff later.'

'But . . .'

'We might only have a short time. I don't want to talk to them about something that might be completely irrelevant.'

Rose sighed. 'I need to get out of the car.'

'Go for a walk. Clear your head.'

He didn't need her there. He wanted her to go away so that he could be on his own. She opened the door.

'Will you be all right?'

He nodded, laying his hands on the steering wheel, gripping it.

She walked away from the car out of the pub car park and turned on to the lane. The rain had stopped but there was no one out. The street had houses on each side but no front gardens, just doors that opened on to a narrow pavement.

The High Street was a single lane road and there were small shops and a couple more pubs. It didn't look as though anywhere was open. Up ahead a man was walking a small black and white dog. He was talking on a mobile phone and stopping at shop windows. The dog was pulling at the lead but the man seemed oblivious. She could hear his voice from where she was. 'So I said to him, "Why not buy second- hand? As soon as you buy a new one it depreciates. That's a couple of thousand quid down the drain!"'

She crossed the road. Pulling her phone out of her bag she saw that it had just gone three thirty. Half an hour until Brendan would come along with her mother. It gave her a jittery feeling and yet at the same time she felt a heaviness about it. It wasn't going to be the big reunion she had sometimes fantasised about in the early days when they'd first gone missing. There was to be no happy ending here, no putting their lives back together or making up for lost time. They wouldn't need to say 'Where have you been? Why did you go?' They already knew the answers to these questions.

She ached for it to be different.

To see her mother after so long.

To be able to touch her, to hold her hand, to hug her.

Rose found herself willing this. Forget about all the things they had learned. Forget that she and Brendan left without a word, without the whisper of a goodbye. Let that sit in the past if she could just have her back, the way it was when she was twelve years old. Even if it was only for a short time.

She'd walked the length of the main street. She turned round to come back and saw the man with his dog still talking on his mobile, the dog still pulling on the lead.

It was time to go to the pub and wait for them to come.

At ten past four they were sitting at a table in the bar of the Three Kings. There were a number of other people in there but they were in a corner by themselves. The door opened and Brendan walked in. He let it close and Rose saw that he was alone. She was immediately thrown. She'd expected her mother to be walking behind him.

Where was she? Had she not been able to come?

He paused to look for them. A woman sitting on a bar stool turned round to see who had just come in. Her eyes stayed on Brendan.

Rose looked him over.

He'd lost weight. His hair was neatly cut and he had round glasses on that made him look like a college lecturer. He wore a leather jacket styled like a suit jacket. He looked smart. The woman at the bar thought so too because her eyes followed him across the room as he came to join Rose and Joshua.

He looked so much *younger* than she remembered.

He took a chair out and sat down opposite them. He pulled it back a little as if he didn't want to be hemmed in. He didn't make eye contact with either of them but looked around from side to side.

'Dad . . .' Joshua started.

Brendan shook his head.

'The name is Ben Markham. That is what you call me now.'

Ben Markham. Another identity. Rose wasn't surprised. He wasn't like Brendan any more. He was a different person. Five years older and yet he seemed like a younger man altogether.

'Where's my mum?'

'*Kate Markham* is outside in the car. She's keeping an eye out for anyone who might be a bit too interested in our little outing. You can see her in a minute. We've agreed that I should explain things to you first. Then, Josh, you can tell me what happened to your face.'

'You don't need to. We know what's been going on. We know why you're working at . . .'

'Enough. You have to listen to me, Josh. There'll be plenty of time for full explanations later. I have two things to say to you. Number one: we did what we did to save your lives.'

Rose frowned. Brendan's eyes met hers and he faltered. For a second she saw the old Brendan, *All right, Petal?*

'Because of Viktor Baranski's death?' Joshua said.

Because of his murder, Rose thought.

'Justice for Baranski left a lot of German gangsters short of money.' Brendan's voice lowered and he looked around the bar. 'Two million pounds. They thought that your mother and I knew where this money was. They would have done anything to get hold of it – kidnap, torture, murder and they would have started with the things that were dearest to us, our children. Your lives were in danger if we stayed. Our disappearance had to look completely real, that is why we had to abandon you. You and the pain you experienced was evidence to them of our deaths. No parent abandons their child. That's why they believed in the car in the reservoir at Childerley Waters. Munroe's story wasn't just made up for you and Rose, it was set up years ago to be leaked to the Germans. We still had to lie low of course.'

'But . . .'

'No, Joshua. No more discussion.'

Rose frowned at Brendan's coldness. Here was his son who he hadn't seen for five years and yet he wasn't even *touching* him. His hands were firmly placed on the rough wood table, his palms down.

'Number two. If you continue to interfere this mission will fail and Kate and myself could end up dead. In five days' time this will be over. There is a party for our employer's birthday up in London. After that we will be gone. Our work finished. We will relocate to another country and then we will send for both of you. It will be up to you whether you come or not.'

Joshua didn't speak. He was holding his glass, his fingers woven into each other. Rose felt herself disorientated by Brendan's delivery, his tone of voice, the lack of emotion in his words. Over by the bar she noticed the woman on the stool was still looking at him from time to time. She appeared to be in her early twenties and yet she was clearly attracted by Brendan. Rose thought of Daisy Lincoln, five years before. Had she too been attracted by Brendan?

'You should go and see your mother, Rose,' Brendan said, the words low.

Rose got up and left her seat without a word. She walked towards the door, her heart seeming to stiffen in her chest. She went slowly. She was steeling herself for a meeting that was similar to the one she had just had with Brendan. Her mother would be firm. Wearing her new heavy-framed glasses she would say the same things that Brendan had said but use slightly different wording. She might number her points. 'Firstly' she might say. 'Secondly' she would continue. She might slice the air with her hand emphasising the fact that Rose and Joshua should keep out of what was happening.

She pulled the pub door open and looked around. Their Ford was parked by the entrance to the car park. There were two cars on the other side. One of them was the black Mercedes they'd seen earlier. Rose saw her mother in the driver's seat. She walked towards it. She imagined herself opening the passenger door and getting into the car and sitting tightly, her hands sandwiched between her legs, waiting to hear what her mother had to say.

She wouldn't cry. She wouldn't be emotional.

She would nod and show her mother how grown-up she was.

She neared the car. It had stopped raining and the sky was crammed with bright white clouds. It hurt her eyes to look at it and she squinted and then looked at the windscreen. Her mother's face stared back at her. She headed for the passenger door but at that moment the driver's door swung open and her mother got out and began to walk towards her. Rose froze. She didn't know what to say. Her mouth opened but no words came out. Her mother came round the bonnet of the car, straight up to her and raised her arms and then she was hugging her fiercely. Rose's arms were clamped to her side and she couldn't move them. Her mother's face was on her shoulder, she felt her hair at the side of her cheek. Her arms were tight around Rose's body and then she felt the trembling, the shaking, as her mother began to cry silently. With heaving sobs she held on to Rose and Rose's eyes filled with tears as she stood awkwardly by the side of the Mercedes. After a few moments her mother's arms slackened and she stood back and Rose realised with surprise that she was the taller one. Her mother was thinner as well and seemed lost in a billowing mac, her glasses looking like they were made to measure for someone much bigger.

'Rosie,' she whispered.

'Mum,' Rose said, her voice trembling.

'You've heard everything that Ben said?'

Rose nodded. Her mum meant *Brendan*.

'Just another few days and all this will be finished. We will contact you. Be ready for us. I *long* to see you, to explain . . .'

A door opened from behind and Rose heard raised voices, people laughing from inside the pub. Brendan and Joshua walked out. Brendan didn't look over to her mother but headed for the Ford. Joshua pointed the keys at the car and the sidelights flashed on and off.

'When will I see you?' Rose said.

'Soon. I promise it will be soon.'

Her mother stepped forward and gave her a kiss on the cheek, her hand grasping on to the fabric of her jacket. Then she stepped away. Turning back to the Ford Rose saw that Brendan had hooked his arm around Joshua's neck and given him a hug. Then he headed back towards the Mercedes. Rose walked past him and as she did she felt his fingers brushing hers. She approached the car and got in. Seconds later, before they'd even got their seat belts on, the Mercedes shot forward and swept out of the car park.

They didn't move.

Joshua's hands rested on the steering wheel and he stared out the front of the car. Rose crossed her arms.

This was what they had dreamed about – finding their parents.

This should be a moment of celebration and yet she felt a sense of desolation. For years she had felt adrift, floating here and there, searching for land. Now they had found it they weren't allowed to dock, to step on to it, to rest. She turned to Joshua wanting to say something but he was lost in his own thoughts. The search for their parents had brought them together. Now that they had found them it seemed to edge them apart.

'I told him about Baranski,' Joshua said. 'I told him to be on the lookout.'

'What did he say?'

'He was angry. He said he would make a point of seeing Baranski before he left England.'

She closed her eyes. More violence. She put her hand in her pocket and felt something. Her fingers poked at the sharp edge of a piece of card. She pulled it out and looked at it. One side was blank. On the other side was a phone number and by the side of it the letter K. The single letter was big, written with a flourish.

Joshua started the car.

It was her mother's number, a way to get in touch with her.

Rose turned it over, a swirl of emotion in her chest.

SEVENTEEN

Rose had an appointment at the Bethnal Green Police Station at twelve. She went to college first. She only had one class and could have missed it but she decided not to. Joshua's appointment had been at ten and she wondered how he'd got on.

The previous evening, getting back from Essex, they'd both been drained. Anna had been at home and wanted to make them a meal. Rose was surprised at Anna's insistence and the three of them sat down to pasta and salad followed by ice cream. Anna had been very talkative throughout the meal, asking Joshua lots of things about his course. Rose knew that her grandmother was making an effort, trying to wipe out the horrible things she'd said about Joshua and Brendan the previous autumn. After the meal she wouldn't let either of them help her to load the dishwasher. She seemed happy, buoyant and told them that she had some busy days ahead. The charity she worked with had a number of important functions that she needed to attend, projects that were coming to fruition. Joshua and Rose listened in silence and Rose managed some conversation but after a while Joshua said he needed a shower and an early night and she watched him go up to the attic. She left Anna in her drawing room and went back to her study and sat quietly looking at the small card which her mother had given her at the phone number that was there.

This morning she was holding it again as the teacher went through the main points of an essay they had to do. She wondered, for the hundredth time, if the card was an invitation or a *prompt* for her to get in touch. Did Brendan know that she'd given it to her? Was it some kind of secret plea? Was her mother doing something behind Brendan's back?

She thought of the moment in the pub when Brendan said *You should go and see your mother, Rose.* She had in fact walked slowly across the bar and looked tentatively around the car park. In her head, though, she wished she had dashed across the room and burst out of the pub door. Once there she pictured herself seeing her mother and her face breaking into a glorious smile as she ran across to the Mercedes.

But she hadn't done these things. She'd acted like a guilty schoolgirl heading for the headteacher's office.

What must her mother have thought?

That she didn't care? That she had no feelings for her?

The classroom door opened and a young woman came into the room and went to speak to the teacher. She wasn't much older than Rose but she was wearing a skirt suit and white shirt and had on high heels which made her walk a little unsteadily. Rose didn't recognise her but she must have been a member of staff because she had an identity tag hanging round her neck. After she spoke the teacher nodded and looked up at the class. The woman left and the lesson went on. When the buzzer went and people started to move out the teacher came across to Rose.

'Someone is waiting to see you in reception,' she said.

'Oh?'

Her first thought was that it was Joshua, having come straight from the police station with something important to tell her.

'A woman. A family friend, she said. The college don't really like it but just this once. It's recess anyway.'

'Thanks,' Rose said.

She went off, weaving through the slow-moving stream of students changing classes. She headed for the reception area where the hard flooring turned to carpet. When she got there she was surprised to see a blonde woman sitting on one of the soft chairs, flicking through a college prospectus. The woman saw her and stood up. Her hair was more white than blonde and she had on a smart trouser suit with a silk scarf at her neck.

It was Margaret Spicer, Munroe's wife.

'Hello, Rose. Could we talk?'

Rose stiffened. 'What do you want?'

'About thirty minutes of your time. A few private words. My car is parked in the street outside.'

'I don't want to speak to you.'

'I'm going away and there are things I need to say to you and Joshua.'

'Joshua came to see you.'

'I can't talk to Joshua. He is too angry.'

'You think I'm not angry?'

'Darren Skeggs was his friend.'

'He was my friend too.'

'I thought you might be prepared to listen for a while. If not to *understand* what happened in Newcastle to at least know the full facts of it.'

Margaret Spicer took a step towards the doors. Rose gave the slightest nod of her head and followed. They walked out of the college and headed for a silver SUV that was parked further down the road on a meter. The sight of the car gave Rose a jolt. The two silver SUVs she'd had associations with over the last months had brought only unhappiness and pain. She came to a stop a few metres away.

'We can just sit inside for privacy,' Margaret said.

'What happened to the dog?'

'The dog has been rehomed.'

'Is that a euphemism for "put down"?'

'Get in, Rose.'

Rose got into the front seat of the SUV. There was enough room to put her rucksack down by her feet. The car smelled heavily of scent. An air freshener hung from the mirror in the shape of a lemon. Margaret's car keys lay on the dashboard. The key ring was in the shape of a small dog, its tail in the air.

'I'm leaving. I won't be known by the name Margaret Spicer any more. That's why I wanted to talk to you.'

'You mean you're relocating. Like my mother and Brendan.'

'Yes. It has to be done. Some of the people we've been involved with are very dangerous.'

'Some of the people you've killed.'

'I'm here to talk to you about Newcastle,' Margaret went on, ignoring Rose's remark, 'because I wanted you to be clear about happened there. You are Kathy's daughter. Kathy and I became friends, close. At least as close as people can be who are involved in this kind of enterprise.'

Rose didn't speak. She was making it sound like a start-up business.

'James and I went to Newcastle to spend Christmas near my family. Well, my elderly mother, who is in a nursing home. She has Alzheimer's and will not last much longer I'm afraid. It was to be our last Christmas in the UK so it seemed the right thing to do. James and I had plans to relocate together, like all of the people in the project. Once the job was done we were all going to have new lives.'

'You're divorcing, though?'

She nodded, looking suddenly fragile. She picked up her car keys and toyed with them. Rose turned away. She wasn't going to feel sorry for her.

'When we got to Newcastle James found out about Stuart Johnson's accident and of course Stuart was always a worry for the project.'

'He started it off.'

Rose thought of the documents that she, Joshua and Skeggsie had found hidden in Brendan's brother's house. His confession to the murder of Simon Lister, the man who killed Judy Greaves. The Butterfly Murder.

'He did something that gave birth to our project. His action in killing Lister stopped other deaths. *The Butterfly Project* we called it.'

There was quiet in the car. Rose looked out of the window at the college buildings. Some students were in a huddle chatting. A couple of boys were looking intently at each other's phones and a girl was leaning against the wall reading a copy of *Death of a Salesman*.

'I was the first officer on scene. I saw Judy Greaves,' Margaret said, replacing her keys on the dashboard.

'I know.'

'An estate agent had an appointment to go and make a valuation of the property. The owner, Timothy Lucas, was in a care home and his house was to be sold to pay for the care. The agent, a man called David Miller, went round to the house. He had keys and he went in and saw the girl's body. He came straight out and phoned the police but as luck would have it I was walking through that street after making a couple of house calls.'

Rose knew all this but she let Margaret talk.

'He came running up to me. He was virtually incoherent and he tugged at my arm and I went into the property and found her in the living room. I'll never forget walking into that room and seeing that little girl on the floor.'

Rose looked down at her lap and saw that she'd woven her fingers together.

'She was clothed and lying flat on her back. She had on an old-fashioned dress, something with frills and flowers like a doll might wear. Her eyes were open and she seemed to be staring at the ceiling. I remember walking across to her, my feet barely touching the ground. I had to make sure she wasn't alive. I *knew* she wasn't but I had to make absolutely sure and I knelt down beside her and placed my fingers on her neck. There was no pulse. She was still warm. She didn't have a mark on her that I could see but her skin was blanched of colour. Then I stepped away and stood at the door of the room. It was a crime scene and I had to make it safe, make sure no one went in there. That was the hardest thing. Standing, looking at her from a distance, waiting for Scene of Crime Officers to arrive. Someone should have been there beside her, so that she wasn't alone.'

Rose heard the muted sound of the college buzzer for the end of recess. Margaret seemed to wait until it had finished and then continued.

'Just as I heard the car sirens nearby I noticed the pictures on the wall. Except they weren't pictures, they were frames full of mounted butterflies. Timothy Lucas had been a prolific collector. By this time most of his furniture and belongings had been moved from the house but these hadn't gone anywhere yet. I don't suppose anybody wanted them. Ghoulish things. Perhaps collectors think they are beautiful but I just saw a lot of dead insects. The beauty is when they're *alive*.'

'Is that when you met James Munroe?'

'It was. But I must get back to the point. When we heard that Stuart Johnson had had a fall we were worried. We were always worried that he might say something and involve Brendan and possibly James and myself. But for five years he didn't. Then the fall. When Joshua and his friend and you came to Newcastle James was concerned that Stuart would say something to him or you. We were just keeping an eye on things and then your friend, Darren Skeggs, was trying to find my registration number.'

'You had his computer cloned?'

'James thought it best to keep an eye on what he was doing. The lad had some powerful equipment and spent hours every day trying to research relevant data. We knew that it was Joshua who wanted to know these things but without his friend's help he wouldn't have got very far.'

'So Munroe decided to get rid of him?'

'No. He just wanted him to stop. James arranged for a local petty criminal to speak to the boy and threaten him. But that was all.'

'You took that thug to the alley,' Rose said bluntly.

'I did. And I deeply regret it. James absolutely assured me that it was just to be a verbal warning. At no point was I informed that anything else was planned.'

'And when Skeggsie came along you said something to him, you prompted him to go into the alley.'

Margaret nodded. She was gripping the steering wheel.

'Then you left.'

'I had no idea what had happened until much later. What I'm trying to tell you is that it was never my intention for the boy to be killed. Never.'

'But it was Munroe's?'

'I can't say. I thought I could but I really don't know any more.'

There was quiet as Rose thought about the things Margaret had said. Was she trying to excuse herself? Or was it true that all the plans had been made by Munroe and she had been used. In the end it didn't really matter. Joshua and she knew who was responsible for Skeggsie's death.

'Is that why you are getting divorced from Munroe?'

'Nothing to do with any of this. James and I . . . have some differences. He has . . . He wants a different kind of marriage than I do . . . Of course it's our business. No one else's.'

Rose didn't say anything. Margaret Spicer's love life was not her problem.

'When are you going away?'

'In a couple of days after the Macon Parker judgement. I intend to start again, somewhere else.'

'What about the project? I'm sure there are still lots of guilty people out there you can punish.'

'We feel we've done enough. Macon Parker was always going to be the last one. That was decided long before your friend was killed. Doing this kind of thing changes a person. We don't want our lives defined by it.'

It is a pity that Skeggsie's life was defined by it, Rose thought.

'How do you get the new identity?'

'James handles that sort of thing. He was a senior policeman. A civil servant. He has contacts in all sorts of places. He sees himself as a kind of enabler. He has never personally been involved in any of the *hands-on* work.'

'You make him sound like a scout leader.'

'If anyone was the leader it was Brendan. It was his passion and sense of moral outrage that got this thing going. He was one of the officers involved in the discovery of the girls in the container lorry in 2003. It was before he went into cold case work. It was the *reason* he went into cold case work.'

Rose hadn't known that.

'Don't judge us too harshly. I know your friend is dead and I know that can never be put right but we did what we did for the right reasons.'

Rose looked at Margaret. Her white-blonde hair wasn't natural, Rose knew that. Would she change it again, go back to brown? Start wearing a different style of clothes and call herself Alice or Sophia or Emily?

Rose opened the passenger door.

'Do you want me to say it's all right? That I accept that Skeggsie's death was an accident and that you are forgiven? I'm not going to do it.'

She closed the door and stepped back from the car as Margaret drove off.

She looked at her phone. It was eleven thirty. She also saw that she had a message from Joshua. **Interview over. No problems. See you at your gran's.**

Now she had her appointment to keep at the Bethnal Green Police Station.

EIGHTEEN

'Sorry I've made you wait.'

Rose looked up to see Wendy Clarke standing smiling at her. The police officer was wearing a long skirt over boots. Her hair was loose. It looked fluffy and flyaway as though she'd just washed it. Rose stood up and managed a weak smile.

'Come through,' Wendy Clarke said brightly, as though she was taking her for a wash and blow dry instead of a formal interview.

Wendy Clarke took her along a narrow corridor then up a flight of stairs. People spoke to her as she went past. 'Morning, Mam!' 'Hello, Wendy.' 'Good day, Mzzz Clarke.' When they got to the interview room Wendy Clarke pulled out a chair out for Rose to sit on. Then she sat down herself and looked expectantly at her. There was a table between them and on it was a file. It had no label but looked ominous. Rose couldn't help frowning at the sight of it.

'Aren't you going to tape the interview?' Rose said, glancing at the recording equipment.

'No, I don't think that will be necessary. I think a chat is what I'd like. Unless you want it to be more formal?'

Rose shook her head. She just wanted to get it over with.

'OK. On Saturday evening we spoke at Joshua Johnson's flat and I was straight with you. I also said it seemed to me as though you and he were hiding something. Keeping something to yourselves. You both have the look of someone who has a good hand of cards and is not playing it yet. If I wanted to lay a wager I'd say that whatever is in that hand of cards might have something to do with my Daisy.'

'*Your* Daisy?' Rose said, shifting about on her seat.

'Daisy Lincoln. Yes, Rose. I think of her as mine. I have to do that, you see, because then this crime is personal to me. Actually I think every crime is personal. Have you heard the line *never send to know for whom the bell tolls, it tolls for thee*?'

'John Donne.'

'Be honest. You didn't think police officers read poetry,' Wendy said.

Rose shook her head.

'John Donne. That's the one. The point is strong. Every time a crime is committed it's a crime against all of us. When someone tied Daisy's hands up, killed her and buried her in your back garden I took it personally as if she was my own daughter. That's why I have to find her killer.'

Rose thought of her conversation with Margaret Spicer an hour or so before. *We did what we did for the right reasons.* What would Wendy Clarke think of this? Wendy Clarke wanted to *own* Daisy Lincoln. She wanted to take personal responsibility for finding her killer. Wasn't that what her mother and Brendan and the others were doing? Owning the victims of murder? They were treating these victims as though they were their own children. The difference between them and Wendy Clarke was that they decided on what constituted *justice*.

'I understand. When someone is killed we are all touched,' Rose said quietly.

'If only that were true. Most people walk by on the other side of the road. It hasn't happened to someone they loved so why should they care?'

'I care about Daisy,' Rose said, her voice barely making it out of her lips.

'Do you, Rose?'

Rose nodded.

'So tell me,' she said, 'what is it that you and Joshua Johnson have up your sleeve?'

Rose shook her head. Had Wendy Clarke asked Joshua this very same question hours before? How had he answered?

'OK, I'll rephrase my question. Does this thing, this knowledge you have, have anything to do with Daisy Lincoln? Just answer that honestly and I'll leave you alone.'

Rose stared at Wendy Clarke. Her hair stood out, wisps of it flying around. Rose half expected to *hear* the electricity coming off it.

'It doesn't,' Rose whispered.

'You do have something, though, some secret? But it's not linked to this? To Daisy?'

'It's not linked to Daisy.'

Rose put her hand in her pocket and felt the card that was there. Her mother's phone number. She ran the tip of her finger along the edge.

'Well, you've said more than your stepbrother did,' Wendy Clarke said, picking up the folder in front of her and holding it to her chest. 'In any case you and Joshua Johnson's secrets are your own affair.'

'Can I go now?' Rose said, standing up.

'Sure. Oh! While you're here, though, I would like you to take a look at these. These are things we found on or around Daisy's body and we're trying to link them to her or rule them out. Maybe items belonging to your family that were lost in the garden at some stage. It won't take you a second to have a look.'

Wendy Clarke laid photos on the table as if she was playing Patience. Rose sat down again, only half on the chair, most of her body turned to the door. There were four items all placed on white backgrounds. The first was a ring. The second were some metal buttons, three in a triangle. The third was a watch face with no strap. The fourth was a picture of a part of a chain and a pendant. The pendant was a silver heart shape and in the middle of it was a red stone. A ruby. Rose's eyes only stayed on it a second. She flicked her glance away but her throat had fired up and her thoughts were running ahead of her. Then she pulled each photograph back taking time to look in detail, her fingers tracing the items.

'No, none of them ring a bell,' Rose said, her voice thickening.

Wendy Clarke gathered the pictures up.

'OK,' she said. 'And I don't need to tell you to contact me if anything comes up.'

Rose stood up and walked to the door.

'I'll take you back to reception,' Wendy Clarke said.

Rose went home. The Ford was parked in the street so she knew that Joshua was in. She went in and up to her rooms hearing the distant sound of music coming from the attic. She put her rucksack down and pulled a packet of gum from the front compartment and took a piece. Chewing gently, she went across to her pinboard and looked at the picture of her mother that she'd put there a couple of weeks before when the clearing out of the Blue

Room started. She pulled the tack out of the corner of the photo and held the picture in her hands. Her mother's smile beamed out and around her neck was the pendant. The silver heart sat on her breastbone, the ruby coloured gem in the centre. The same one that was in the photo which Wendy Clarke showed her.

Rose felt a crushing feeling in her chest.

She thought of that last summer when they were together as a family. In her mind those days had been perfect, halcyon. But now she had learned other stuff about that time: her mother and Brendan at odds, a miscarriage, time spent apart. Then there were the other factors: Daisy Lincoln's older boyfriend, her hands tied up with Brendan's tie.

Now her mother's pendant had been found *on* or *near* Daisy's body. Brendan had given this to her mother as a gift, she was sure. She had a picture in her mind of her mum opening a box and taking it out. Had Brendan been there? She couldn't quite remember. She knew her mother hadn't liked it much.

From upstairs she heard Joshua's footsteps cross the ceiling.

She felt a cloying anxiety. She'd told Joshua none of this. She'd kept the story about the miscarriage and Brendan's letters from him. Then the card with the phone number. Now the pendant. Why was she doing this? Hadn't he a right to know about these developments?

196

She went out of her room and up the stairs. She was holding the photo flat against her chest.

She would make a clean breast of it. Tell him everything.

She knocked on the attic door and he shouted, 'Come in!'

She went in.

He was standing facing the wall opposite his bed. He had papered the surface of the wall with articles and pictures. The images were all of one girl. Rose remembered her from Joshua's explanation of Macon Parker's activities. Polina Bokun, a nineteen year old from Belarus. She'd come to England as a student, part of some deal for the removal of an organ, Joshua had said. Then she'd disappeared, her body turning up weeks later in the Thames estuary minus her liver and kidneys.

'How was it?' she said.

'What?'

'At the police station.'

'Oh, she kept going on about how well had I known Daisy,' Joshua said. 'If I'd seen her with Brendan. Whether Kathy was away a lot. Stuff like that.'

'They're trying to link Daisy to Brendan.'

'She asked me if Daisy and *I* had spent time together. I laughed at her. *In my dreams*, I said. How about you?'

'That's what I wanted to talk to you about partly . . .'

'But look at all this,' he said, not seeming to register what she'd said. 'I printed this stuff off the internet. It's important to know this story. It's important to read the detail behind the headlines.'

Rose walked across to the wall. There were newspaper articles pinned side by side. One said *Belarus Teenager Wanted to Be a Nurse*. Another said *Polina's Mother Suffering From Breast Cancer*. Another, a magazine article, showed a small photo of Polina with a male friend. *She Was My Soulmate*, the heading said. *Poverty forces the young to flee abroad*, was a subheading further down the page.

In the middle of it all was the police photo of Polina.

In some way it reminded her of the photo of Daisy that had been in the newspapers. The hair was dark although not as long, the expression blank. They were passport photos, maybe. She focused a little longer so that the girl's facial features seemed to dissolve. Polina and Daisy. Now she was on first-name terms with two dead girls.

'This is a girl's life that has been snuffed out. That's why they're going after Macon Parker!'

Rose turned to him. He was moving about, looking from one article to another. He was like an enthusiastic teacher in front of a classroom display, pleased with his work.

He stepped across and put his hand on her shoulder.

'We have to keep this clear in our minds. So that when it happens we know why they did it.'

He meant the *execution* of Macon Parker.

'What's that?' he said, pointing to the photograph of her mother wearing the pendant.

'Nothing,' she said, folding it in half and half again.

He turned back to the display. He was building up a case for murder. On the wall were pictures of a girl whose life had been taken. He was amassing evidence of waste, of loss and despair. She couldn't tell him about the pendant or the other stuff about her mother and Brendan's relationship. None of that would be important to him. All he was interested in was this. In his head this murder would balance whatever their parents were going to do to Macon Parker.

Oh,' she said, tucking the photo in her pocket. 'Margaret Spicer came to my college today. She wanted to speak to me, to tell me that Skeggsie's death really was nothing to do with her. She seemed to be distancing herself from Munroe.'

'Yes?'

'And she's leaving. Getting a new identity. Starting a new life.'

Joshua's face hardened. 'Right. Pity Skeggsie will never be able to do that.'

'You know what she called it? *The Butterfly Project*.'

'Yeah, well, I've moved on from Margaret Spicer. I'm not interested in her any more.'

Rose stood for a moment and watched him tidying up his wall display.

'I'll go. I've got some work to do.'

She left him in the attic and went back down to her room.

She sat on the edge of her bed, the wrinkled photo of her mother on the bedside table. In her hand was the card with the telephone number.

She composed a text. **I need to see you urgently. Let's meet. Just you and I. No one else needs to know. xxxx**

She pressed *Send*.

After a short while came a reply. **Liverpool Street Station Cafe Black Tuesday 1 p.m.**

She had just under twenty-four hours to wait.

NINETEEN

At ten to one Liverpool Street Station was busy. A rush of faces passed her by, moving in different directions. Coming off the tube escalator, she sidestepped travellers who were heading for different platforms, their shoulders down, their faces pinched with determination. Rose felt herself being pulled here and there with the flow. After searching round for several moments she saw Cafe Black on a mezzanine floor. She headed for the stairs and went up. Inside the cafe it seemed soundproofed. The announcements and collective noise of the station were hushed. One wall had screens which were full of listings of departing and arriving trains. There was a counter and also a self-service area packed with rolls and sandwiches. There were circular tables, most of which were occupied. Rose bought a coffee and found an empty seat by the window and waited.

At one thirty she'd long finished her drink and was wondering what to do.

Could something have happened to detain her mother?

She looked out of the window at the people below heading for the platforms. Many of the men had on suits and overcoats, carrying computer bags. She was reminded of James Munroe in his Crombie overcoat. He always looked so respectable. An ex-policeman, now a civil servant, who had a sideline in assassination. She thought about him hurting her hand and warning her off. Margaret Spicer said that it was he who organised all the new identities. He had contacts so he was able to get hold of new papers, passports and so on. He would be doing this for her mother and Brendan, which meant that he would know where they would relocate and their new names. They would always be dependent on him.

'Rose.'

She looked up. Her mother was there.

Her face broke into a smile. She stood up and her arms moved upwards as if to hug her as her mother had done in the car park of the pub in Great Dunmow. Her mother stepped back, though, glancing from side to side. She looked stiff as if standing to attention. She was wearing a dark jacket and trousers and had a pink silk scarf wound around her neck a number of times. It had fringes at the end and looked out of place against her sober suit.

'I'm getting a coffee. Do you want one?'

Rose shook her head. Dismayed, she watched as her mother went up to the counter and waited to be served.

She wasn't wearing any glasses and she was scrabbling about in her purse for money to pay. The barista must have made a joke because he laughed and handed her a tall cup. Her mother gave a weak smile and walked back towards her then sat in the seat beside Rose.

'I haven't got long,' she said, placing a hand on the table.

Rose saw her nails then. Long and manicured, painted a pearlised white. It reminded her of Anna, who spent many hours having her nails shaped and coloured. Rose frowned. This was not something her mother had ever done before.

'Why aren't you wearing your glasses?'

'Contact lenses.'

Her mother's words were spare as though she was paying a bill and had just the right money. She seemed angry that Rose had called her there so soon. The phone number she'd given her was possibly just a gesture, a token which Rose had used up. She felt like she was on the brink of crying but then her mother placed her hand lightly on top of hers. It was warm and firm.

'Rose, I'm getting the two o'clock train back. There are things I need to tell you but first you have to promise you will not try to contact us again and you will not come out to the house.'

The house. She meant the mansion owned by Macon Parker, the man who stole people's organs.

'Ben and I work there. He manages the grounds and the cars and I am the housekeeper. We've been there for over a year now and are trusted.'

'How can you call him *Ben*?'

'That is his name just as mine is Kate Markham. We are different people now, you have to respect that. We have a job to do. It's our last one and although it is unpalatable and hard for you to understand we must do it to the best of our ability. All I would say to you is that you have not seen the things that Brend– Ben and I have seen. You have not walked in our shoes. You cannot know what made us do this.'

Rose looked down at the table. A couple had just come into the cafe and sat next to them. They were young with giant rucksacks which they struggled out of, laughing. The rucksacks sat on the floor, discarded shells, as the couple went up for their drinks. Rose looked and saw labels on them. They were heading off on a journey, carefree. No doubt their parents were at home doing *normal* things.

She turned back to her mum. She should ask her about the last summer and Daisy Lincoln, how she and Brendan had been getting on, about the miscarriage. Then she could mention Brendan's tie and the pendant. The words were there, in her mouth, practised frequently over the last twenty-four hours. Is it possible that Brendan was having a relationship with Daisy Lincoln? This is what she would say.

Instead she said something quite different.

'How could you leave me?'

Her mother's eyebrows crinkled. Rose noticed deep lines between her brows. Worry lines.

'I thought . . . Ben explained this yesterday?'

'I want to hear it from you.'

The white nails tapped on the table and her mother picked her cup up and drank from it. When she put it back down again her face had reddened.

'It started with Judy Greaves.'

The Butterfly Murder. Rose nodded.

'I knew nothing about it until a year after Stuart killed Simon Lister. That was when Brendan told me everything. He showed me the things that had been on the man's computer. The pictures, the plans to kill another girl. Judy Greaves was ten. You were ten. I just looked at it all and thought of you and it seemed as though some sort of rough justice had taken place and that was just the beginning.'

'But to kill someone . . .'

'We worked in cold cases,' her mother said, lowering her voice, looking carefully round the cafe. 'We saw lots of killing that went unpunished. We decided on two things, we would only pass judgement on killers if there was no chance that they would ever be caught by the authorities. And we would only pass judgement if it seemed that they might do it again. That way we were saving lives.'

Pass judgement. Rose had heard Brendan use these words. She'd seen the word *judgement* in the back of the notebooks. She wondered if they did it in a formal way, a group of people sitting round saying 'Guilty?' or 'Not Guilty?'

Her mother was holding her hand now. Her scarf had come undone, the end of it slithering on to the table. Rose was afraid for a moment that it might dip into some coffee that had been spilled.

'This is our last case. We want to move on and have a new life. We can do that. There's a place in British Columbia where we can go.'

Rose sat back and pulled her hand away.

'You're going to leave again?'

'We have to. There's no life for us here. We will get settled. Then send for you and Josh. That was always the plan. To start a new life.'

'We have a life here. We all had a life here, in Brewster Road.'

Brewster Road. Hadn't Rose called her mother here to talk about precisely that? To ask her about what might have happened to Daisy Lincoln?

'We did,' her mother said. 'But we had to leave. We had serious gangsters after us. The judgement on Baranski was carried out in 2006. In May 2007 one of our group, a man called Jason Butler, went missing. He was never found but things started to happen through that summer and we had to assume that he had given information about us to the Germans who were looking for the money that Baranski owed them. Whether this information was given for money or whether it was forced from him we will never know but it became clear that they knew who had killed Baranski and they were coming for us. Leaving you? It was the hardest thing I've ever done in my life. The other stuff? The killings?' Her mother shook her head. 'These things are distasteful, brutal, but nothing ever clawed at me like leaving you.'

'But Munroe told us that those German gangsters had been arrested. Weeks, months, after you went away. Why didn't you come home then?'

Rose felt her throat drying, her voice thinning.

'That was part of the story he fabricated about our bodies being found in a submerged car. It was an attempt to persuade you and Joshua that we were dead. The Germans in question were killed just months ago actually. This was nothing to do with us, it's just a fact of life for these people. They live by violence. Sometimes they die by it. This is why we are able to finish our work now. Move on with our lives. We have rid the world of some very nasty people, Rose.'

Rose sat back in her chair. She folded her arms across her chest. She wasn't hearing what she'd wanted to hear.

'I always thought that maybe you'd just gone along with it all because of Brendan,' she said. 'I never thought, for one minute, that you left voluntarily. You left me clues – the glasses case in the restaurant, your signature in the B and B. You wanted me to find you . . .'

'Oh, Rosie . . .'

Her mother moved her chair around the small table. She put an arm around Rose's shoulder and pulled her close. Rose felt the silky scarf rub against her face. Her mother spoke in her ear.

'I was a willing participant. Brendan didn't force me. At least he didn't force me to go along with the judgements. I agreed to those. He had to force me to leave you behind. I admit to that.'

'But have you . . . Have you actually *killed* someone?'

'That's something that none of us will talk about. How it's done, who does it. Those things are drawn randomly.'

'Viktor Baranski?'

'I can't say. It doesn't matter *who* did it. We are all responsible. The judgement is the *deed* and we all make that. The act is inconsequential.'

'You know about Skeggsie?'

'The boy? Josh's friend? It was a terrible mistake. James Munroe was very upset by what happened. It's what happens when outsiders are involved.'

'I saw Margaret Spicer. She seemed less sure that Munroe hadn't intended Skeggsie to die.'

'You saw Margaret?'

'She came to see me. She wanted to explain.'

'Well, she and James are splitting up. She is very upset. Very bitter. But we trust James Munroe. He is a good man.'

Rose didn't know what to say. Her mum sounded so certain, so positive about what they were doing. It wasn't what she'd wanted to hear. She watched as her mother rearranged her scarf, tucking the fringed end into her jacket.

'Did you have a miscarriage?' Rose blurted out.

Her mother looked startled. 'How did you know about that?'

'I found some of Brendan's letters to you. It sounded as though you weren't happy.'

'For a while we weren't. We were under a lot of pressure from the German situation. It wouldn't have been right for me to have another baby but I was so sad when I lost it. It meant that Brendan and I had differences for a while. At one time I even thought . . .'

Rose waited.

'I even thought we might separate. But we didn't.'

'And now there is this dead girl in the back garden. Daisy Lincoln. You know the press have linked her death with your disappearance?'

'I did see some press about it . . .'

'Did you know her? Did Brendan know her?'

Her mother looked puzzled. 'I don't think we did know her. I might have passed her in the street and known her by sight but I couldn't have put a name to her face.'

'The detective I spoke to said that her hands were tied behind her back. Then she was killed and buried.'

'It's awful. An innocent girl with her life ahead of her.'

'Mum, her hands were tied behind her back with Brendan's tie.'

Her mother's face dropped. Her eyes crinkled, the deep line between her eyebrows darkening. She looked as though she was about to speak but didn't say anything.

'Why do you think that was?' Rose said nervously.

'Are you sure that's what they said? A tie *like* one that Brendan had? Wasn't that what they meant?'

'They have his DNA.'

'I don't understand. Wait . . . Something is making sense to me now. Something that happened that summer. In August Brendan and I went away for a long weekend. We went on the Thursday night and came back on the Tuesday. You and Josh stayed with friends. I don't remember the exact date but when we got back the back door was unlocked. I thought someone had been in the house. Brendan said I was overwrought. I even thought it might have been the Germans but . . .'

It wasn't a believable explanation. Rose slumped back in the chair.

'You think someone *might* have broken into the house and used Brendan's tie.'

'Rose, I don't know. But it wasn't Brendan or me.

Whatever happened to this poor Daisy girl is nothing to do with our mission.'

The pendant. How did Daisy get the pendant? Rose thought.

Rose didn't ask the question. It would only have elicited the same answer. If the police were right about it being Brendan's tie then the person to ask was *Brendan*.

'Now I really must go.'

Rose stood up. Her mother hugged her.

'You wait to hear from us,' she whispered.

And then she was gone. She slipped out of the cafe and Rose watched her go down the stairs until she merged into the crowds, only her pink scarf visible, and then after a few moments she couldn't even see that. Behind her the young couple were talking about Berlin.

'It's a great place for nightlife, so we'll spend a few days there!' the young man was saying.

Rose couldn't listen any more. She left the cafe and headed out of the station.

TWENTY

Rose went back to college. She stayed in the library after her classes to finish an essay that had to be in. Sarah and Maggie were also there, further along the table. From time to time she looked at the screen of her phone to see if she had a message. Sarah and Maggie gave each other knowing looks.

'You waiting for a text from Jamie?' Sarah whispered loudly.

'He really likes you,' Maggie said, smiling.

Rose shook her head and they both nudged each other.

What *was* she looking for? A message from her mother?

The librarian looked up and gave them a glare. Rose put her phone away and carried on with the essay. A while later she printed it off.

'See you tomorrow,' she said to Sarah and Maggie.

'You catching the train?' Sarah called after her.

'Jamie catches that train!' Maggie called.

Rose ignored them and dropped the essay in the

teacher's pigeonhole outside the staff room. Then she walked off towards the station. She was relieved to see that Jamie was not on the platform.

She caught the twenty-two minutes past five train and sat at a window seat. She was tired. It had been a long and emotional day. Disappointment hung around her. She had built up a story in her head which had her mother as some kind of passive follower, sucked into this *mission* through her love for Brendan. And yet it was not true. Her mother was committed. She was not making excuses or trying to shift blame. She did not even seem to accept *blame*. It was as though this had become part of her role as a policewoman. She was no longer employed as a police officer but her heart was still firmly wedded to the job only with a view of sentencing and retribution far beyond what was allowed.

And yet the people they had killed were rotten to the core.

Did they deserve to be sentenced to death as they had surely sentenced other people to death? She thought of Simon Lister, The Butterfly Killer. He had been a builder, a man who had easy access to people's houses. He had watched ten-year-old Judy Greaves weeks before he took her. She had been alive for five days before he killed her. All the time he knew what he was going to do, maybe even from the first moment he set eyes on her. Did this man deserve to live?

Who was she to say?

She stared out at the urban landscape – the backs of houses, garages, building yards and apartments that sided on to the railway line. Her eyes flicked around the carriage to see a number of students lolling across the seats, some of them with their feet up daring any of the other travellers to say something. Rose looked away. There was a man sitting across the aisle. She hadn't noticed him before. He was wearing jeans and boots and had a holdall on the floor. It was red and had a chequered flag on it.

The sight of it startled her.

She looked harder and saw it was definitely there, in the shadow of the seat in front of the man. She glanced at the man's face. He was wearing a hoodie and because he was older it seemed wrong. She recognised him immediately.

He turned round.

'Hello, Rose,' he said.

He picked up his bag and shuffled across the seat and then he was sitting next to her. It was Frank Richards. She'd seen him in Wickby, the ex-policeman who had been sacked from the force. And months before he had killed a boy that she had known. In cold blood.

'What are you doing here?' she said. 'Have you been following me?'

'Just looking out for you, Rose, making sure you're all right. I thought you looked a little strained last week.'

The train stopped and most of the students got out. A woman with a pushchair got on and sat down a few seats away. Rose stared at the window. Had he followed her? Did he know she'd been with her mother just hours before? She was disconcerted by his presence. He seemed to hang around the edges of *The Butterfly Project* like a disconnected ghost. What was his part in it? What was he doing here? Days before he'd sent the remaining notebooks to Joshua.

'Why did you send the notebooks? Did Munroe tell you to?'

'My records? They have nothing to do with Munroe or anyone else.'

'But why send them to Joshua? What's the point?'

'He saw the others – stole them from me. Now that it's all coming to an end he might as well have those. It's all there. Everything we did. I was a good policeman. I made notes. I recorded every move.'

'In code.'

'Easy to break,' he said, lowering his voice. 'It's up to Joshua if he wants to or not. I thought that as he was Brendan's son he would be the best person to have them. They are evidence of why we came to our judgements and what we did. I'm not ashamed of my actions and neither is anyone else. Joshua can get rid of them if he wants to or he can keep them for posterity.'

'Aren't you concerned that he will give them to the authorities?'

'His father is there on every page.'

That was the reason for Frank Richards' confidence. He wanted Joshua to have the information *as a record* but he knew for sure that Joshua wouldn't reveal it because it meant his father would get into trouble. She remembered then how disdainful Munroe had been about Frank Richards. *He's a loose cannon, a maverick. He doesn't know what he's talking about.*

'Aren't you worried that Munroe will be angry?'

Frank Richards' voice rose and he made a dismissive gesture with his hand. 'Munroe is not in charge of me. I don't have a boss in all this and if I did it would be Brendan not Munroe.'

The woman with the pushchair looked up. She frowned at Frank Richards. The train was approaching Rose's stop, Parkway East.

'I have to go,' she said.

She stood up and walked away towards the doors, holding on to the seat handles to keep her balance. Even though she didn't look back she felt Frank Richards coming after her. It made her feel anxious. When the train stopped she got out and began to walk along the platform but seconds later felt a hand on her arm.

'Just five minutes, Rose. I just want you to sit with me for five minutes.'

Her instinct was to walk away. Although Frank Richards was involved in *The Butterfly Project* and worked with her mum and Brendan there was something creepy about him. She headed for a bench, though, and sat down, her feet tightly together, her rucksack on her knees. She leant forward and stared down the railway line.

'What do you want, Frank?'

'I want to talk to you about the boy.'

Frank Richards looked up at the bridge over the tracks. She followed his gaze. There were some people coming across it. She could hear them talking in loud voices and laughing and then they appeared at the top of the stairs, two teenage boys and a girl. They came down heavily, clattering on the steps. She remembered the night last autumn when she had been here on this very platform. She'd met up with a boy from her college. He'd been unpleasant to her. Then he'd changed his mind about using the train and walked off up the stairs and come face to face with Frank Richards.

He'd died on that bridge of a single stab wound. Rose didn't particularly want to hear about that night again. She sat still, though, and listened as he talked.

'The boy said things about you, Rose. Disgusting things and I couldn't ignore it. I tried to talk to him. I told him that if he didn't wash his mouth out with soap and water that I'd do it for him. He was a nasty piece of work. No one liked him much. You knew that, Rose. You knew what he was like at college. Kathy had asked me to look out for you and here was this filthy-mouthed boy running you down. Then he pulled his knife out. He thought he was acting like a man. When I took it off him he had this babyish expression like I'd just taken his rattle.'

Rose closed her eyes. She didn't want to be reminded about what happened. A boy murdered because of her.

'His expression changed when I put the knife in . . .'

She stood up. She began to walk away and heard Frank Richards coming after her. There was noise from the bridge, footsteps, heavy and slow. She looked up. It was a police officer. He peered over the side at her.

'Everything all right there, miss?'

She looked round at Frank Richards. His face had frozen. Maybe it wasn't too late to give him up for killing Ricky Harris. She heard the sound of the policeman coming down the stairs. She could say, 'Officer, I was a witness to a stabbing here in this station last autumn. This is the man who did it. I recognise him.'

'Don't do it, Rose,' Frank Richards said, under his breath. 'Don't betray me.'

Betray him! He was living in some kind of fantasy world and saw her as part of this quest. She pictured him sitting in a room on his own, writing in the notebooks, night after night. Every letter had to be in code. Painstakingly he recorded what had happened like the policeman he had once been. He thought it was important. Amid all the murders he had principles. He was deluded. Maybe, for once, Munroe was right.

'I don't ever want to see you again.'

'You won't. I'm going abroad.'

She turned just as the policeman came on to the platform.

'Everything OK, miss?'

'Sure,' Rose said. 'No problem.'

She walked past him up on to the walkway. Halfway across she paused and looked back down. Frank was talking to the policeman. The tone was light-hearted, two men passing the time of day. Further along the platform the three teenagers were standing together, one of the boys whispering something in the girl's ear.

It was the second time that she'd failed to give Frank Richards up to the police. Why hadn't she done it? Because Frank Richards was part of the fabric of *The Butterfly Project*. He was a loose cannon and couldn't be trusted. Once in police custody the whole thing may begin to unravel and how would that leave her mother and Brendan? No, Frank Richards, like James Munroe, was a compromise she had to make to keep her mum and Brendan safe.

TWENTY-ONE

Rose walked in the direction of Anna's.

She wondered if her mother even *knew* about Ricky Harris.

She tried to push it out of her mind and headed along the road, sidestepping passers-by. Although it was getting dark the High Street was busy. Shop windows were illuminated and the traffic lights were bright. The cars were queuing and there was the sound of muffled music coming from inside stationary vehicles. It was cold, the air sharp against her face. She pulled her coat tighter as she turned the corner into Anna's road. All at once there was a change. The road seemed darker and the sounds of the High Street receded as she walked further along.

Up ahead a figure stepped out from behind a car.

Rose continued walking although she felt a little apprehensive. The figure was a man and was standing very still. She sensed that he was looking at her but then he turned away as if to open the door of an adjacent car and she felt herself relax momentarily.

Then she felt hands gripping her arms from behind and she was pushed rapidly towards the hedge of a front garden, her face shoved roughly into the foliage. She closed her eyes, certain that the person behind her was Mikey. She felt one of his hands in her hair, grabbing it tightly and with the other he pulled her rucksack off her shoulder and let it drop on the ground. His front was sandwiched against her back. She could smell cigarettes and aftershave. Just then she heard Lev Baranski's voice at her ear. He was calm, enunciating each word.

'You tell the Johnson boy that we have your mother. You tell him to tell his father that.'

Her mother?

Rose struggled but Mikey held her tightly.

'We have her and we will kill her if he does not give himself up to us. Tell him to be at London Eye tomorrow at midday. On his own. Then I will let her go. If he doesn't come then I will take her in a boat out to sea, tie her hands behind her back and throw her in. Is only fair after all . . .'

Rose felt herself go weak. If Mikey hadn't been holding her tightly she would have slid on to the ground.

'If he doesn't come, not only will I kill this woman, I will also find him and kill him. This way only one of them dies.'

Mikey drove her head further into the hedge. Rose felt the twigs scratching the side of her face. Then he let go of her hair and wound something round her neck, pulling it tight, constricting her throat. He gave her a sideways push and she staggered but kept her footing. Her hands were free but she didn't move. She stood rigid with her face in the foliage for a few seconds then turned round to see the two figures walking off toward the High Street. She was shaking. She put her fingers up to her neck and felt a soft silk scarf there. She pulled it, off knowing that it was the one her mother had worn when she met her earlier that day. She ruffled the fringes.

She felt nauseous. The pavement beneath her feet seemed to slope away from her, the parked cars at an angle. She bent over, feeling a gagging in her throat. Her blood was hammering in her ears. If only Frank Richards had been watching out for her then. After a few moments she straightened up, steadied herself, picked her rucksack up off the pavement and ran into the house.

Anna wasn't at home. Rose went straight up to her room. All the time her thoughts were racing. Had they followed her? To the station? Seen her with her mother? Had she made it possible for them to snatch her mother when she was walking away, heading for the two o'clock train?

She threw her bag down and pulled her coat off.

She found herself crying.

They had her *mother*. They would tie her hands up and throw her out of a boat unless Brendan went to the London Eye and turned himself over to them and certain death.

And it was her fault.

She was walking up and down, hiccupping sobs, using her knuckles to wipe the tears from the corners of her eyes. She went to the door of her room and called out Joshua's name. Her voice cracked, though, and the sound didn't carry. She walked out on to the landing and called again. She thought she heard footsteps but then there was nothing. She stood at the bottom of the stairwell. She was crying loudly, her nose running, her shoulders shaking.

They had her mother.

'Josh!' she shouted. 'Josh. JOSH.'

She waited. The door of the attic opened and his head appeared at the top of the stairs. He smiled and then his face dropped.

'What's wrong? What's happened?'

She sank on to the bottom stair and let her head fall into her hands. When he reached her he pulled her up to a standing position.

'What? What? What's happened? Your face is grazed. What's happened to you? Tell me!'

She was limp. Like a doll. She had no shape. She just hung over his arm.

'They've got my mum,' she said, through cries. 'Baranski has got my mum.'

'Try and stay calm,' Joshua said, holding a wet flannel up to the side of Rose's face. 'We have to think. We have to work out what to do.'

Rose took the flannel. She had stopped crying. She had told him about the meeting with her mother and the things she had said. He had listened without giving away his feelings. He hadn't admonished her for not telling him about the card with the phone number on it. He hadn't got angry. He prompted her to tell it all, nodding, giving reassuring sounds.

She hadn't told him about the other stuff – the pendant, the letters from Brendan, the fact that they hadn't been getting on. All of that seemed irrelevant in the face of what had happened.

'We can work something out,' he said.

Joshua looked pained. He was walking up and down. She noticed then that he was wearing his father's jumper again, the sleeves rolled up, the hem on one side fraying. *Brendan's jumper*. Brendan who would have to go to the London Eye tomorrow in order to save her mother's life.

'We have to contact Brendan.'

'How?' Joshua said.

'We have to get in the car and go there now! To Two Oaks!'

'No. We can't do that. It's too direct. We don't know what sort of situation we might put him into.'

'Maybe we should ring Frank Richards. I still have his number . . .'

She remembered Frank Richards, an hour or so before. She hadn't yet told Joshua about seeing him. The man had seemed creepy, odd, overwrought. Did they have to depend on *him* to save her mother?

'No, we'll contact Dad through Munroe.'

'*James Munroe?*' Rose said, startled.

'This isn't just about Dad and Kathy. This is about the organisation. *The Butterfly Project.* Wasn't that what you said Margaret Spicer called it? Whatever they did to Baranski was a joint decision. So the group should know that one of their own has been taken. It's up to the group to deal with it. Not just Dad.'

'But there isn't time.'

'There is time. We go and see James Munroe now, tonight. I know where he lives, remember?'

'How can we ask that man to help us? After what he did to Skeggsie? We can't deal with him!'

'We're not asking him for help – we're telling him what's about to happen to one of his people. He has power, Rosie. You remember how they cleared the cottage in Stiffkey? At the time we were amazed at their resources? Well, let him use those resources to set up this meeting at the London Eye tomorrow. Let him look after his own people.'

'I don't know'

'We can't deal with this. You and me, we've stumbled around in this mess for months now but *this* is something we cannot deal with. Lives are at stake here and if it means dealing with Munroe then I'll put my feelings aside and do it.'

He was right. There was nothing they could do to save her mother or Brendan on their own. James Munroe, on the other hand, was ruthless and had the power to make things happen.

'We'll go to Munroe's now. We should leave a note for your gran. Tell her we're staying at the Camden flat tonight.'

Rose nodded. Pulling herself together she packed some clothes into her rucksack and paused to write the note.

Dear Anna, Josh has some IT equipment at the Camden flat which will help with one of my assignments. I'll probably stay over there and go straight to college in the morning. See you tomorrow. Rose

She placed it on the hall table as they left the house.

TWENTY-TWO

James Munroe's home was close to Surrey Quays station in Docklands. They got off the train and walked along a well lit but deserted street. On one side of it was a long apartment block, a glass and steel structure which had been recently built and was not quite finished. Overhanging the street were rows of apartments with balconies which all sat in darkness awaiting occupiers. The only lights were those along the wooden security fence.

'The docks are on the other side of those houses,' Joshua said, pointing as if she'd asked. 'Munroe lives a few streets over there. His apartment block is not as close to the water as these but it's still pretty smart.'

They walked on and turned off the main street into a small paved square.

'There.'

Across the square was a brick building that looked like an old primary school. It was three storeys high and had a high wall around it. Rose followed Joshua to the corner of the square and along a narrow street. About ten metres ahead was an entrance for cars and pedestrians. There was a keypad and audio box. She was reminded of Macon Parker's home in the country. She lifted her eyes and saw that on the wall, angled down to the entrance, were two CCTV cameras.

'How do you know which apartment he has?'

'The surnames are there. His is number three.'

They went close to the row of numbers and buttons and Rose saw *Munroe* next to number three. Joshua put his finger on it and Rose waited. There was a low buzzing sound. Then they stood back. Nothing happened. There was no voice, no movement of the gate. Joshua stepped forward and pressed the button again, holding it for longer.

'What if he's not in?'

'Let's just hope he is.'

Joshua took his finger off the buzzer and looked up at the building.

'It's that apartment on the third floor, on the right-hand side.'

Rose looked up as a pair of headlights came along the narrow lane. She turned to see. A dark car was moving towards them.

'Look,' she said.

As the car came closer she could see James Munroe inside it. He was alone. He approached the entrance and stopped. His window slid down.

'What are you doing here?' he said testily.

'We need to talk,' Joshua said, leaning down to the window, then lowering his voice, he added, 'Lev Baranski has taken Kathy.'

'What! How on earth . . .'

'It's a long story.'

'I'll park the car then I'll buzz you in.'

There was a lift to the third floor. It was modern and tiny and Rose and Joshua stood face to face waiting for it. Rose touched Joshua's cheek where the plaster had been.

'Is it still painful?'

'I've forgotten about it.'

The lift doors opened. James Munroe was standing outside his apartment waiting for them. They walked into a room that had once been a classroom. The ceiling was high, the floor parquet, and the wall space seemed empty as if it was missing a display of children's pictures and stories. There was a leather sofa and an armchair. In the corner was a large television. Across the far wall was a fitted kitchen and in between the two areas a wooden table. James Munroe had taken his coat off and rested it over the back of a chair. On the table were car keys, a BlackBerry and a smartphone. There was also a briefcase on a chair. Munroe walked across and stood with his back against a kitchen cupboard. He looked at each of them coldly.

'Your father's already been in contact with me. Kathy was due back in Essex this afternoon and she hasn't turned up. You say you know what's happened to her?'

'Mum's been taken by Baranski. He says he'll kill her if Brendan doesn't go to the London Eye tomorrow at twelve. I think he wants to take Brendan in exchange for Mum . . .'

'Hang on,' he said, exasperated. 'Kathy and Brendan have been undercover for over a year. How did he find them? And how do you know about this?'

'I found them,' Joshua said. '*We* found them.'

Munroe looked at Joshua with hostility.

'I told you we wouldn't stop until we found them. Perhaps Dad didn't tell you about seeing us.'

Joshua said it with relish. Rose frowned. It was misplaced bravado. They had found them and then put them in danger. Munroe stared at him unfazed. There was real *dislike* in his expression. Joshua held his look. Rose pulled the conversation back to the reason they had come.

'My mum might be killed. If she is working for you then you should do something about it!'

Munroe's voice was steely. 'You couldn't just leave things alone. Wasn't it enough that your friend was killed because of your interference?'

Joshua bristled. 'His death is down to you.'

'I'm not repeating the conversation I had with you in Newcastle. You two have meddled and put everyone in danger. You're a couple of kids and you should have kept your noses out of it. I wonder what your father will make of this latest disaster!'

Joshua stepped forward. 'Don't you tell me or Rose what to do. It's because of you that we lost our parents five years ago.'

'Because of me? How ridiculous. Who do you think started all this? Your father. Brendan Johnson, covering up for his brother's stupidity,' Munroe said, pointing his finger at Joshua.

'He thought he was doing the right thing . . .'

Rose shook her head. 'There's no time for arguments now!'

Munroe turned his fury on Rose. 'Then maybe you should have heeded what I said when I visited your grand-mother. I warned that this might end badly and now look what you've done!'

'Don't shout at her!'

'Ever the gentleman. Just like your father. Protecting the ladies!'

Joshua lunged at Munroe. He collided with him, push-ing him further along the kitchen units, knocking over a fruit bowl, oranges falling out and bouncing dully on to the wooden floor. Munroe steadied himself and grabbed Joshua's jacket and shoved him backwards.

'You have got in my way once too often. This time you will not interfere. This judgement was made almost two years ago. It's taken us this long to get everything in place and now here we are days away from completion and you barge in and ruin everything and leave it to me to pick up the pieces.'

Joshua's back was at the wall. He was taller than Munroe but the older man was stocky and strong. Munroe's face was rigid, his eyes like slits as he pinned Joshua harder against the wall. Then without warning he let him go and Joshua slid down to an almost sitting position. Munroe walked away, rubbing his palms together. Joshua struggled up, looking shaken and angry. Rose tried to help him but he shrugged her off. She picked up the oranges instead, placing them back in the bowl.

'What happened to your ear?' Munroe said, his voice calm.

'Baranski's man, Mikey. He did it,' Rose said.

Munroe shook his head. 'Baranski – like father like son. Getting rid of him was a good judgement. Now, you need to tell me what has happened since Newcastle so that when I call your father I have all the information. Then we'll see how to deal with this.'

Joshua turned away as if he couldn't bear to look at Munroe. Rose knew that it was she who would have to tell the story. In a stuttering voice she explained it as clearly as she could. She left out the irrelevant stuff about

Brewster Road and the murder of Daisy Lincoln. She ignored Munroe's expression of distaste and annoyance and told it in order ending with Baranski's threat to kill her mother.

Munroe picked up his phone and BlackBerry.

'I'm going to call your father in the other room. I need to sort some things out with him then I will get him to speak to you.'

He closed the door to what Rose supposed was a bedroom.

'What do you think he'll say? What will they do?'

Joshua shrugged.

They sat at the table and Joshua shook his head slowly.

'He'll go down for Skeggsie. One day he will.'

Rose didn't answer. In a just world he would. But maybe this wasn't essentially a just world. Maybe her mother had been right when she said *You have not walked in our shoes. You cannot know what made us do this.* Can any person ever walk in another person's shoes? There was the sound of talking from next door, rapid words, low and emphatic. There were gaps followed by more talk. Rose looked around the living area. It was uncluttered, like a show flat. There was nothing she could see that indicated a female presence. Either it had only ever been a place for Munroe to sleep over in the city or Margaret Spicer had already stripped the place of her belongings.

The bedroom door opened and Munroe came out holding his phone. Without a word he gave it to Joshua. Joshua walked away towards the window and stood with his back to them. Rose felt uncomfortable standing near Munroe. She too moved across the room and heard Joshua speak.

'I didn't know about Kathy giving Rose the phone number.'

'I didn't know they were going to meet.'

'Kathy must have decided for herself . . .'

'I'm not going to stay away tomorrow.'

'Rose and I will be there . . .'

'We will not stay away so there's no point in . . .'

'You don't have the right to order me . . . Not now, not after everything.'

Joshua went quiet. Rose could hear the hum of the voice on the other end of the phone. She saw Joshua nodding and wondered if Brendan was taking charge, laying down the law. After what seemed like a long time Joshua ended the call and handed the phone back to Munroe.

'Go home now. Leave it to us,' Munroe said.

'I'll be nearby tomorrow,' Joshua said.

'Just go home.'

Rose took Joshua's arm and led him out of the living room towards the door of the flat. Munroe didn't follow them.

* * *

234

Back in the Camden flat they both sat on the sofa in the living room. It had been an almost silent journey back from Docklands. Joshua was speaking now, giving instructions about the next day. In his hands he had a Google Map of the area around the London Eye.

'We get to the London Eye about eleven thirty. Dad says we should try and disguise ourselves.'

'What?'

'Just slightly. You know, wear something more formal, carry a briefcase, umbrella or wear a hat, just some small thing to alter the way we look. And we shouldn't stay together. I thought you could stand on Hungerford Bridge, here.' He pointed to the map. 'I've got some binoculars you can use. You'll be like a tourist looking at the Houses of Parliament or the boats on the river. I'm going to be around County Hall. There are a lot of places there where I can merge in with the crowds. Dad says we just have to stay away from him and Baranski and Mikey. And of course there might be other Baranski people there.'

'What can we do? I mean to help?'

'Nothing. Dad says to leave it all to them. We can just watch. There'll be a switch at some point. Dad taking the place of Kathy. Munroe will be looking after Kathy so we should keep our eye on Dad and whoever has him. Mikey maybe. I think, if you can, you should swing from side to side with the binoculars and when you see that they've taken Dad you should keep the binoculars on him. Dad says he'll wear a light blue padded jacket. You'll be able to see which direction they take him in. I'll call you when I go off to County Hall and we'll keep the line open so we can be in touch. All we can do is watch from a distance. I think Munroe and Dad and maybe some others will have to handle it.'

'Frank Richards?' Rose said.

Joshua shrugged. 'I don't know.'

'It seems so . . . theatrical. Like a movie. It seems unreal.'

'Yeah, well . . .'

Joshua said something under his breath.

'What?' she said sharply.

'It should never have come to this.'

'How do you mean?'

'If you hadn't had that meeting. If you hadn't gone behind my back . . .'

Rose bridled. 'I didn't intend for this to happen!'

''Course not. No one intends something like this to happen but it should have been obvious to you that meeting Kathy was a dangerous thing to do. Especially after what Baranski did to me!'

'Why are you saying this?'

'I don't know. Maybe it just needs to be said.'

Rose stood up. 'I'll go back to Anna's. I'll see you at the London Eye in the morning.'

'No! We said we'd stay here.'

'You didn't say any of this when I first told you. When we went to Munroe's?'

'Because it's just beginning to dawn on me how dangerous tomorrow is going to be. If it all goes wrong Baranski will have my dad.'

'You mean like he's got my mum now?'

'But Kathy put herself in danger. She took a chance . . .'

'So she's to blame for Baranski taking her?' Rose said angrily. 'Maybe if Brendan hadn't killed Baranski's father none of this might be happening.'

Rose walked out of the room to the hallway and put her coat on. Joshua came out after her.

'This is not the time to argue,' he said, laying his hand on her arm.

'Why is it that you have to decide on every single thing that happens to us? You wanted to find them. We found them. My mother wanted to see me so she gave me her phone number secretly. What is it you're upset about, Josh? That I went to see my mother without you knowing or that your father didn't give you his phone number at all?'

'Rose!'

'I'm sick of always doing what you want when you want it. Go to Wickby, go to Two Oaks, stay in Camden, hire a car, make a website. Do it your way. I wanted to do it my way for once.'

'And look where it's got us! Your mum's in Baranski's hands now.'

Rose flinched. She turned away. He grabbed her arm and pulled her back. His other hand was on the wall preventing her from moving.

They were both wedged in the narrow hallway.

Neither of them spoke.

Then Rose leant against him, her body heavy with worry.

'I'm sorry,' she said.

He kissed the side of her hair and she felt her skin prickle. He put his arms around her and pulled her towards him and kissed her on her face and then her mouth. Her eyes were closed and she moved her head so that she could feel his lips on hers. His hands were moving up and down her back and she raised her arms to clasp him round the neck.

'I'm not sure how right this is, you and me . . .' he whispered.

'It is right,' she said, pressing into him.

He kissed her again for a long time. When he stopped she felt breathless.

'It's late – let's go in here,' he said.

He led her towards his bedroom door.

TWENTY-THREE

The London Eye seemed utterly still against a brilliant blue sky. Rose saw it as soon as they came out of the tube exit. They went up some steps and stood at the north end of Hungerford Bridge. It sat like a sombre fairground ride on the bank of the river.

Joshua was wearing a dark overcoat and around his neck was a red cashmere scarf that he said he'd been given by his uncle years before but never worn. The dressing was off his ear and all he had was a flesh-coloured plaster on the wound. The strangest thing of all was that he was wearing Skeggsie's glasses. There was glass in the frames but he insisted he could still see through them. It made him seem like a different person.

Rose had on a Union Jack baseball cap of Joshua's which had been left over from the Olympics. It covered her head and forehead. Underneath the peak she could hold the binoculars. It wasn't much of a disguise but it was enough to make her look like a tourist. She had her hands-free earphones in, the remote hanging by her throat, most of it hidden by her hair.

It was 11.32 a.m.

'I'm going across to the County Hall building. I'll find a vantage point and I'll call you. Once you get my call don't disconnect even if you don't hear me speak for a while,' Joshua said.

She nodded and grabbed his sleeve suddenly fearful of what might happen.

'Just look as though you're a tourist and remember Dad's wearing a light blue padded jacket.'

He gave her a hug and then walked off. She thought, fleetingly, of the night before. So much was happening between them and yet it had to be pushed to the back of her mind. This was the important thing, getting her mum back safe. There was lots of time to think about the two of them when this was all over. She took some gum out and put it into her mouth. The chewing calmed her and made her mouth less dry. She looked around. The bridge wasn't crowded, just a few couples walking across. Parallel to the walkways was the train line which sliced through the centre of the bridge. Every now and again Rose could hear and feel the deep rumble of a train heading for Charing Cross. Looking across the water she couldn't see any crowds at the base of the London Eye. There were trees alongside the river blocking her view.

She walked along the bridge, holding the peak of her cap down. That morning Joshua had taken a long call from Brendan giving them more information. He had told his employer that his wife, Kate, had been in London to visit her elderly father and found him fragile and rather unwell. She'd decided to stay with him for a few days and might not be available for Macon's birthday celebrations. It meant that Brendan and her mother's cover with Macon Parker was still intact.

As if that mattered to Rose – all she cared about was getting her mother safely back from Lev Baranski.

Halfway across the bridge she stopped and took the binoculars out and lifted them up to her eyes. She pointed them at the Houses of Parliament and Big Ben. She stood looking at these historical sites for some minutes, playing her part as a tourist, panning the binoculars slowly to the left as though she was trying to take in every detail of the horizon. When she got to the London Eye she paused. She could see the queues of people in and around the trees that lined the river. There were a couple of buskers performing to the people awaiting their turn. Behind the London Eye was a green space, the size of a small park. There were some white marquees on it and a carousel. Rose let the glasses focus on one of the horses on the fairground ride. It was white and its mane was jet black. There were painted jewels on its bridle and its mouth was open slightly as if caught in a neigh. Rose let the glasses sweep past the queues to the left again and saw the concrete buildings of the Royal Festival Hall. She remembered then that Joshua was on the far side of the Eye at County Hall. She swivelled the glasses back and looked for him against the chunky grey building but she couldn't see him. She decided to walk a bit further across the bridge. A train went chugging by, slowing down, its great weight seeming to fan out across the walkway. A group of tourists were lining up for a photograph and Rose waited so that she didn't spoil the shot. They all headed off towards the Eye and she attached herself to the group, listening as they spoke rapidly to each other in Spanish. When she was three quarters of the way across the bridge she stood still and held the binoculars up to her eyes again.

She saw Brendan.

He was wearing the blue padded jacket. It was a light blue, like a skiing jacket, and he was standing by the front of the queue for the Eye. He was apart from it though as if he was deliberately placing himself in full view so that someone could see him. She had a squirming feeling in her stomach. Whatever Munroe and Brendan had planned had to go right. Her mum had to come back safely but Brendan too. She moved the binoculars back to the river so that it seemed as though she was looking everywhere and not focusing on the Eye.

Her phone vibrated. She put her hand in her pocket and accessed the call.

'Keep the line open, Rosie,' Joshua said, his voice in her ear.

'All right,' she said, adjusting the volume.

It was 11.48.

Now that she'd seen Brendan in his bright jacket she didn't need the glasses so she shoved them in her pocket for a moment. She looked towards the building behind the London Eye. She knew that there was a road behind it and that that was the most likely place for Lev Baranski to get out of a car and bring her mother. Unless he changed his mind and came alone. Joshua had said that was always a possibility. He might tell Brendan to go somewhere with him, threatening her mother in some way if he did not. On the other hand he might just bring her mother out into the open and swap her for Brendan. Baranski knew that no police could be involved. There would be no sharpshooters perched on the tops of buildings watching for him.

'Rosie?' Joshua said, his voice scratchy.

'Yes?'

'I'm by the corner of County Hall. I can't see Munroe anywhere. Can you see him?'

'I'll look for him.'

She took the binoculars out of her pocket and scanned the area around the Eye. She pictured Munroe in his Crombie overcoat and looked for it for a few moments but then, by chance, she saw Munroe's face. He was standing by one of the marquees. She had to look twice because he was wearing a dark, boxy jacket and light-coloured trousers. He turned to the side and she could see that on his back he had a rucksack which looked as though it had a French flag sewn on the side. He too was attempting to look like a tourist. She saw him lift the inside of his wrist up to his mouth and speak. He looked like a secret service man guarding a politician. She glanced quickly at Brendan who wasn't speaking to anyone, just eyeing his watch and looking round.

'Munroe's by the marquees on the grass,' she said quietly, angling her voice down to her neck.

A few moments later she heard his voice in her ear.

'I see him.'

It was 11.57. Rose pulled the front of her cap down and stretched her arms, feeling her joints click. She took the chewing gum out of her mouth and wrapped it in a tissue and put it in the zip compartment of her bag. When she looked back to the green behind the Eye she saw three figures walking across the grass. Two men and a woman. Her jaw tightened. Even though she knew it was her mother she used the binoculars to see who else was there.

'Baranski's coming with Mum. Mikey's there too. They're heading towards Brendan.'

'I see them,' Joshua said, his voice in a whisper as if they might hear him.

Rose lowered the glasses and watched the trio go past the marquees and past the place where James Munroe had been standing. She wondered where he had gone. Mikey had his arm around her mother's shoulder and one of his hands was in her mother's pocket, Joshua must have seen it clearly as well.

'I think Mikey's got a gun on Kathy.'

'I see it.'

Rose felt her stomach contract. She put the binoculars in her pocket and walked closer to the south end of the Hungerford Bridge. She saw that the three had slowed as they came up to Brendan. Brendan gave them a scowl, not seeming to pay any attention to her mum. Baranski stood apart from the couple and spoke to Brendan pointing towards the Royal Festival Hall. Brendan shook his head.

'He must be asking Dad to go with him,' Joshua said.

Rose lifted the binoculars again. She focused on the four faces. Her mother's face was calm but Mikey looked annoyed. Baranski was gesticulating with his hands, pointing up the embankment as though he wanted Brendan to walk there. Looking through the group, she thought she saw Joshua mingling on the other side of the queue, Skeggsie's heavy-framed glasses standing out. She hoped he wasn't going to try and do anything – they'd promised to leave it to James Munroe.

Where was James Munroe?

Brendan and Baranski started to walk away from her mum and Mikey. She heard Joshua's voice.

'Mikey's staying with Kathy. Maybe he's not going to let her go until he gets a call from Baranski to say that Dad's got into a car. I don't like this. I don't see Munroe. I don't like the idea of Dad getting into a car. Rosie, follow them, keep your eye on where Baranski takes Dad.'

Rose headed for the stairs. She had to wait as a party of tourists meandered up before she could get off the bridge on to the South Bank of the river. All the while she kept her eye on Brendan's blue jacket. Once off the bridge she saw them up ahead. Brendan was lagging behind Baranski. Baranski wasn't touching him or holding him and didn't seem to have a weapon of any sort. It was her mother who had a gun pointed at her. That was the only reason why Brendan was going quietly.

'I see them. I'm following,' she said breathlessly.

'I'm staying with Mikey. Cut the call for now.'

Rose ended the call. She continued to follow Brendan and Baranski. They walked ahead, like dozens of other tourists and sightseers, passing the Royal Festival Hall and the shops and restaurants that fronted the river. Brendan stopped for a moment and tied his shoelaces while Baranski appeared to be berating him. Rose stopped for a second. Was Brendan trying to slow Baranski down? She leant her elbows on the river wall, as if looking at the beach below. Then she continued after them. Up ahead was Waterloo Bridge. Rose wondered where Baranski was heading – somewhere where there was a car waiting, she thought. The man was clearly losing patience. He was tugging at Brendan's arm, hurrying him along.

Someone bumped into her. Something hit her ankle, making her gasp with pain. She turned round but by then the person had gone past.

It was a man pulling a small suitcase on wheels. A tall man in a flowing overcoat walking swiftly as if he was terribly late for something. It was the suitcase that had mounted her ankle and he hadn't seemed to notice.

She kept going, panicking as her view of Brendan and Baranski became obscured by other people. She side-stepped them and quickened up just as the pair went under Waterloo Bridge. The man with the suitcase had caught up with them. He was walking alongside Baranski. He seemed to have slowed down as if he was joining the pair.

Rose watched.

The man did an unexpected thing.

He raised his left arm straight out until it was level with his own shoulder. He seemed to be pointing a finger at Baranski's head. A moment passed and Rose suddenly *knew* what was going to happen.

Her mouth opened with shock. She was just stepping under Waterloo Bridge when she heard the sound like a whip, a loud crack echoing. It came from the man's hand.

The man with the suitcase on wheels. Baranski's head jerked to one side and there was a puff of vapour in the air, so slight that it vanished in an instant.

Baranski collapsed.

Brendan stepped away from him and carried on walking.

The man with the suitcase kept on going as if nothing had happened. She knew then and there that the man was Frank Richards. Maybe he had bumped into her deliberately, to slow her up, to keep her back. Now he veered to the right, pulling his suitcase with him.

People stopped and looked round not sure what the sound had been. Rose couldn't move. Frank Richards had executed Baranski, coldly and efficiently. Her eyes dropped down to the Russian who had fallen untidily, his head at an odd angle to his neck, a dark viscous shape expanding beneath his head.

Rose felt her legs tremble.

She turned and saw a few metres away the figure of Mikey running towards the bridge. He was sprinting, his face hard and angry.

Rose pulled the earpiece from her ear and walked away, passing Mikey before he reached his boss. Other people were heading towards the bridge, some breaking into a run. Behind her she heard people shouting, 'He's been shot!' 'Someone has shot this man!' 'Call the police, a man's been killed!' She glanced round and saw Mikey on his knees beside Baranski's body. She quickened her step staggering towards the river wall, pulling off the Union Jack cap and letting it drop by her feet. Just then she felt a heavy hand on her shoulder.

She spun round.

It was Joshua. She grabbed his wrist.

'Frank Richards killed Baranski. I saw him. I *know* it was him,' she said, her voice high-pitched, squeaky.

Joshua put his arms round her and shushed her.

'He shot him in the head. It was horrible,' she whispered.

'He was going to kill my dad, Rosie,' he said, manoeuvring her, moving her further along the wall.

'What about Mum?' she said.

'Safe. She's gone with Munroe.'

There was the sound of sirens in the distance and Rose could see a policeman hurrying along the pathway in the direction of Waterloo Bridge. Rose's eyes stayed on him as he approached the bloody mess on the ground that was Baranski. Her eyes searched the area for Mikey but it didn't look as though he was there any more. She looked back to Joshua's face. He didn't seem upset in the slightest.

'It was perfectly organised,' he was saying with awe. 'And it happened in seconds. Mikey was holding Kathy's arm at the London Eye when she seemed to swoon. Her legs gave way and she just crumpled on to the ground.

He had to try and pull her up and then Munroe was there behind him. Munroe must have been holding a knife or gun at his back because Mikey seemed to freeze and Kathy stepped away from him. Then Mikey gave Munroe his gun and at that minute Frank Richards came past and Munroe handed it to him. No one saw a thing. The man walked on, pulling his suitcase. Just like any other tourist.'

Rose remembered Frank Richards moving quickly and purposefully. Like a relay runner he'd already picked up the baton and then overtook everyone until he got level with Baranski.

'Munroe held Mikey there for a few minutes. He was talking in his ear and Mikey was getting more and more angry. It was like holding a dog on a leash and then letting it go. Munroe must have put his weapon away because Mikey shot off after Baranski. Maybe he thought he could get there in time.'

Rose didn't want to hear any more but Joshua went on.

'The gun will have Mikey's prints on it.'

Crowds were gathering and the police siren sounded as if it was close. Rose felt unwell.

'I want to see Mum.'

'Soon. For the moment we're joining in with the shocked public. We're onlookers. Give us a chance to calm down.'

Rose stood while other people surrounded her. She felt

Joshua's arm around her waist, holding her up. There were people talking excitedly. 'Murder! In daylight!'

Rose's stomach churned with nerves. Joshua wanted her to calm down. She doubted she would ever be calm again.

TWENTY-FOUR

An hour later they were in a cafe a couple of streets away from Liverpool Street Station. Munroe had told them to meet there. Rose was drinking black coffee. It wasn't a drink she liked much but she needed a jolt of something to shake her out of the malaise that was gripping her. She was in a corner seat and Joshua was across from her. She needed to adjust, to rearrange all the things in her head. Her mum was alive, so was Brendan. That was the important thing. She could smell food cooking and felt pangs of hunger but she couldn't imagine herself eating a thing.

The door of the cafe opened and James Munroe came in. Brendan was following him. They were both wearing macs. Munroe's was a dark colour, black maybe, Brendan's was beige. Munroe spoke to Brendan then walked towards the counter.

'Where's Mum?' Rose said as soon as Brendan got to them.

'She's at the hotel sleeping it off. She's had a bad night,' he said, sitting down, pushing his chair back from the table a bit as if he wanted to distance himself.

Rose felt pained. She'd been so worried about her mother, so desperate to see her, and yet her mother had gone back to a hotel room rather than come and see Rose. She couldn't understand why she wasn't there sitting next to her. She couldn't bring herself to ask. It would seem churlish.

Joshua reached across and put his hand on his father's.

'Dad, I'm so glad you're all right,' he said.

Rose wondered what had happened to the blue ski jacket. Had it been splattered when Baranski was shot? Had Brendan got rid of it, left it somewhere because it might identify him in some way?

'I think we all need to discuss what happens next,' Munroe said, putting two hot drinks on the table and sitting down.

'Was Mum hurt?' Rose said.

'They tied her up and left her in an empty room. She's a bit bruised and her wrists are chafed but apart from that . . .'

'Kathy's OK. There are other pressing matters here . . .' Munroe said. 'Brendan, I'll leave it to you.'

Rose noticed that no one was using code names any more. Brendan seemed to think for a moment then began to speak.

'I know that you two have had your differences with James but you should understand that we're all on the same side here. What happened to your friend was an awful mistake and it happened because James was trying to protect Kathy and me. Perhaps after this Baranski business you will see that the threat we were under was very real.'

'Skeggsie is still dead,' Joshua said sullenly.

'That's true and no one regrets it more than James or Kathy or me. And it's all the more reason for us to finish our work with Parker. Otherwise it seems that your friend's death will really have been for nothing.'

Brendan was speaking in a low voice, looking round at people sitting at nearby tables. He picked his drink up and sipped it. Rose could see his hand was shaking slightly.

'Dad, I don't think you should do this.'

'I told you both when I saw you on Sunday that we were going to carry this through.'

'But things are different now. Now that we've found the two of you. Now that Baranski's . . . gone.'

'Parker's crimes are still the same as they were when we made the judgement. He is still a killer who has evaded the law.'

'You shouldn't go back there.'

'Your mother will stay at the hotel. Tomorrow evening she'll join me for Parker's birthday celebrations at Tate Modern.'

'The art gallery?'

'Private party on the seventh floor. I drive Parker and his wife up from Essex and then I will finish this business. I have to be sure that you will not interfere any more. The time for a deeper, more thorough explanation is later when our work is finished.'

Brendan looked at Rose and Joshua for some sort of confirmation. Joshua nodded his head in a dejected way. Rose just stared at Brendan. He was definitely thinner than when they had lived together – then he was always on a diet. *Lose a few pounds, eh, Petal.* Then he was soft round the edges and looked like someone's dad. Now he looked slim, harder, angular.

'I have to go now,' Brendan said, pushing his cup away untouched. 'I need to get back.'

'Isn't anyone going to talk about what just happened?' Rose said, her voice lowered to an angry whisper. 'I just watched a man being executed under Waterloo Bridge.'

'Baranski brought that on himself, Rosie,' Brendan said. 'He might have killed Kathy. Or me. Or both. We had to do something.'

'And Mikey? Won't he come looking for you? Tit for tat?'

'Mikey won't be able to do a thing. The gun which killed his boss has his fingerprints on it.'

'But people nearby will have seen *you*. And Frank Richards. They'll remember.'

'No. They'll recall a blue jacket but not the man in it,' Brendan said. 'They'll remember a tourist with a suitcase on wheels but not the face, not the man. And the police have a recording of an anonymous call from a Russian voice who said they saw Mikhail Gavlik shooting his boss under Waterloo Bridge. They'll either catch him or he'll go on the run. My bet is he'll go back to Russia.'

Mikhail Gavlik. Mikey's real name.

'You need to get off,' Munroe said. 'I'll bring the hardware to Kathy before tomorrow night.'

'Good,' Brendan said.

'When can I see Mum?'

'Now if you like. The hotel's in Bloomsbury. She's there under Kate Markham. It's the Lord Buckingham, room eighteen. Holborn is the closest tube station.'

Brendan stood up and buttoned up the mac he was wearing. It looked brand new. Had he actually bought it in preparation for the aftermath of the shooting? Joshua stepped across to hug him. Then Brendan walked away. When the cafe door shut behind him she turned and stared at Munroe. He immediately made eye contact with her.

'Why does Brendan have to do this?'

'To finish what we started.'

'Why tomorrow night? Why not do it in Essex tonight? Why have you waited a whole year for this?' Joshua said.

'That's a lot of questions.'

'I think we deserve to know.'

'Do you?'

Munroe sat back and folded his arms. He looked pleased with himself. 'Time was you didn't want to breathe the same air as me. Now that I've saved your father you feel differently.'

'Just explain,' Joshua said, irritation in his voice.

'The judgement will take place tomorrow night because there will be many of Parker's friends and associates there. Some from Denver, some from Florida. Brendan will use American hardware, which I have procured.'

'Hardware?' Rose said.

'He means a gun, Rose.'

'That's right. Then the blame for this will rest on one of Parker's associates. At least the *suspicion* will rest there. It will just seem as though there's been a falling-out between rich gangsters.'

'But why did Mum and Brendan have to be there for a year?'

'They have to be completely and utterly trusted. That way when Brendan takes Macon Parker aside to deal with some fictional problem Parker won't hesitate. Neither will Parker's minders. They won't feel the need to protect their boss because they think that Brendan and Kathy are part of the family.'

'But when it's done won't they suspect Brendan?'

'Brendan will be gone. Parker's associates will all suspect each other for planting Brendan. They'll be rushing off back to the States and your father and your mother will turn into different people. Which reminds me. I have to go soon and give Frank Richards his new papers.'

Munroe took a slim envelope from his pocket and put it on the table. He looked pleased with himself as though it was a winning card. Rose knew he expected her to look at it but she wouldn't. It would be a new passport for the man who shot Baranski. A new name, a new life. Clearly he wasn't to be involved in Macon Parker's death. Rose pulled some chewing gum from her bag. She put it in her mouth and chewed it slowly. Her stomach was empty but she didn't dare swallow anything in case it made her sick.

'Why were they in Cromer last summer?' Joshua said.

'How did you know that?'

Joshua shrugged.

'Parker insisted they have a week's holiday. He knew someone who owned a seafront property and set it up for them. They had no choice but to go along with it. They couldn't be sure that one of Parker's associates might not check up on them. They had to look like normal holiday-makers.'

Rose remembered the photographs taken by Rachel Bliss, her one-time friend. Her mum and Brendan in deck-chairs looking out to sea. How overjoyed she'd been when she saw those pictures – proof of life.

'Now I will say goodbye,' Munroe said. He picked up the envelope and slid it into his pocket. 'I doubt we will meet again. I wish you both well.'

He walked away. Rose didn't watch him go but when she heard the street door close she felt the tension falling from her shoulders. She put her hand on Joshua's arm and felt the tightness in his muscles.

'I'll never give up trying to link him to Skeggsie's murder. He might think that he's got away with it. He might think that what nearly happened to Dad has made me change my mind but it isn't true. He'll slip up or I'll find some evidence. One way or another he'll pay for killing Skeggs.'

Rose didn't speak. These were just brave words. Joshua had no choice but to accept what Munroe did. Munroe had made it clear that if he was ever arrested he would make sure that her mum and Brendan were put in danger. Rose remembered the notebooks, the list of names Joshua had shown her. Someone attached to one of those men would want to take revenge and Munroe would know their parents' new identities and where they had relocated.

Because of this Munroe would always be safe.

Rose found the Lord Buckingham Hotel easily. The receptionist phoned through to her mother's room. It was on the first floor. Rose used the stairs and knocked gently on the door. Her mother opened it and pulled Rose inside, giving her a tight hug. When she let go Rose took her hand and walked her across to the window to look at her. She was wearing her glasses and looked like her old self. She had on a jumper over jeans and boots. Brendan must have brought her things up from Essex the previous evening. She took her mother's wrists and looked at the red marks, the skin broken in places.

'Does it hurt? Are you all right?'

'I'm fine. What about you, though? Those grazes on your face!'

Rose put her fingers up to her cheeks. She'd forgotten about Mikey pushing her into the privet the previous evening. So much had happened since then.

'I was so worried about you.'

'Sit down,' her mother said, pulling out a chair from a desk and edging it towards the bed. 'Don't let's go over this stuff that's just happened. There's the future to think about.'

'But there's still tomorrow . . .'

Before the future could come Brendan and her mum had to kill a man. Her mother shook her head and put a finger on her lips. She wasn't going to talk about it. She looked tired but there was hardness around her eyes, a tightness to her jaw. It was a barrier between them. Rose didn't feel she could cross it.

'Oh, Rosie, it's so good to see you. So grown-up. Taller

than me. There's so much I want to ask you, so much I've missed. Tell me about school . . . About living with your gran . . . Now you're at college . . .'

Rose shook her head. She couldn't talk about any of those things as if her mother had just returned from working abroad for a few months. She couldn't just act as if this was a normal kind of reunion. There was an elephant sitting in the corner of the room and it was staring hard at her.

'I wish you wouldn't do this . . . thing. Just for me . . .'

'I'm doing this thing *for* you. For you and other people. For a girl who was brought to this country with the promise of a better life . . .'

'Polina Bokun.'

'Yes. For poor Polina and for all the others who are victims.'

For a fleeting moment Rose thought of Daisy Lincoln. Daisy wearing her mother's pendant, her hands tied behind her back with Brendan's tie. How was she ever going to be able to talk about that?

'Just think about the day *after* tomorrow. That's when everything will change,' her mother said. 'James is organising a new life for us.'

'I don't trust him.'

'But we do.'

Rose remembered the first time she saw Munroe. He came to talk to her after her mother and Brendan went missing. She'd been twelve years old, sitting in Anna's drawing room. He'd been in uniform, respectful, sympathetic. He'd known her mother before, he'd said. He'd never stop trying to find her, he'd said. He'd told her his name and made her trust him. His lies poured out like honey.

'Joshua hates him.'

'I know. James has told us what Joshua's feelings are. But you know I have a lot to be grateful to James for. It was because of him that I came to London. I met him on a training course in Manchester just after I joined up. He encouraged me to become a detective and transfer. It was really hard to get on in the police with such a macho culture. As well as that I was a single mother. I was on my own. Your gran and I hadn't spoken for years. I had no help from anywhere and James offered to let me live in Brewster Road.'

'How come?'

'He owned it. He'd moved out and was thinking of renting it. He let me have it for a nominal rent and that meant I could pay for really good childcare. I owe him a lot.'

'I didn't know that.'

'No reason why you should.'

'But he wasn't part of the Butterfly Murder?'

'No, he was sent up to Newcastle to oversee the local investigations. The Newcastle force weren't getting anywhere finding the killer of Simon Lister and they wanted an independent officer to look over the case. Someone from another force. Brendan decided to tell him what had happened. James was prepared to turn a blind eye and later on he got involved in the project.'

Rose was quiet. It wasn't the Munroe she knew. She thought of him hurting her hand, threatening to expose her parents. Should she tell her mother this?

'Joshua will calm down. Grief fades. He'll begin to realise what a terrible mistake it all was.'

That will never happen, Rose thought.

'You didn't know Skeggsie. I didn't really get on with him that well. He was self-contained, not exactly a warm person but Josh . . . He was like a brother to Josh.'

She was tearful suddenly. Why was she crying for Skeggsie when she had all this bigger stuff to cry about? She grabbed her mother's hand.

'This is why I don't think you should *do* this thing. When you kill someone you hurt other people as well and those people never forget. They carry that poison with them for ever. All your life you'll be looking over your shoulder for people like Baranski.'

'I'm used to that.'

'It nearly got you killed.'

'But it won't happen this time. In a few days we'll be in another country and if you want, in a while, we can make arrangements for you to join us. James will do that for us.

It's important to him that he makes us all a family again. We trust him with our lives. Look how he got me away from Baranski. He's made mistakes but he's a good man.'

Rose shook her head. Her mother stood up.

'You have to go home now Rose. Let us finish our work. I will contact you in a couple of days.'

Her mother was by the window. She had her back to the room. Rose looked at her. She was standing tall like a sentry. She was determined. There was nothing Rose could do to change her mind.

TWENTY-FIVE

The next morning Anna made breakfast for Rose.

'Was Joshua well enough to go home the other night? He still looked a bit peaky to me.'

'He was feeling a lot better.'

Anna put a plate of toast in front of Rose. The slices had been cut into triangles and there was a pat of butter in a dish and a small glass pot of jam. Rose spent a long time buttering a piece while Anna talked.

'I'm sorry I've not been around much over the last few days. As you know our function was last night and it was very successful. We raised over thirty thousand pounds. We're thinking of doing it on a yearly basis. The most successful aspect of it was the auction. Oh, look, I picked up something for you.'

Anna placed a small plain brown bag on the table.

'Oh.'

'Have a look.'

Rose pulled out a black lace scarf. She unfolded it. It

was long and dropped to the floor but it was narrow and would have to be wound round and round the neck. The lacework was intricate with single white pearls woven in here and there.

'I know you like to wear black and white. It's a beautiful piece. Nineteen-twenties, I think.'

'It's great,' Rose choked out the words. 'I like it lots. Thank you.'

'Good. In a couple of days we'll get the decorator in to look at the Blue Room. Have a think about colours and furniture.'

Rose heard Anna's heels tapping along the hall floor. She sat alone in the kitchen, only half of her toast eaten. In her hands she held the lace scarf. Anna had really thought about what she would like. It was fragile and lovely and looking at it gave her a lump in her throat.

At college she sat alongside Jamie Roberts. The class was Law and the tutor was talking about the morality of restorative justice.

'Really like the scarf,' Jamie said. 'You don't normally wear stuff like that. Girly stuff.'

'It's vintage,' she whispered back as if that was some kind of excuse.

Rose made notes. She glanced at the textbook and then up at the whiteboard. She did it methodically without looking at the classroom clock. She wanted the lesson to be over. Then there would be another and lunch and then a further two classes. Then she would go home and maybe spend some time with Anna in the Blue Room and that way the day would pass and it would be time to go to bed.

Not that she would sleep much.

The previous night had been a wakeful one.

After eating with Joshua at the Camden flat she'd gone back to Belsize Park. Anna had been out so she'd gone up to the attic. She saw traces of Blu Tack on the wall where Joshua had had his display of Polina Bokun. She spent a bit of time edging it off with her nail, trying not to leave a mark on the wall. Then she'd gone downstairs to her rooms and put the television on and sat watching it mindlessly. At some point she went to bed and had a broken night's sleep. She'd thought of texting or ringing Joshua but really didn't know what to say to him. It was just a day they had to get through. Just twenty-four hours to tick by until this whole thing would be over.

'You're miles away,' Jamie said, interrupting her thoughts.

She looked around to see that students were packing up, talking quietly amongst themselves. The teacher was sitting down at the desk, looking through some paperwork.

The session was over. Another hour had passed.

In the corridor she and Jamie were joined by Sara and Maggie. The two of them talked about going to the Pink

Parrot the next night and asked her if she wanted to go along.

'Jamie's coming, aren't you?' Sara said.

'Go on, Rose. You'll enjoy it.'

Rose gave a vague nod. It wasn't worth refusing even though she had no intention of going.

'Look, PC Plod,' Sara said.

'That copper is, like, always around college!' Maggie said.

Rose looked down the corridor. Henry was there, moving slowly forward. Rose felt apprehensive. It didn't mean he was there for her. A moment later, though, he saw her and began to walk towards her. Something had happened. Henry was only ever the bearer of bad news.

'I've got to go. See you guys later.'

Rose walked towards Henry. She edged around groups of students who were on their way to classes. When she got to him she could barely ask. She didn't need to. He took her elbow and steered her to the edge of the thoroughfare.

'What?' she said.

'Wendy Clarke? That detective from East London? She's arrested Joshua.'

'Why?'

'In connection with the death of Daisy Lincoln.'

'I don't understand. Why? Because he couldn't

268

remember anything from that time? Because he was a bit off with her?'

'Rose, it's more serious than that. She's had him picked up and brought to the station in Bethnal Green. He's there now. She's talking to him about the death of Daisy Lincoln.'

Rose stared at Henry in disbelief. She started to say something but then his words seemed to fall into place. Joshua was being questioned as a *suspect*. Wendy Clarke thought that he had something to do with Daisy's killing.

'Oh no! This is not right,' she said. 'Joshua was fourteen. He was not capable of anything like that . . .'

She pulled her phone out of her bag. There was a missed call from Joshua. She tutted. She'd had it on *Silent* for the lesson and not turned it on again. Henry was still talking.

'Wendy Clarke rang me this morning about this. She said that her officers had been re-interviewing the family and friends of Daisy, trying to jog their memories, and a couple of them mentioned a local lad who Daisy had said had a crush on her. The newsagent's who she worked for said it was the boy from your address. He knew because he came into the shop to pay the paper bill and he used to see him mooning after her.'

Rose remembered Joshua's story about being in the shop as Daisy was finishing a shift. She was looking in the mirror, using her fingers to do her hair. Then she turned round to Joshua and put her lipstick on in front of him. He'd liked her, Rose knew that. He was fourteen. Maybe he spent more time looking at her, seeking her out, than he knew himself. But Joshua was a soft boy who liked fixing bikes. He would never have hurt anyone.

'Have they stopped looking for the older boyfriend?'

There were fewer students in the corridor, most having gone to their classes. Rose's voice sounded loud.

'No. They're not doubting that that there was someone else involved. Her sister confirmed that. They're looking at the fact that she was buried in the garden of Joshua's old house. How would this older boyfriend have had access to someone's house? And then there's his father's tie.'

And the pendant, thought Rose.

'The way in which she was buried throws up questions as well.'

'What do you mean?'

'Well, it wasn't done in a hurry. They're thinking it was dug by someone who had all the time in the world. Someone who knew they weren't going to be discovered. Someone who lived there?'

'This is just mad!' Rose said.

'The police in Bethnal Green have gone through your parents' work records and it looks as though they were independently off work for holidays and on work courses that summer. So the house was empty from time to time and Joshua made the point to DI Clarke that he stayed at a friend's house during those times. So it was possible that one of those times Joshua could have used the empty house to bring a girl back. Perhaps Daisy Lincoln.'

'She was eighteen. He was fourteen.'

'It has been known. Fourteen-year-old boys can father babies,' Henry said, looking round in an embarrassed way.

'This is insane!'

'I'm not saying I believe it but it's the reason he's been pulled in for questioning. DI Clarke is right to pursue it. She suggested that I let you know.'

Rose tugged at the lace scarf. Was DI Clarke serious about suspecting Joshua? Or was she just punishing the two of them for not being more forthcoming in their interviews? Did she really think that Joshua could have done this? Or was she trying to get him to let something out about his father and Daisy? Whatever it was Rose felt completely exasperated. What else was going to happen to her and Joshua?

'I have to go,' she said.

'I'm seeing one of the staff here about another matter. Otherwise I'd walk along with you.'

She shook her head. 'You've been a real friend, Henry. More than a friend. Don't think I don't know that.'

She walked off towards the exit. She made her way to the station, her head down, unaware of people passing by. She sat alone on the platform waiting for her train. All the while she was picturing Joshua in an interview room, Wendy Clarke asking him if he'd tied Daisy's hands up with his father's tie and killed her. Joshua would be angry and upset. His best friend had died in his arms and yet the policewoman would be asking him if he was capable of such a thing.

Yet the most unexpected people were capable of murder. Her own mother was at that moment in the possession of an American gun that would kill Macon Parker later tonight.

The train came into the station. Rose got on. The journey went by in a blur but still she noticed the cemetery as they slowed down to stop at Parkway East. St Michael's RC Cemetery. It had been opened in 1868. It was twenty-three acres of gravestones, mausoleums and plaster angels and saints. Rose had spent time there the previous autumn. Then she thought she'd seen enough death.

She half walked half ran down the street towards her grandmother's house. She pulled out her key and opened the door. Her grandmother was in the drawing room at her desk. She looked round. Rose hiccupped out a sob.

'You have to help me to help Joshua,' she said.

Her grandmother stood up, puzzled.

'What's wrong?'

'You have to get a solicitor for Joshua. They're going to try and charge him with the murder of that girl who died at our old house. He didn't do it. He couldn't do such a thing. Please, Anna . . .'

'My dear . . .'

'I have no one else to turn to,' Rose said.

Rose stepped across and put her arms around her grandmother. Anna seemed surprised, ambushed by this emotion. She was stiff and awkward and Rose felt her reluctance. She held on, though. Anna softened, bit by bit, her back and her shoulders becoming fluid. Then she lifted her arms and encircled Rose, hugging her back.

'Of course I'll help you, Rose.'

Once Rose was sure that her grandmother's solicitor was on his way to the police station she went up to her room. She paced up and down.

'Think, think, Rose,' she said under her breath.

Daisy had an older boyfriend, Sandy had said. Wendy Clarke had also said it. Joshua had seen her getting into a Saab car. A Swedish car, not something that a younger driver would have. Her hands were tied up with Brendan's tie. Rose's mother's pendant was found on or near her body. She had been with this man to a cottage in Norfolk. These were things that pointed to Brendan.

Except Brendan didn't own a Saab car. Rose wouldn't have noticed at the time but Joshua would have known and when he told the story about Daisy getting into the Saab he would have said, *a car just like my dad's*. But he didn't.

Was the Saab car nothing to do with it?

Could it have been Brendan who was Daisy's older boyfriend? Could he have borrowed a car to take her out, fearful of being seen in his own car?

Rose sat down at her desk. She didn't know.

She got her mobile out. She'd taken Sandy's number on the day she went to visit her. Sandy hadn't had any information about the older boyfriend. She remembered her words. *I wasn't a close friend. Her sister, Esther, might have known*. Rose scrolled down her list of contacts. She stopped when she got to Sandy's name. She composed a text. **Hi Sandy, I'd like to talk to Daisy Lincoln's sister. Which school does she work at?**

It was twenty minutes before she got a reply. **St Peter's Primary in Walthamstow. She's nice. Hope you r well!**

Rose looked at the time. It was two o'clock. She could get there in time for the end of the school day.

TWENTY-SIX

The school was five minutes' walk from Walthamstow Central tube station. When Rose got there the children were still inside the classrooms but there were small groups of mothers dotted around the playground waiting for them to finish. On the pavement outside the gates a couple were standing apart smoking. It was three thirty. She wondered what was happening at the police station. How long would it be before Joshua was allowed to leave?

One of the women in the playground was holding a small black dog which looked a poodle. She was older than the other mums – possibly someone's grandmother. She had blonde hair pulled up in a bun at the back. Another woman was saying something to her and pointing at the dog.

Just then there was the sound of children coming out of the building and some big wooden doors opened. Children came running out, holding coats and bags and making loud end of school noises. Rose expected them to run across to their parents but they didn't. They went to the far side of the playground and lined up. Rose watched while class after class spilled out of the building followed by teachers.

Rose wondered which of them was the sister of Daisy Lincoln.

When it seemed as though the whole school had lined up parents began to walk towards them.

'Excuse me,' Rose asked a nearby parent, 'do you know which is Miss Lincoln?'

The woman shook her head and then it occurred to Rose that Daisy's sister could be married and have a different surname. As the ranks of children were dismissed Rose looked from teacher to teacher. She would have to go over and ask.

But then the older woman with the small dog in her arms called out to her.

'Miss Lincoln is the dark-haired lady on the end. The pregnant one. Now she's called Mrs Beatty. But she used to be Lincoln.'

'Thanks,' Rose said.

Daisy Lincoln's sister was a tall slim woman with a tiny bump at her middle. She had on a blouse and narrow trousers. Her hair was long and dark with a heavy fringe. Most of her class had been claimed and she was left talking to a small girl. Rose walked towards her as a man came from the car park end of the playground and took the girl's hand and spoke briefly to Mrs Beatty before leaving.

Rose paused for a moment then she went across to her.

'Are you Esther, Daisy Lincoln's sister?' Rose said.

The woman's face hardened. 'Are you the press? I'm not speaking to any press about anything.'

'I'm not. My name is Rose Smith and I lived in the house in Brewster Road when your sister was . . .'

Rose couldn't quite bring herself to say *murdered*.

'Rose? The kid who Sandy babysat for?'

Rose nodded.

'What do you want?'

'Look, Esther, what happened to your sister was a terrible thing. I . . . obviously had no idea and of course it makes me feel terrible . . .'

Rose raised her hands in a gesture of helplessness. She had deliberately not mentioned Joshua, unsure whether the police had told the family of their intentions to question him.

'You're the girl whose parents disappeared?'

Rose nodded.

Esther let out a sigh. She placed one of her hands on her bump.

'This is a mess. Why have you come?'

'I wanted to talk to you about her. The police have asked us . . . me, if I can remember anything from that summer. All I can recall is that it was the last summer before my mother vanished. I think if I could talk to someone who was around . . . I've already spoken to Sandy.'

'I'm not sure what more I can say but you might as well come into my classroom,' Esther said, walking off and pulling Rose in her wake.

It was on the ground floor of the building. Outside was a line of hooks and a big wooden shelving unit divided into squares with names on each one. Above it were handwritten signs that said *Coats*, *PE Kit*, *Cooking*, *Science Aprons*. Rose went inside and was faced with tiny tables and chairs, a playhouse and a reading corner. Esther pulled her chair out and sat down, straightening her blouse over her expanded midriff.

'When's your baby due?' Rose said.

'June. I finish work at the end of this term.'

Rose sat on the corner of one of the tables nearby.

'It's your first?'

Esther nodded, looking proudly down at her stomach.

'Boy or girl?'

'Girl. I wasn't sure I wanted to know but then I asked a couple of weeks ago.'

Somehow that seemed sad to Rose. Just now, when her sister's body is discovered, she finds out the sex of her baby. Esther smiled at her, giving a shrug of her shoulders, as if she thought the same thing.

'I didn't know your family at all when I lived in Brewster Road,' she said after a moment. 'It was only when they went missing that I remembered that Sandy had babysat for some police officers. My family, Daisy, all of us had moved to Chingford in the summer – you probably know – so we were away from the street when the news of your parents' disappearance hit the newspapers. I rang Sandy to see what had happened. She said you were really sweet kids. At the time I remembered feeling that we had a kind of link even though both cases were completely different. You lost your mother, I lost my sister. Of course your parents' disappearance made the national newspapers. When Daisy left home she took a case of belongings with her. She had a history of storming off, staying at friends' houses. She'd told friends that she was going to run away with her lover. Everyone, my parents, me, our family, we all expected her to turn up any day.'

Rose listened to Esther with a growing feeling of sadness. She had wanted to dash in and out of this school, to pick up some piece of information that would prove that Joshua had nothing whatsoever to do with Daisy's death. But Daisy's story had to be heard.

There was the sound of children from the playground. A name bring called over and over – 'Gerry, Gerry, GERRY!'

'Daisy's disappearance was like a slow burn. For the first few days we expected her to turn up shamefaced, saying sorry. Then weeks went by. The police kept in touch but there was no search for her. Why would there be with bits and pieces of evidence that said she went of her own accord. You know she took her passport? And all her jewellery and her favourite clothes. She took *five* pairs of shoes. She *loved* shoes. She had tiny feet, size three, and she bought shoes in charity shops and sales. She loved heels. *What do you think of these*? she'd say. I laughed at her. It wasn't even possible to walk in some of those shoes.'

'I didn't know her,' Rose said, trying hard to pull together the one image she had of Daisy walking along Brewster Road. Possibly Rose had been getting out of her mother's car and seen her with Sandy. 'I only knew Sandy because she babysat for me.'

'In the first couple of weeks after she left she used her cash card, or at least we thought she had. *Someone* used her cash card five times in places around London. That told my family that she was still alive. Then it stopped and there was nothing. After that we didn't know what to think. We thought maybe she'd gone abroad. The police just shrugged their shoulders. People go missing, it's a fact of life. They don't like the life they're leading, they find a different life. Teenagers especially. They told us to keep abreast of the Missing websites and organisations, and that maybe Daisy would try and contact us. I remember the last time I spoke to a detective. It was on the one-year anniversary of when she left home. After that nothing.'

Rose didn't know what to say.

'But this isn't helping you to remember things from those days!'

Rose couldn't go on pretending. 'Look, I'm not going to lie to you. I *am* trying to remember that summer but the real reason I'm here is that the detective in charge of the case made it clear that she suspected that Brendan Johnson, my mother's partner, was involved with Daisy. Now she's questioning his son, Joshua. He was fourteen at the time and he admitted to me that he had a crush on Daisy but this police officer is actually questioning him about her murder.'

'Oh.'

'I know it doesn't matter to you and the family who they question. You just want the guilty person put away. But Joshua, my stepbrother, is not guilty of anything other than having a crush on someone who was older than him and out of his reach.'

'And his father?'

'I can't say. He was my mother's partner and I cared for him a lot but whether I really knew him or not I don't know.'

'Well, you are being honest. What do you want to ask me?'

'Sandy mentioned that Daisy said her boyfriend was older. Do you remember anything about him?'

'I don't know if it was this Brendan. I never met this mystery man. No one did. I wasn't around much that summer. I'd just graduated and was on holiday some of the time and working the rest. I saw Daisy lots of course but it was unremarkable. Just sister stuff – chats, arguments, swapping clothes. She'd been out of college a year and was working in the newsagent's.'

'Near Roman Road.'

'Just part-time at first. Early mornings, some half-days. Then it was full-time. She was a bright girl, Daisy, but she had no ambition. She could have done better. I spent a lot of time that year helping her to apply for jobs.'

'Wendy Clarke, the detective, told me that you said she'd gone away for a weekend with him.'

'No, I said she *told me* she was going to go away for a weekend and she wanted me to cover for her. Look, Rose, I'm not sure how this is helping you but Daisy could tell a few fibs and I never really knew if there was an older boyfriend or whether she was making it up. She'd come in and tell me stuff, like the plans for the weekend away. He'd got this cottage in Norfolk, she said. They were having sex, she said, and she'd had to go and get the morning after pill from the chemist once. She showed me the pendant she said he bought for her.'

'I know about that.'

Rose pictured the pendant hanging round her mother's neck.

'It looked like something an older person would buy. Not something I would have worn. I was surprised she liked it. She did tell me he had a tattoo of a butterfly. I thought it was an odd thing for an older man to have.'

'A butterfly?'

'Yes. Weird.'

Rose hugged herself. She thought of Brendan with a cringing feeling. He had a butterfly tattooed on his ankle.

'You know the worst thing about all this? At first I really thought she'd gone off with a boyfriend. I had a *to hell with her* kind of attitude. Then after a couple of weeks when we didn't hear anything I began to get worried. She was too much of a show-off not to come round flaunting her independence or parading her holiday photos or whatever. After that first anniversary I got really depressed, couldn't get up for work, that kind of thing. But because they never found a body I convinced myself that she must be alive, living somewhere else, that she'd just washed her hands of us and I got on with my life. Then a couple of weeks ago this policewoman came to my mother's house. I was there at the time. She came in and said to my mother, *Don't upset yourself, Mrs Lincoln, but we think we've found Daisy's body.*'

Rose felt her phone vibrate. She ignored it.

'Esther, thank you. I can't tell you how sorry I am about your sister. I have to go now.'

Rose walked towards the door.

283

'One thing,' Esther said, just as she was leaving, 'Daisy told me her boyfriend was a landlord, which made him sound about sixty years old.'

'A property developer? That kind of thing?' Rose said.

'She just said *landlord*. That's all.'

Rose felt her mouth go dry. A landlord.

Esther looked at her quizzically. 'Are you all right?'

Hadn't her mother told her that James Munroe had been *their* landlord. That he had owned 49 Brewster Road?

'I'm sorry, Esther, I have to go,' Rose said. 'I hope your baby makes you very happy.'

She walked swiftly out of the building. Once outside she took her phone out. She had a message from Joshua. She read it in a distracted way. **Where R U? I'm out of the police station now. The lawyer was great. Thank your gran. Am back at the flat. Come round.**

James Munroe had been their landlord. He had a key to their house. He knew when her mother and Brendan were away. Was he was Daisy's older boyfriend, the man driving the green Saab?

Overwhelmed, she sat on the brick wall of a front garden. She stared at her mobile phone. Then she found her mother's number and composed a text, her fingers jabbing at the letters, missing now and then so that she had to go back and correct it. **Mum, please just answer this question. Then I won't contact you again today. It's important. Did James Munroe ever own a Saab car?**

She waited. Maybe her mother wouldn't answer, would just dismiss her message without even opening it up. Possibly she would think that it was another appeal from Rose for her not to go ahead with the events that evening.

A beep sounded. It was a text from her. She opened it. **I asked you not to contact me!! But anyway, yes. James owned a green Saab car. No more messages. Not today.**

Rose felt a heavy weight on her shoulders.

Whenever they started uncovering secrets James Munroe seemed to be at the heart of them. She stood and walked in the direction of the tube station.

TWENTY-SEVEN

Joshua was agitated. He kept walking up and down the kitchen of the Camden flat. He told her about the interview with DI Clarke at the police station and the intervention of the lawyer. 'They were never going to charge me with anything,' he said. 'It was just a fishing trip. The lawyer knew it. DI Clarke knew it. That's why they had to let me go.'

He seemed relieved to be home yet he couldn't stay still.

Then she told him what she had found out about James Munroe.

He was surprised, shocked. She explained the things she'd heard from Daisy's sister and what her mother had said about the car.

'I just can't get my head round it,' he said, sitting down at the table, leaning back in the chair, using his hand to massage the back of his neck.

Rose sat opposite him. She could hardly believe it herself.

'It makes sense. James Munroe was the older boyfriend. Daisy told her sister that he was a *landlord*. Well, in a way he was. He owned the house we lived in in Brewster Road.'

'I never knew that,' Joshua said.

'Neither did I until yesterday. That's why he came to my gran's house after Daisy's body was found. He said that he'd heard about it from the press but he must have been contacted by the police. He owned the house in 2007. They would have wanted to speak to him. That's how he knew what had happened.'

'You think *he* took Daisy there?'

'He would have had access to it. Keys for the house. He also knew the times when Mum and Brendan weren't going to be there. He knew that you and I would be staying over with friends. It was an empty house where he could take his young girlfriend.'

'But he didn't live round here. How did he meet her, hook up with her?

'He was visiting Brendan and Mum? Maybe he just chatted to her out in the street. She might have been with Sandy and Sandy spoke to Brendan. Then he saw her in the newsagent's or pulled up in his car and asked her the way. I don't know.'

It was what Rose had been puzzling about all the way back from Walthamstow. How had Munroe met up with Daisy Lincoln? Munroe had still been a policeman then. Had she come into contact with him in that way?

'But I never knew Munroe so he couldn't have come to the house.'

Rose had never seen him either. Not before her parents went missing. She would have remembered a visit from him, she was sure. But then she had never seen Frank Richards either.

'Maybe, once *The Butterfly Project* started, they avoided going to each other's houses.'

'Except that Munroe used the house for somewhere to take his girlfriend.'

'But wouldn't someone have seen them going in?'

'He used the back gate? Or waited until it was dark?'

'And the cottage in Stiffkey.'

'Daisy was eighteen. Why would she be interested in a man of his age?'

Joshua said it with distaste. Rose remembered his infatuation for her, the crush he had had.

'How old is Munroe?'

'In his forties? Forty-five?'

'This was six years ago next August. Munroe would have been in his late thirties then. It's not unheard of for a man of that age to get involved with a young woman,' she said.

'He was married.'

'This could be why he and Margaret Spicer are splitting up.'

'He killed her, Rosie. It wasn't an accident.'

Rose was quiet. Joshua was right. It couldn't have been an accident. Daisy had had her hands tied behind her back.

'He used my dad's tie to stop her struggling,' Joshua said thoughtfully.

Rose watched as he got up, walked across to the window and looked down into the street. He had his back to her. She wondered what he was thinking.

'Do you think he tried to set my dad up?' he suddenly said.

Rose didn't answer straight away. She pictured Munroe in his smart clothes, in his apartment by the river. She remembered how cold he had been in Newcastle. Then a week or so before he had hurt her hand and threatened her parents with an *ugly* end.

'Deliberately make it look as though Dad killed her?' Joshua went on, turning round to face her.

'Why would he? He was his friend. They were involved in *The Butterfly Project* together.'

'He used Dad's tie, though. He could have taken it off the girl's hands afterwards, disposed of it but he left it there. And he buried Daisy in Dad's garden. He could have waited until dark and taken her body away.'

'Maybe he panicked?'

'That grave took a long time to dig. There was no panic there.'

'But why?'

'So he could never get charged with it?'

'And if the grave was found someone else would be suspected?'

Joshua swore gently, under his breath. 'So Munroe gets away with Daisy's murder as well as Skeggsie.'

'No. He won't get away with it. Let's go and see him,' Rose said. 'I know he won't get arrested for it but maybe we could get something out of this. Something that will help Mum and Brendan.'

But it won't help Daisy, Rose thought, but didn't say it.

They took the Mini and drove to Surrey Quays and parked a couple of streets away from Munroe's flat. They talked for a few moments going over the things they were going to say. Then they got out of the car and walked through the tiny square across to the building that had once been a primary school. It was the second primary school building that Rose had been in that day. She rang his bell. His voice came through the speaker, curt.

'Yes?'

'It's Rose and Joshua. We need to speak to you.'

There was a sigh from Munroe.

'I'm going out shortly. Can't this wait until tomorrow?'

'No.'

'Well, my dear Rose, it will have to. I have an important engagement tonight . . .'

'It's about Daisy Lincoln,' Rose said.

There was silence. Rose was about to repeat herself when the speaker clicked off and the wooden gate began to slide open. Rose and Joshua walked inside and headed up to Munroe's apartment. When they got out of the lift Munroe was standing at his front door and stared sullenly at both of them as they walked along the passageway. When they got to his door he stepped back a fraction making them both squeeze past him.

There was music playing. It was low, classical. It was like something Anna would play while she was having breakfast. On the table Munroe's things were laid out – cufflinks, rings, a coin purse, wallet, phone. There was a thick white card with gold embossed print. Over the back of one of the chairs were three ties. A jacket hung over another. Munroe hadn't been lying when he said he was going out somewhere. Joshua picked up the white card and read it out loud.

'The Metropolitan Police Senior Officers' Reunion. An invitation to James Munroe. Please attend the Barnaby Suite at the Royal Swan Hotel, Hyde Park. Drinks at nine p.m. Lounge suits. This doesn't start until nine. You have plenty of time.'

'I have someone else to see beforehand,' he said tersely.

'We're just wondering how you actually met Daisy Lincoln?'

'What?'

'The girl who you had an affair with.'

'You are referring to the girl whose body was found?'

'Let's not waste time. I saw her get into your car. A green Saab. I didn't know it was your car at the time . . .'

'Is this a joke?'

'I saw her.'

'I am not the only person in London to have owned a green Saab . . .'

'And a cottage in Stiffkey.'

'The landlord of the Brewster Road house.'

'A man with a tattoo of a butterfly. I'm assuming you have the tattoo!'

'This is ridiculous.'

'It's true. Why don't you just explain it to us? There's no point in lying. It's not like we can go to the police with the information. The *law* doesn't apply here. You've told us that already. You know where Mum and Brendan are going. You hold their future in your hands. We've got nothing on you.'

'Then why can't you both leave things alone?'

Rose stared at Munroe. She suddenly thought of the day Margaret Spicer had come to her college. She'd sat in the silver SUV and heard her speak sadly about him.

'Did Margaret Spicer find out about you and Daisy? Is that why she left you?'

Munroe's expression cracked. He seemed upset.

'She must have heard about the discovery of the body.' Rose continued. 'Maybe she saw a picture of the dead girl in the newspapers. She recognised her, didn't she? From 2007? She'd seen you together.'

Munroe looked down at the ground. Then, seconds later, he seemed to straighten up. He picked up one of his cufflinks and began to put it on. He fiddled with it, pulling the cuffs together awkwardly.

'Margaret knows, doesn't she? That's why she came to see me. She wanted me to know that *she* wasn't involved in Skeggsie's death. *She* never intended that Skeggsie should die. That's what she wanted to tell me because she knew that what happened to Daisy was intended. That you meant to kill her. Margaret knew. As soon as Daisy's body was discovered she knew you'd killed her.'

'Why do you meddle!' Munroe said, folding his cuff back and picking up the second cufflink. 'The girl came for a job at Margaret's security company. Margaret was out that day. I interviewed her. Sadly she was too young to work for us. I told her and she was disappointed. I saw her address and obviously it got us talking. She lived in the road where I owned a house. As she left the interview she said *If you're in my street you could take me out for a drink . . .* She walked off but then came back moments later and gave me her mobile number on a piece of paper. This was a direct invitation to me and I took it up.'

'She was eighteen.'

'She did all the running, I can assure you. We spent some time together. I took her to Norfolk. I took her to a few London hotels but then she became tiresome. She said she was in love.'

Munroe straightened his cuffs and walked along the table to the chair that held the ties. He picked one up and held it under the light. He put it back on the chair and then took another. He lifted his collar up and draped the tie around his neck.

'That summer was difficult,' he said, finally turning back to look at them. 'There was a lot going on. There was the fallout from the Baranski judgement. In July there was the Michael McCall judgement. A quick case, dealt with by Frank. I had to keep a cool head, had to arrange things for him and for your mother and father. New passports do not come easy. Strings have to be pulled, people have to be paid and every time I had a free moment there was a text on my phone from this girl. And then Margaret saw us together. I swore to Margaret that it was over. But the girl kept on calling. I gave in. I agreed to meet her at the house in Brewster Road. We met there three times.'

'You gave her my mother's pendant.'

'No, she took it. She stole it. It was one of the reasons that I got so angry with her. She was . . . unstable. The last time we met I knew I had to put a stop to it. I never intended to kill her. Things just got out of hand.'

Joshua made a snorting sound. 'You never mean to kill anyone. You didn't mean to kill Skeggsie either . . .'

'I'm tired of you and your whining. You've heard what you came to hear. Now leave me alone.'

'You tied her hands with Brendan's tie. You were trying to make it seem as though he'd killed her.'

'Don't be ridiculous. I picked up the first thing that came to hand.'

'That's not true. You used his tie so that it would look like he'd done it. Just in case my dad ever got to be a problem for you. It was a perfect crime to fit him up for.'

'This is nonsense. What does it matter what I used? It happened. I intended to frighten her. But she said things . . . that I couldn't allow. She spoke about telling Margaret . . .'

'And you buried her in our garden.'

'Strictly speaking, Rose, it was my garden. Now, if you don't mind, I have somewhere to go.'

'Let's get out of here, Rose.'

'Yes, please go.'

Joshua walked off. Rose heard him at the front door.

'How can you be so unfeeling about Daisy?'

'Don't think I did not suffer after what happened to Daisy,' Munroe said, looking drawn. 'I did suffer. I saw my role as an avenger of crime. Not a perpetrator. Maybe it's why I've been so determined to carry out the judgements. To rid the world of people who commit murder without a whiff of conscience.'

'But aren't you just like them?'

'A world of difference. You should go now. And remember what I said about your parents. After tonight they can have a very nice life in British Columbia. As long as you both keep your mouths shut.'

'What about Margaret? Aren't you worried that she will go to the police?

'Margaret will never betray me.'

'Come on, Rose,' Joshua called.

She watched Munroe putting his rings on. The music came to an end and the apartment seemed unnaturally quiet. She closed the door without a sound.

Joshua drove. After a few minutes he pulled over to the side. They were far enough away from Munroe's apartment. He turned off the ignition and they sat for a moment. He undid his seat belt. Rose was nervous.

'Do you think it worked?'

'Hope so,' he said.

He turned on the inside light and pulled Skeggsie's tiny recording machine from his pocket. He fiddled with the buttons and then held it out.

'"... *Strings have to be pulled, people have to be paid and every time I had a free moment there was a text on my phone from this girl. And then Margaret saw us together. I swore to Margaret that it was over. But the* girl kept on calling. I gave in. I agreed to meet her at the house in Brewster Road. We met there three times."

"You gave her my mother's pendant."

"No, she took it. She stole it. It was one of the reasons that I got so angry with her. She was . . . unstable. The last time we met I knew I had to put a stop to it. I never intended to kill her. Things just got out of hand."'

Joshua smiled at Rose.

'Let's see what Dad and Kathy think of Munroe now.'

TWENTY-EIGHT

The Lord Buckingham Hotel was busy. A coach of tourists had arrived and their cases were clogging up the reception area. Rose went round them and headed for the stairs. Joshua followed her. The staff were occupied and no one seemed to notice them or question why they were going up to the rooms. Rose had no idea if her mother would still be here or whether she would have already left for Tate Modern.

When her mother's room door opened she was surprised to see Brendan standing there. He was wearing a smart dark suit.

'What are you doing here?' he said, holding the door ajar.

'We've come to see you. There's something important you have to hear.'

Rose pushed at the door but Brendan seemed to be blocking it.

'Let us in, Dad.'

Brendan stood back. When Rose walked in she saw her mother sitting on the bed, her face red and puffy from crying. She was wearing a dressing gown and had a bunched handkerchief at her nose.

'Mum,' she said, alarmed.

'Your mother always gets like this before a judgement. I shouldn't really be here but she called me . . .'

Her mother was patting her face and sniffing. She straightened her back and seemed as though she was trying to pull herself together.

'You can't do this. You can't go and kill in this cold-blooded way. It's not right.'

'We can't have this conversation, Rose. Not again. We have a job to do.'

Her mother's clothes were on a hanger hooked to the outside of a wardrobe – a dark skirt, jacket and white shirt. Black and white. These were the colours that Rose insisted on wearing. She looked at them now with a feeling of dread. An executioner's uniform.

'Dad, your group, this project, whatever you want to call it, you all feel that everything you've done has been for completely *just* reasons?'

'Of course. Everything we've done has been shaped by principles, by rules. We are not some bunch of renegades. We are police officers carrying out justice. Tonight will be the very same. We have rules, guidelines. It is planned to the letter.'

Brendan pointed to a zip-up bag that was sitting on the bed. It was small, a bag that might carry a camera and a tourist guide. Instantly she knew it held the gun, the American hardware that Munroe had provided for the killing.

'But Skeggsie's death . . .'

'We've explained this over and over. What happened to your friend was not planned. Indeed it is an example of exactly how we haven't operated. Then James was in a corner and felt he had to use local help. Someone outside the organisation who didn't adhere to the rules. It was a moment of bad judgement.'

'So was the killing of Daisy Lincoln a moment of bad judgement as well?' Rose said.

'What?'

'What do you mean?' her mother said.

'Daisy Lincoln?'

Brendan said the name in a distracted way. As if he had *no idea* who she was. As if he'd been working undercover and had not allowed anything to penetrate his world in Essex. No wonder he'd been so shocked and aloof when he first saw them.

'The girl whose body was found in the Brewster Road garden,' her mother said.

'James Munroe had a relationship with this girl. He took her to our old house when he knew there would be no one there. When she began to threaten him he killed her.'

'This is a joke!' Brendan said.

They finally had his full attention.

'It's not true. James is a good man,' Kathy said.

'He killed her, Mum. He told us.'

'This is ridiculous. James would not do such a thing. I've known him for years . . . He is a real stickler when it comes to rules and doing things properly.'

'If you don't believe us, hear it in his own words.'

Joshua produced the recorder. He placed it on the bed and it started to play. Rose heard her own voice and then Munroe's answers. His voice boomed out of the recorder, arrogant, confident that he was untouchable.

'Oh my goodness,' her mother whispered.

'No, no . . .' Brendan said, his voice gravelly, his face shocked.

Brendan insisted on hearing the recorded conversation twice again. The second time he sat on the bed next to Kathy with his elbows on his knees and his forehead resting on his hands. Kathy was shaking her head at Munroe's words.

'This is extraordinary . . .' Brendan said when the recording finished for the third time.

'He's not the person you thought he was, Dad. While you were doing this for some ideal of justice he had no problem getting rid of people who were a nuisance. He didn't care about Skeggsie and he didn't care about Daisy.'

'He doesn't care that we know,' Rose said. 'He's in a position of power over you, over Frank Richards.'

'And Margaret,' her mum said in a whisper.

'Were there other people involved?'

'Three others. Their work is finished and they have been relocated.'

'So, you shouldn't do this,' Rose pointed to the canvas bag on the bed. 'Now that you know about Munroe you *should not* do this.'

'But this makes no difference to Macon Parker and the things he does. He's a murderer and he'll do it again . . .' Brendan said.

'You can't carry out the judgement now, Dad. Your actions are tainted by what Munroe has done. You didn't know before. Now you do. Killing this man – whatever he's done – doesn't put you on the moral high ground any more.'

'They are right, Bren . . .' her mum said.

'Macon Parker doesn't deserve a reprieve . . . Munroe may have made a mistake with this girl . . .' Brendan said, shaking his head.

'He planned Daisy's killing, Dad. He tied her hands with your tie. He tried to make it look as though *you* were the killer.'

'He wouldn't do that,' Brendan said.

'It's true. The police have you as their number one suspect in this murder. Munroe left enough evidence. He was saving himself by putting the suspicion on you.'

Brendan was silent. On the bed beside him was the bag that held the gun. He frowned at it.

Rose hurried on. 'And when they couldn't talk to you they turned their attention to Joshua. He's been in the police station this morning. Anna got him a lawyer. That's why he's here now and not in police custody.'

'I can't believe it. Munroe . . . How could he do this? After all we've been through. After the things that we've done,' Brendan said.

'You can't trust him any more,' Joshua said.

'Daisy was just a girl. A year older than me when she was killed,' Rose said.

'I should go and see him. Have it out with him.'

'No.' Her mother stood up. 'No, he is finished for us. We don't carry out the judgement. We get away from here before Munroe knows that we haven't done it. We use the new passports and get a flight somewhere. Then we disappear and use different aliases. Live quietly for a while. Let the whole thing die down. There are people we can contact in British Columbia who might help us with new papers.'

'I don't know.'

'Brendan, we can't continue. Not now that we've heard this from James's own mouth. He is not what we thought. We've always been one hundred per cent sure of what we were doing. We did what we did for a better world. But if James did this then we cannot trust him. We don't know who he is any more, Brendan. He murdered an innocent girl and it looks as though he tried to frame you for it.'

Brendan was nodding his head slowly.

Rose felt the tension drain away. They were listening. They had been persuaded. They were not going to do this awful thing. She glanced along the bed at the canvas bag. The gun would not be used tonight and her mother and Brendan would cut all links with Munroe. She felt herself well up suddenly. It was as if she and Joshua had *saved* Brendan and Kathy. Now there was a choice they had turned their back on violence. She pulled out a tissue and blew her nose.

'OK . . .' Brendan said, standing up, looking a little dazed. 'OK. What we do now is . . . What we have to do . . .'

'Dad, you have to get your things together and call a taxi for Heathrow. When you get there you get an earlier flight. You get out of Britain.'

'What about Macon Parker? I don't want to raise any suspicions there. It's almost seven thirty. We're both due at the Tate at eight. Macon leaves his hotel at eight thirty. He'll be expecting us. It will look odd . . .'

'Does it matter? If you're never going to see him again?'

'Ring him and tell him Kathy's . . . *Kate's* father has died. He won't question that. Then you just disappear,' Rose said.

Brendan sat down on the bed again, looking hopeless. It was as if someone had punched him in the chest.

'Dad, you need to get going!'

Brendan looked at the canvas bag. 'I have to dispose of the gun. I have to do that properly.'

'I'll do it, Dad. I'll take it with me, stop the car along by the river and I'll chuck it in. Don't you worry. You just get away, both of you. Just get your stuff and go.'

'Brendan, we have to do this,' Kathy said.

Brendan stood up. He looked like a drunk man. Kathy took charge.

'You go, both of you. Let us deal with this ourselves. We'll contact you. I have my phone for any absolute emergencies. Go, Rose.'

'Mum . . .'

'Go now.'

Brendan seemed to come to a decision. 'No, Kathy, let Josh take the gun. Go to a bridge and drop it in from the centre otherwise it'll just wash up too soon.'

'I will.'

He plucked the bag from the bed.

'Come on, Josh,' Rose said and pulled him out of the room.

In the car she was elated. She felt herself smiling stupidly. They had stopped their parents from getting any more blood on their hands. It was a small victory and yet it meant everything. The finish of this horrible thing they had started. She tried to explain it to Joshua but the tone of his voice told her that he wasn't happy. Not at all.

'Munroe gets away with it.'

'Not exactly.'

'He does. All the people involved will have moved to other countries. He stays in his flat in Docklands, drives his expensive car, has new girlfriends. He's got shares in the security company, he works as a civil servant. He has a perfect life. Oh, and don't forget he got away with murder. Twice.'

'Mum and Brendan are out of it. We must be grateful for that.'

'But Skeggsie is dead, Rose. That's something I can never forget.'

'I know.'

There was quiet in the car and Rose reached out and grabbed Joshua's arm and squeezed it. He nodded, seeming to pull himself together, and turned the car ignition on.

'We'll take the gun to Waterloo Bridge. It's the closest.'

'Won't it be a bit public there? Full of commuters?'

'They'll be too busy heading home. No one will notice us.'

She felt a prickle of apprehension. Waterloo Bridge was where Lev Baranski had been shot. It wasn't somewhere she ever wanted to be again. Still this was different – a drive to the middle of the bridge, get out of the car and throw the canvas bag into the water. As Joshua began to edge his way through the West End traffic Rose noticed the recorder lying on the dashboard. She got hold of it and pushed it into the front pocket of her rucksack. It was important to keep it safe. It was the only evidence they had about Munroe. Then she checked her phone, wondering if her mother might send her one last message. There was nothing so she put that in with the recorder. The canvas bag and her rucksack were filling the footwell so she hauled her rucksack up and hoisted it over to the back seat.

They were stuck in traffic moving slowly forward towards Aldwych. Joshua was staring out of the windscreen, his face expressionless. She went to say something but thought it was better to just keep quiet. Joshua had to deal with his own thoughts. They'd done the best they could and achieved one major thing. There would be no more killing. Joshua would realise that himself. In the long run.

They pulled away from the traffic lights. Up ahead was Waterloo Bridge. It had gone eight so the rush hour traffic was easing but there were still a good number of commuters. Joshua kept a steady speed and began to slow down as they got to the centre of the bridge.

'We're not supposed to stop here. Aren't we just drawing attention to ourselves?' Rose said.

'It won't take any time at all. I'll pull over,' he said. 'You get out. Have a look at the river. Make sure there are no dredgers or riverboats going by. Check along the bridge for police cars or any nearby pedestrians. When you think it's clear come back and tell me and I'll bring the bag.'

307

'I can do it,' Rose said. 'Then you won't need to get out of the car.'

Joshua had his indicator on to move in towards the pavement.

'Do you mind if I do it? Dad asked me. I'd like to do it for him.'

'Sure, I didn't think.'

They came to a stop. A car tooted behind them.

'Go on,' Joshua said.

Rose got out and walked across the pavement towards the parapet. She looked from right to left. There were some pedestrians but most were staring straight ahead walking swiftly towards the other side of the bridge. She looked along the road first towards the north and couldn't see any flashing lights that might indicate a police car. It was the same in the other direction. Then she leant across the parapet and looked down at the river. There was a riverboat some distance away but it was on the far side of the river and wouldn't come anywhere near them. The lights along the embankment gave it a festive feel but did not spill on to the river.

It was the right time to dispose of the American hardware.

She turned to make her way over to the Mini but stopped in her tracks.

It wasn't there. The Mini had gone.

Joshua had driven off and left her.

Why?

It only took moments for it to fall into place. Rose felt her insides churn. Joshua was never going to throw the gun into the river. He had driven her here to get her out of the car. It was all a ruse to get rid of her.

He intended to find James Munroe.

He was going to punish him for what he'd done to Skeggsie.

TWENTY-NINE

Rose shivered in the dark. She was shocked that Joshua would leave her there. Shake her off. Abandon her. She stared at the traffic going past. A stream of yellow head-lights blurred and sharpened and blurred again. A cyclist, whose light was blinking on and off, sped past her, weaving in and out of slow-moving cars and vans. The Mini was far away. She couldn't be sure how long she had stood there because she didn't have her phone so didn't know exactly what time it was. She found herself close to tears. Joshua had left her there so that he could head for the hotel in Hyde Park where Munroe was attending a police social event. She was sure of it.

The gun was in the canvas bag. It was loaded and it wouldn't take much know-how to take off a safety catch and pull a trigger. Joshua was good with mechanical things; he'd spent years fixing bits of bikes in the box room of Brewster Road.

Rose walked back to the parapet. Underneath the

bridge the river was black and gel-like and seemed to ooze along. The riverboat she had seen before was going past, too far away to notice anyone ditching a weapon into the water.

What are you doing, Josh? Rose thought.

Without Rose holding him back Joshua would be able to let go of the feelings of frustration he had about Munroe. He would park his car and sling the canvas bag over his shoulder and walk towards the Royal Swan Hotel. He would wait outside for Munroe.

Rose walked up and down. She was stuck. She couldn't ring him because her phone was in her rucksack in the back of the car. She had no money to call a cab or get on the tube or hop on a bus. She was on Waterloo Bridge and Joshua was in a car heading for Hyde Park, two or three miles across London.

She had no idea what to do next.

She turned back across the bridge and began to walk. She shoved her hands in her pockets and put one foot in front of another and went as quickly as she could. At the edge of the bridge she stopped a woman passing by and asked the time. 'Twenty past eight, my dear.'

She strode on, heading west. She wasn't that familiar with the streets of London but she knew that Hyde Park was near Green Park and that was close to Piccadilly. A bus went past. She looked at the front. It was heading for Piccadilly Circus. It was the right direction but she had no Oyster card and no money. She ran a dozen steps to the stop and waited until a few people had got on and went up to the driver.

'I've lost my pass,' she said, looking pleadingly at him.

'No pass, no ride,' he said, sighing with impatience.

'You could just take my name and address . . .'

'You're holding these passengers up . . .'

The driver flicked his hand in the direction of the door. Rose got off and watched the bus move away. She walked swiftly on. At a crossroads she asked a woman the directions for Piccadilly Circus. She continued, her thoughts full of Joshua outside the hotel building in Hyde Park. Maybe he would discard the canvas bag and have the gun in his pocket. In her mind she saw him hunched over, looking for Munroe, his face screwed up with worry. His hand would be in or near his pocket. Maybe he would be forcing himself to think of Skeggsie and the way he was murdered in the alleyway. He might have to go over and over this to psych himself up. Or maybe it was all there, the well of grief that he'd felt over the last months, just waiting for a time like this. These thoughts would spur him on, his finger twitching, his heart full of hatred for Munroe.

How calm Frank Richards had seemed when he'd pulled the trigger of a gun. She remembered him under Waterloo Bridge, one hand pulling his suitcase on wheels, the other holding the weapon. Frank Richards had raised his arm elegantly, like a dancer. After the shot he'd dropped the weapon and glided off. Had it taken anything from him? Cost him in an emotional way? Rose had no idea. She knew for sure, though, that if Joshua succeeded in killing Munroe it would destroy him. He would never be the same person again. Even if he were to drop the gun and fade away into the darkness unseen it would warp his life for ever.

She couldn't let Munroe do that to Joshua.

Even if it meant him getting away with two murders.

Up ahead she could see the neon lights that peppered the buildings around Piccadilly Circus. She quickened her pace. She must have been walking for fifteen or twenty minutes already. Munroe was due at the Royal Swan Hotel at nine. She simply wasn't going to get there in time. She saw a London Underground sign and headed for it. At the top of the stairs there was a group of young people standing round, a couple smoking, the others talking, looking at phones. She had nothing to lose except her pride.

'Guys, can anyone lend me some money?'

'What? Get lost!'

'My bag's been stolen, my phone, everything. I just need a tube ride home. I can write down my mobile number and tomorrow you can ring and I'll give you double, treble what you give me.'

'It's a scam.'

'I'm stuck up here otherwise. I've got no way of getting home.'

'Go to the police,' a boy said, looking at her in a puzzled way.

'I don't trust the police.'

Several of them turned away but the boy continued to stare at her.

'Please,' she said. 'I'm desperate.'

He put his hand in his pocket and came out with a pen. He held his arm out and pushed the sleeve of his jacket and jumper back.

'Write your number there.'

She wrote it, holding the pen softly so it didn't dig into his skin. He looked at the number, then back at her. He put his hand in his trouser pocket and pulled out a five pound note and gave it to her. Some of the others saw it and started to laugh.

'I always said Tony would have to pay for sex!'

Rose took the money and mouthed the words, 'Thank you.'

She ran down the steps of the station and in minutes was on a Piccadilly Line train to Hyde Park Corner. Then she just had to find the Royal Swan Hotel. The journey was just two stops and she dashed off and up the escalator until she was outside the station and standing by a busy road. Across the road was Hyde Park, huge, dark and quiet. Behind her was a line of glass buildings, some apartment blocks and hotels. She ducked into the half-moon drive of a hotel. The concierge was standing on the front steps.

'Excuse me, I'm looking for the Royal Swan Hotel?'

He sighed and looked away from her. 'Four buildings along, madam.'

She hurried away, quickly passing the other buildings. When she came up to the Royal Swan Hotel she saw that it was smaller and older than the others. It had a recess for coaches and cars to pull in. Then there was a garden area. Along the front of it was a line of trees and benches dividing the hotel off from the busy road. Rose looked round at the grass and shrubs that grew there. It was mostly dark but the lights from the traffic illuminated parts of it.

She saw Joshua. He was sitting forward on one of the benches, his hands in his coat pockets. She was sure it was nine or thereabouts. She had no idea which direction Munroe would be coming from. He had said he had somewhere else to go before coming to the hotel. She walked over to the bench. Joshua saw her coming. He was surprised. He stood up.

'Leave me alone, Rosie,' he said, looking from side to side.

'Don't do this. It makes you just like him,' she said, putting her arm through his.

'No, it doesn't,' he said, shaking her off, stepping away from her. 'It evens things out. It rids the world of a killer. Wasn't that what *The Butterfly Project* was all about?'

'It will taint you. It'll change you.'

'It'll make me happier. I haven't been happy since Christmas Eve. It'll pay back for Skeggsie.'

And Daisy? Rose thought.

'You'll get caught. This is a public place.'

'I don't care.'

Joshua stiffened, looking over her shoulder. Rose turned round. Munroe was walking towards the hotel. He had on his Crombie overcoat. It wasn't buttoned up, it was flying out behind him and he seemed to be moving quickly as if he was late. Joshua stepped past her but she grabbed on to his jacket.

'Josh, don't do this thing,' she said, her voice cracking.

But he shook her off. He walked forward to the edge of the garden. Munroe was coming up to the hotel, striding briskly along the pavement. He looked at his watch and seemed to be smiling at something. Rose stood transfixed as Joshua edged close to a tree, took the gun out of his pocket and raised his arm.

'No,' she said, her hand over her mouth.

Seconds later a shot rang out, like a car backfiring. Everything seemed to stand utterly still as Munroe jolted and twisted as if he'd had some kind of electric shock. Then he fell to the ground. Rose ran up to Joshua.

'Oh my God,' she said.

Joshua was shaking his head and Rose burst into tears.

'Oh, what have you done?' she cried.

'Nothing. Nothing,' he said.

Munroe was lying on his back. He seemed to be twitching, his arm moving for a second then he stopped. People were walking towards him. A man at the front of the hotel was pointing towards the park.

'We have to get away from here,' Rose said through sobs.

But the man wasn't pointing in their direction. He was shouting and gesturing to a spot further along the garden. Rose spun round and looked.

'I didn't do anything,' Joshua said. 'I didn't have time to fire.'

Margaret Spicer was standing by a tree. She stared at Rose. She dropped something from her hand. She took a pale raincoat off and let it fall to the ground. Underneath she was dressed in a black trouser suit. She walked towards them, peeling off some gloves and letting them drop on to the grass.

'Margaret did it,' Rose whispered.

Rose stared horrified as Margaret Spicer walked up to them.

'That was for Daisy,' she said.

Margaret walked away from the hotel. Rose saw her cross the traffic, her head high. Then she disappeared into the darkness of Hyde Park.

'We have to get away from here,' Rose said, taking the gun from Joshua and holding it under her coat. 'Where's the car?'

Joshua mumbled something.

'Where's the car!' she said, sharply pushing his arm.

He walked off. She held her coat tight and stayed behind him. A siren sounded and she put her head down as they cut off into side streets and walked for a while until they came to the Mini parked half up on the pavement, a parking ticket wedged under one of the windscreen wipers. Joshua took it out silently. He tossed it into the back seat.

'Let's go back to Waterloo Bridge and finish what we started.'

Waterloo Bridge was quieter. Rose had wiped the gun clean and replaced it in the canvas bag. Joshua pulled the car up in almost the same spot as he had an hour or so earlier. Before they got out he looked at the news on his phone. He read it out. 'Man shot dead outside London hotel. '

There were only a few details. James Munroe was not named. Rose thought all of that would come later, perhaps in the late night news and the morning papers. Her mother and Brendan would be on a plane by then and so, most probably, would Margaret Spicer.

She got out her phone and accessed her mother's number. She wrote a text, short and to the point. **Munroe dead**. Then she pressed *Send*.

They got out of the car and walked to the parapet. Further up on the South Bank Rose could see Tate Modern, its chimney lit up with purple neon. On the seventh floor a party was taking place for Macon Parker, the man who stole people's organs. He would be wondering where his housekeepers were. He would never know how close he had been to death. His notebook, back at the Camden flat, would never be completed.

The river was bright. Two riverboats were passing in opposite directions. They waited until both had gone by and then dropped the canvas bag. There was no sound for a few moments then a distant splash.

'Will it wash up?'

'Eventually but there won't be any prints on it.'

'Let's go back to the flat.'

Joshua took Rose's hand and they walked back to the car.

THIRTY

Anna had allowed Rose and Joshua to light a bonfire at the bottom of the garden. It was in a space adjacent to her studio, the building that had once been an unused garage. They had cleared away the remains of old garden rubbish to make room for the blaze. Rose had told Anna that she was burning old papers of her mother's and Anna had nodded supportively. 'It's best to move on with your life,' she said.

Joshua was trying to get the fire going using bunched up newspapers and scraps of wood that had been lying around.

Rose looked up to the house and saw her grandmother at the window of the Blue Room. She was busy talking to the decorator. They had chosen furniture and rugs and blinds and Rose was to have a television and stereo. In the past week she'd spent a lot of time with Joshua at the Camden flat but that would end in the summer. Skeggsie's dad was going to sell the flat and Joshua would have to find a room in a shared house. So maybe the Blue Room would be a good place for them to use.

The fire was taking a while and Joshua was looking puzzled.

'Maybe we should use some firelighters?' Rose said.

'It'll catch,' he said. 'It's not like we haven't got enough flammable stuff to keep it going.'

Joshua pointed to the carrier bags he'd brought in the car earlier. They were full of all the stuff they'd ever used or printed off to do with the notebooks and *The Butterfly Project*. In another bag were the notebooks themselves.

The front door bell sounded; maybe it was the decorator's mate, a lad in his twenties who wore headphones all the time and went pink whenever Rose came near. She looked back at the fire. Joshua's face was rapt in concentration.

'It's coming,' he said.

He still had plasters over his ear but his face had healed and was looking normal again. Rose put her hand up to her cheek where her skin had been grazed and scratched. It too was getting better. A week had passed since Munroe's death and she and Joshua were recovering.

'Oh good,' she said, seeing a flame lick around a piece of wood.

Just then she heard Anna call her name as Joshua fed some computer printouts on to the fire.

'I'll be back,' she said.

Anna was in the kitchen. 'There's a policewoman to see you. She won't come into the house. Nothing I should be worried about?'

'No, definitely not. It's probably someone bringing a message from Henry. He sent me a text asking me to help in his club.'

Her grandmother went back upstairs and Rose went to the front door. Wendy Clarke was standing in the street next to a parked police car. Rose picked up her key from the hall table and went out of the house to join her. There was a uniformed officer in the driving seat. Wendy was leaning back against the car, her unruly hair held back with a hair-band. She was smoking a cigarette. It was not one of her roll-ups but a filter tip. Under her arm she was holding a padded envelope. Rose recognised it immediately.

'Hello, Rose. How are you?'

'Fine.'

'Not got anything to tell me?'

'About what?'

Wendy held out the cigarette and tapped it. The ash dropped off.

'I received this yesterday.'

She showed the envelope. On the front of it was the address of Bethnal Green Police Station and it was made out for the attention of Wendy Clarke. Rose stared at it.

'Imagine my surprise when I opened it and a small black recorder dropped out.'

'A recorder?'

'Yes, you know. You turn them on, they record what's being said. You turn them off, they stop. Now I'd say that you and your stepbrother had something to do with this.'

Rose's face was very still.

'As well as the recorder there's this piece of paper which has a name and address typed on it. This name turns out to be a Mr James Munroe – the same James Munroe who was a victim of a sensational shooting in central London a week ago. This is the man who was the owner of the property in Brewster Road at the time that Daisy Lincoln was murdered. During the recording this man, James Munroe, confesses to the killing of Daisy Lincoln. I say confess but there are several sections of the tape which have been wiped clean so it's only half a conversation that I'm hearing.'

'I knew James Munroe,' Rose said.

'Oh, I know that. This man was a colleague of your mother's so I'm guessing you may have met him once or twice.'

Rose shook her head. 'Only after my parents disappeared. I didn't like him. Ever.'

'So, we've gone to this Mr James Munroe's London address and we found a letter from his wife, Mrs Margaret Spicer. This letter is a suicide note and gives, as a reason, her discovery of the affair that her husband had with

Daisy Lincoln and her belief that it was he who killed the girl.'

'Suicide?' Rose said, alarmed.

'It's a suicide note. And yes, some items of clothing and a shoulder bag full of documents has been found on Beachy Head but no body as of yet. So it's a very strange case. These two bits of evidence coming together so neatly.'

'But you'll be able to close the case. To tell the family what happened to Daisy.'

'I will. What I won't be able to tell them is how I found out.'

'But at least justice is done.'

'Someone shot James Munroe outside the Royal Swan Hotel. CCTV footage shows a woman walking away from the scene about that time. That woman could be Margaret Spicer, his wife. What's your view, Rose?'

'I don't know.'

'You know nothing. *Nada*.'

'I don't have a view.'

''Course the officers who looked through the CCTV footage may have missed something. They may have missed other interesting bystanders. What do you think?'

'I can't say.'

'Another one of your secrets. You lied to me, Rose. You told me your secret had nothing to do with Daisy Lincoln.'

'My secret doesn't. This,' she said, gesturing towards the envelope, 'was not my secret.'

Wendy Clarke looked at her without speaking. Then she opened the passenger door and got into the car. She let the window slide down.

'Look after yourself, Rose. Keep out of my way.'

The car drove off. Rose watched it go down the street and then went back into the house. As she walked into the kitchen she could see smoke rising up from the garden. She stepped outside and headed for the fire. Joshua was standing next to it looking pleased with himself. There were several empty carrier bags weighed down by a stone on the ground. There was just one bag of papers left.

'The notebooks,' Joshua said. 'I thought we'd do them together.'

He picked out the first one.

'2005 George Usher.'

He let it drop into the flames. Rose picked up the next one.

'2007 Michael McCall.'

'2008 Ronnie Binyon.'

'2010 James Barker.'

'Oh,' she said, remembering. 'There's one more thing I want to put on the fire. Keep it going for me.'

She went inside the house and up to her bedroom. From her desk drawer she picked out the envelope that had

Myers and Goodwood written on it. She tipped out the red notebook that contained her statement. It would be the first time that Joshua had seen it. And the last. She took it downstairs and while Joshua was moving the wood around and adding more scraps she threw the notebook on top of the fire. She watched it join the remains of the four other notebooks. It sat at an angle. Its edges seemed to catch, first curling and turning brown, and then the fire seemed to eat it greedily until it was black ashes just like the others.

'What was that?'

'Just some notes I was making. Not important any more.'

Afterwards they sat side by side on the sofa in the studio.

'What about your gran? Will you ever tell her?'

Rose had thought about this for some days.

'I will. I will tell her that Kathy and Brendan were working undercover and have left the country. Now that Munroe is dead I can say that they were working for him hence the lies and cover-ups. She has a right to know that her daughter is alive.'

'That'll be an interesting conversation.'

'I can't say I'm looking forward to it.'

Rose had her laptop on her knees. She opened up her mail. There was the email she had received that morning after six days of silence.

Dear Rose and Joshua, We arrived safely in British Columbia via a direct flight to Seattle. We appreciated the text you sent on the night of our flight. It certainly makes our lives a lot easier having that information to hand. We are staying with friends outside a town called Kelowna. We will be involved in various conservation projects based around Shuswap Lake, north of where we are now. In the autumn we will look into renting a property on the outskirts of Calvary. We long to see you both. Maybe you could come in August? Then things can be explained at length and you can both get back to England in time to continue your studies. Jenny and Gareth Somers.

Rose had read this email many times. Jenny and Gareth Somers – she wondered who had thought that name up.

'Do you think we'll go, Rosie? To Canada? In the summer?'

'I don't know,' she said. 'Maybe that's too soon. Maybe we need time to let this all settle. To think it through. To work out what we really feel about what they did. Then we can go later. In a year or two.'

'That's what I was thinking,' he said, grabbing her hand, holding it tightly. 'There's lots for us to do in the next couple of years. Most of it we can do *together*.'

She stared at him and found herself smiling. His haircut didn't look so severe and he seemed relaxed, his hard edges softened. For the first time in months he looked like the boy she had first met the previous September after a five-year break.

She leant forward and kissed him lightly on the lips.

'The main thing is,' he whispered, 'that they're safe and the killing is over.'

That was the main thing. The killing was over.

THE MURDER NOTEBOOKS

**Your parents are dead – or so everyone says.
How much would you risk to find out the truth?**

OUT NOW